CAROLINE COURTNEY

The Courier of Love

Columbine House
King Street, St. James's
London

THE COURIER OF LOVE
First published 1984 by
Columbine House
the romantic side of
Arlington Books (Publishers) Ltd
15–17 King Street, St. James's
London SW1

© Caroline Courtney 1984

Typeset by Inforum Ltd, Portsmouth
Printed in Great Britain at The Pitman Press, Bath

ISBN 0 85140 640 8

1

"Hey, you there! What the deuce d'you think you're doing?"

Startled by the sound of the man's angry voice, the dark-haired girl in the river spun round, hastily ducking her shoulders under the water. It was a prudent precaution, for her tall, slender frame was adorned by nothing more than a fine gold chain around her throat.

Unabashed, she stared up at the tall, ruggedly handsome man on the river bank and replied, in characteristically spirited fashion, "I should have thought it was obvious what I am doing! I was, until your most noisy arrival on the scene, enjoying a refreshing bathe in the river."

The fair-haired man stood arms akimbo and shouted furiously, "What damned impertinence!"

"But I am doing no harm!" she protested hotly, pushing a strand of damp, raven hair from her brow.

"First, you are trespassing on private property," the man informed her in cutting tones. "And secondly, my dear girl, you are disturbing my trout."

The girl's green eyes blazed. "How dare you address me as *my dear girl*, in that patronising manner! My name is Lady Francesca de Lisle. I am the only daughter of the *Fifth* Earl of Marlow, of Marlow Manor near Shaftesbury."

The glimmer of a smile touched the man's deep blue eyes as he regarded the impressive *hauteur* frosting Lady Francesca's attractive countenance. To present such a diginified demeanour was no mean feat, he reflected, when one is standing, totally unclothed, in over five feet of water.

He executed a graceful bow and declared, "Aidan Langley. *Eighth* Duke of Wexford, of Wexford Hall, King's Langley." He strolled along the river bank which was lush with fresh spring grass, and remarked, "Now we have formally introduced ourselves, Lady Francesca, perhaps you would be good enough to explain your most unwelcome presence in my river. Is there, perhaps, a shortage of water for washing in Shaftesbury? Or could it be that plunging into other people's rivers is a quaint, ancient custom of you Dorsetshire girls. A Maytime ritual, perchance, when unmarried maidens symbolically shrug off the shackles of convention, and offer themselves . . . "

Laughing, the Duke stepped quickly sideways to avoid the lump of wet weed flung at him by a livid Francesca.

She said furiously, "Clearly, you Hampshire gentlemen are pedantic creatures who require every 't' crossed and every 'i' dotted. I really cannot undersand why my presence in your river gives you such cause for concern. However, it is simply explained."

Deliberately, Francesca adopted the slow, patient tone one would employ with the village idiot. "I have ridden this morning all the way from Salisbury. That's S-a-l-i-s-b-u-r-y. As the weather is unseasonably warm, I found myself considerably fatigued with the heat. Then I espied the temptingly cool water of your river and . . . "

Her voice tailed away as the Duke's sapphire blue eyes bored into her. When at last he spoke, his tone was edged with steel. "Don't ever dare address me in that manner again!" he instructed her harshly.

To her horror, Francesca saw that he had picked up her claret-coloured riding habit which she had laid over a branch. His mouth was set in a tight, hard line and Francesca realised she had made him so angry that he now intended to throw all her clothes into the water!

"This is yours, I take it?" the Duke enquired coldly.

Francesca knew that it would be politic now to give him her sweetest smile and flutter her eyelashes — tried and trusty feminine wiles to cool his anger, win him over and prevent him transforming her riding habit into a sodden, unwearable lump of wool.

But Francesca had not been born with a submissive spirit. Although perfectly well aware that this was a time when feminine charm should hold sway, she nevertheless found herself answering the Duke's question with an exaggerated glance to left and to right, and a sarcastic, "Indeed, to the best of my knowledge the river is not swarming with unclothed ladies. Therefore I am happy to confirm your most intelligent assumption that the garment you are holding is my very own."

The Duke's eyes narrowed dangerously as he regarded her. Francesca, observing his long fingers tighten round the skirt of her riding habit, tossed back her raven tresses and glared at him defiantly.

Quite suddenly the Duke threw the claret-coloured garment back on the branch and began striding down the grassy river bank. "If you've ridden from Salisbury this morning, you must have been up at dawn." he remarked levelly.

Taken aback by his change of attitude, Francesca stammered, "Oh . . . why yes. As I rode out of the White Hart Inn, I was in time to witness the most beautiful sunrise."

"In that case you must be famished. You will join me up at the Hall for breakfast," commanded the Duke.

Infuriated by his imperious tone, Francesca replied coldly, "You are most kind, Your Grace. But as you have already most articulately pointed out, I have trespassed on your hospitality for far too long already."

A frown creased the Duke's handsome face. "Don't argue with me! We shall take breakfast together."

"But I am not hungry," flared Francesca. "And even if I were, after your arrogant treatment of me here this morning, you are the last person in the world I should desire to gaze at across a breakfast table!"

The Duke proceeded down the river bank, and replied calmly, "You may not be hungry, but your horse most certainly deserves some refreshment. He will be well looked-after in my stables." Swiftly, the Duke untethered Francesca's chestnut from the shade of a willow tree, and led him towards a path through the bushes. He did not look back, but called over his shoulder to Francesca, "I shall expect you in twenty minutes. Do try not to be late."

Francesca was in such a boiling rage at his cavalier behaviour that she was surprised the water all around her was not beginning to steam.

"How dare he!" she stormed, wading out of the water and reaching for her shift with which to dry herself. "First he had the impertinence to interrogate me on my presence in his precious river. And now he has stolen my horse! Well I hope there are poached eggs on the Duke's breakfast table. For if he crosses me one more time I shall take great pleasure in pulping the eggs all over his arrogant head!"

Twenty minutes later Francesca was walking up the broad sweep of drive that led to Wexford Hall. As she gazed for the first time on the timbered, Elizabethan house and watched the sun glinting on the lovely leaded windows, Francesca was forced to admit that she was impressed. Her own house, Marlow Manor, was of the same period as

Wexford. But whereas at Marlow the ancient timbers were rotting with damp, the roof leaked and the garden was a wilderness, here at Wexford everything was in immaculate condition.

The Duke must clearly be an extremely wealthy man, Francesca realised, her trained eye observing the absence of missing slates from the roof; the new stable block; the freshly painted carriage at the door and the beautifully kept expanse of tiered lawns, each ribboned by well trimmed low yew hedges. Francesca was painfully aware of the enormous expense involved in the upkeep of a large house such as this. Her own father, the Earl of Marlow, had long ago given up the struggle, with the result that year by year Marlow Manor was gradually crumbling away.

Francesca could not repress a sigh as she entered the imposing hall dominated by a broad dark oak staircase, guarded by two gleaming suits of armour. Above the stone fireplace were two pairs of crossed swords, and between them was displayed the Wexford coat of arms.

A masculine hall, well suited to its owner, Francesca decided. But she was intrigued to notice, on a small round satinwood table, a display of cheerful anemones, arranged in a copper bowl.

A footman, smartly clad in dark blue livery, led Francesca through to the sunny Breakfast Room, where the Duke was seated at a table set with fresh blue and white china. He rose to his feet as Francesca entered and smiled in surprise.

"Why, you are taller than I had imagined!"

Francesca stood straightbacked before him, her head held high. Her mother had taught her to be proud of her height, and never to stoop or slouch.

"I am aware that I am unfashionably tall," she said, "but I confess I find it a pleasant sensation being able to look down on most of the rest of the world!"

The Duke laughed, and said softly, "How infuriating for you, then, to be obliged to look up to me!"

"Your Grace, you read my thoughts exactly," declared Francesca sweetly, reflecting that this maddening man must stand at least six feet four inches tall. Yes, oh *how* it pained her to be required to look up to him!

Courteously, the Duke waited until Francesca was seated, then he returned to his chair and proceeded to immerse himself in an issue of the *Winchester Courier*. His silence did not affect Francesca in the least. It was the habit of both her father and brother to eat their breakfast in total silence, the only sound being the rustle of the pages of *The Times*.

Besides, thought Francesca, smiling her thanks as a footman served her with a thick slice of cold ham, it is not as if the Duke and I have anything to say to one another. I regard him as an arrogant bully, and he sees me as no more than a trespassing nuisance.

But the main reason why Francesca was delighted to be ignored by her host was that, contrary to her earlier protestations, she was in truth quite ravenously hungry. She had downed a few mouthfuls of strong scalding tea before she left the White Hart Inn at daybreak, but between then and the present hour of ten o'clock, she had taken no other nourishment.

As she tucked gratefully into the delicious ham, then later spread golden toast with a generous layer of blackcurrant jam, Francesca found it impossible to forget the reproving voice of old Nanny Peters.

"Now my lady, you know full well that it is unseemly to attack your food like a starving dog. Especially in the presence of a gentleman who is not your kin! Ladies should always eat sparingly, and preserve an ethereal aura . . ."

Ethereal aura! thought Francesca in despair, biting into her third slice of buttered toast. That was all very well if you were born small boned and delicate, like all Nanny Peters' previous charges, but I am a tall, strong girl! If I pecked in a ladylike manner at my food I should simply fade away.

At last, with her hunger sated, Francesca sat back in the tapestried chair with her second cup of tea and contemplated the view from the open window. The lawn was dominated by a magnificent spreading oak tree, which Francesca guessed had probably been planted when the house was built. The oval flower beds were a riot of Spring colour, leading the eye to the first curve of an avenue lined with purple and white lilac.

Francesca was so entranced with the colour and scent of the scene outside that she completely forgot about her host. A restful half hour passed without either of them uttering a word.

The Duke sat at the head of the rosewood table, but his fair head was no longer bent over the pages of the *Winchester Courier*. Instead his deep blue eyes were appraising the dark-haired girl who sat lost in thought as she gazed out on his estate.

Her damp hair had dried in the sun, and had feathered into light waves and curls around her face. It was an interesting face, the Duke decided, striking rather than conventionally pretty, with strong bones, a firm jaw and magnificent grey-green eyes.

She turned her head now and enquired coolly, "Is there anything of interest in the newspaper?"

The Duke shook his head, and impatiently threw the newspaper onto a sidetable. "The proprietor of the *Winchester Courier* seems increasingly obsessed with the trivial doings of the Winchester elite. News of Napoleon and our brave army is crushed into a single column. Whereas Lady Sombourne's forthcoming charity ball merits over half a page!"

"Perhaps Lady Sombourne is raising funds for our brave army?" suggested Francesca.

"If she is, then that is entirely incidental," snapped the Duke. "The main purpose of her ball will be to increase the social prestige of Lady Sombourne." with an expressive wave of his hands he dismissed the despised Winchester elite. Giving Francesca a frank smile he enquired, "What about you, my raven-haired water nymph? What are you doing, rising at dawn to ride unchaperoned through the Hampshire countryside?"

"I am on my way to visit my aunt in Winchester," Francesca explained. "The family carriage brought me as far as Salisbury where I lodged for the night. But when I was awakened — in the early hours of the morning by some late arrivals at the inn — I knew I could not abide another day in that stuffy jolting prison of a carriage. So I ordered my box to be sent on to Winchester, and I set forth on horseback, along the straight Roman road that leads I believe right down into the city. "Oh", she sighed, her lovely eyes sparkling, "the views were simply glorious!"

The Duke sat back in his chair and crossed his long, powerful legs. "Did it not occur to you that it was rather foolhardy for a young girl like yourself to ride unchaperoned along a lonely country road?"

Francesca's dark curls danced in the sun as she tossed her head. "I am hardly a young girl, Your Grace. I was twenty-one last February!"

"Twenty-one! My, you are ancient indeed," was the sardonic response.

Francesca flushed, "I assure you, I am quite capable of taking care of myself. At home in Dorset I am accustomed to riding wherever I please without the ball and chain of a chaperone by my side."

"Mmm, I am well aware that you are accustomed to

behaving just as you please," he murmured. "And what of your parents? Have you their permission to roam the countryside in such an abandoned manner?"

"Permission?" cried Francesca, bursting into astonished laughter. "My, how amusing you are, my lord Duke!"

His mouth tightened. "I am delighted to find you are so easily entertained. But do pray tell me what I have said to cause you such uncontrollable mirth." The words were lightly said, but the icy expression in his eyes sent a chill through Francesca. She turned away, and pretended to be absorbed in throwing some toast crumbs to the robin perched on the terrace wall.

"My mother died five years ago," she said quietly. "I came straight from the schoolroom to the position of mistress of my father's house. Of course I have also endeavoured to be a second mother to my young brother Edward."

An affectionate smile touched Francesca's face as she thought of the sixteen-year-old Edward, with his tousled tawny hair and impish smile. It was my intention when Mama died to set you a good example in life, Edward. But I fear I have failed, Francesca reflected wryly.

Oh, I should so like to have been like Mama — graceful, unhurried, never discomposed. But sadly, nature did not fashion me in that mould. So instead of speaking to you softly, Edward, and giving you gentle guidance on music, art and all the civilised things of life . . . instead of that, I was to be found indulging in hilarious pillow fights with you on Sunday mornings, or shrieking with laughter as I picked up my skirts and chased you round the orchard. And do you remember the time we went skating on the frozen pond and fell through a hole in the ice?

Francesca stood with her hand to her mouth at the open window as she recalled her father's gamekeeper rushing to their rescue, sliding a branch across the ice for the errant brother and sister to cling on to.

"You look quite transformed," the Duke's voice cut through Francesca's reverie. "Do tell me of what, or of whom you are thinking?"

"My brother Edward," smiled Francesca, sitting down and smoothing the worn claret cloth of her skirt. "He is up at Eton now, so I don't see as much of him as I would like."

"Does he resemble you?" enquired the Duke.

Francesca tilted her head to one side and considered the matter. "In looks, no. He is fair and I am dark. But in temperament, yes, I do believe we have much in common."

"In that case, his masters at Eton have my total sympathy," remarked the Duke dryly. "I should not be at all surprised to open *The Times* one morning and read that one of England's most celebrated establishments had been blown up on the whim of the heir to the Earl of Marlow." His long fingers drummed on the carved arm of his chair. "But of course," he said softly, "your family name is de Lisle . . . and your father is the Earl of Marlow. Yes . . . I see . . ."

The Duke stood up and enquired in a kindly tone, "Have you had sufficient to eat, lady Francesca? Would it amuse you to walk through the Long Gallery and divert yourself at the expense of my dead ancestors hanging on the walls?"

Francesca stared stonily up at him, "Your civility is over-excessive, Your Grace. I assure you, my circumstances no longer cause me the least embarrassment, Why, all England must be aware by now that my grandfather drank and gambled the de Lisle fortune away. My father's income does no more than pay the servants and feed and clothe his family. There is not a penny left over for repairs to the house — ".

The Duke cleared his throat and said abruptly, "I beg

your pardon. I was tactless, I should not have made it so obvious that I remembered your grandfather's . . . over-indulgence."

"Over-indulgence!" Francesca's laugh was bitter. "He was a drunkard and a womaniser. Yes," the grey-green eyes flared, "I am aware of his penchant for dancers and actresses. Women of good looks but little talent who felt the chilling breath of younger, prettier girls on their necks and realised that their salvation lay in a rich patron. Someone who would feed, clothe and bejewel them in return for the precious gift of their bodies once or twice a week."

As the torrent of words spilled out, Francesca was staring with unseeing eyes at the thick Axminster carpet. The linen napkin in her hands had been fiercely twisted into three knots.

"No doubt it shocks you, my lord Duke, to hear a lady speak thus."

The Duke seated himself beside her. Through the blur of her wrathful tears she was aware of the deep blue of his morning coat and the high gloss on his boots.

"No," he said quietly, "I am not shocked. I am ten years older than you, Francesca, and I have drunk deep of many of the dark wells of life. But I am saddened, and intrigued, that a girl of twenty-one should have been made so painful-ly aware of the weaknesses of men. How did you discover such things about your grandfather?"

Francesca lifted her eyes to his. "After my mother died, it was left to me to sift through all the family papers and accounts. My father is a dear man but his books, his library, and his old maps are his life. When I took on the responsibil-ity of running the household, I examined all the old accounts in an attempt to discover why we were in such desperate financial straits. And then I learnt that my grand-father had squandered our fortune. There were details of old gambling debts, and bills pertaining to houses he had leased for his dancer friends. There were details of lavish entertainments, jewels, wine, clothes . . . nothing but bills, bills, bills!"

The Duke nodded. "And when your grandfather died, your father was left to pay the debts."

"At the end of it all, there was very little left," said Francesca, "But I should not like you to think that Edward and I were ever unhappy. We live a simple country life, it is true, but there has always been much love in our house. My father finds a deep contentment in his books, and Edward and I have a rare time together when he is released from Eton."

"But now the outside world is suddenly too much with you," commented the Duke.

Francesca smiled in appreciation of his understanding of her situation. "Yes. I have received an invitation from my Aunt Cecilia in Winchester. The tone of her letter made it perfectly clear that I am invited not on my own merits, but more because she feels it her duty to bestow benevolence on one of the family's charity cousins."

The Duke said thoughtfully, "I must confess, I am acquainted with no lady of the name of Cecilia de Lisle in Winchester."

"No, no, she is my mother's sister. My Aunt Cecilia is married to the Earl of Rothersay, and they have a daughter Aithne."

Francesca raised a delicate, arched eyebrow as the Duke threw back his head and gave a shout of laughter. "Now it is evidently my turn to amuse you," said Francesca coldly, arising from her chair and turning her back on her laughing host.

When at last he spoke, it was apparent that he was quite unrepentant of his outburst. "Let us get this quite clear," he persisted. "You, Lady Francesca de Lisle, whom I found swimming in the most abandoned fashion in my river this morning, you are intending to reside with Lady Rothersay?"

"You are to be complimented on your swift comprehension of the situation," said Francesca bitingly.

"I take it," the Duke went on, his blue eyes agleam with laughter, "that you are not intimately acquainted with your aunt?"

"I believe we met once, very briefly, when I was but a child" Francesca turned to face him, her head held high, her countenance a frozen mask. "Now if you have quite finished mocking my family, I should be glad if you would summon a footman to escort me to your stables. I am expected in Winchester, and I am quite sure that you have many demands on your time this morning."

The Duke strode across the room and flung open the doors. "By a fortunate co-incidence, I have matters to attend to in Winchester today. It will be my pleasure to escort you into the city."

"I assure you," said Francesca firmly as she preceded him out of the Breakfast Room, "I am quite capable of riding into Winchester on my own. I have come all this way without accident. Surely nothing terrible can befall me on the few remaining miles into the city?"

He made no answer, but took a commanding grip on her arm and guided her down the passage and through the front hall of the house. Furious at being treated like an incompetent twelve-year-old, Francesca stared rigidly ahead, unbending only to murmur a thank you to the footman who handed her her riding hat and gloves.

As she drew on her gloves, her eye was caught once again by the pretty pink and blue of the anemones in the round copper bowl in the hall. Once again she found herself wondering which feminine hand had placed them there . . .

The housekeeper of course, she decided. She felt suddenly irritated with herself. Why on earth should I care who arranged the flowers for this arrogant man, she wondered, stepping out into the sunny May day.

At the stables, a groom led out her chestnut. She was pleased to see that the horse was well rested, and bright-eyed. Francesca stroked his silken mane, and murmured, "Not far now, boy. Just a few more miles along the Roman road to Winchester."

"Five miles, to be precise," said the Duke, swinging himself up onto a magnificent grey.

Francesca glared up at him. "For the last time, Your Grace, I wish it to be understood that I desire to travel alone."

"And I, my dear Lady Francesca, am perfectly convinced that it will be in your best interests if I escort you to your aunt's house."

His patronising tone brought Francesca close to screaming point. But for the moment she had no choice but to trot her horse obediently beside his down the long drive. They passed through the huge wrought iron gates of Wexford Hall and a few minutes later traversed a stone bridge.

"In future," said the Duke, with a wave of his hand, "you may find it useful to bear in mind that this river marks the boundary of my estate. I have no objection to your swimming in my river, you understand, but I should be glad if another time you would choose a stretch of water uninhabited by my trout fry."

"Pray do not alarm yourself," retorted Francesca, "after today, I shall ensure that I do not come within spitting distance of either you or your wretched trout."

He grinned, and turned the grey onto the chalk path which led up through the woods to the Roman road on top of the Downs. The sky was blue, the air was fresh and the leafy wood was filled with birdsong. But Francesca, chafing at the bit, was aware of none of Nature's delights. Her grey-green eyes burned into the broad back of the man riding in front.

I won't be escorted to my aunt's like a naughty little girl, she fumed. I *won't*! But how can I rid myself of the Duke's odious presence? Impossible to spur on my horse and attempt to out-distance him. He is clearly an expert horseman. And the grey is a swifter, more spirited steed than my faithful chestnut.

Through a clearing in the trees, the road now lay ahead of them. The Duke turned to her, his handsome face alight with enthusiasm. "You'll have the most marvellous view down to Winchester from up here. It's a splendid city in any season, but especially so in the Spring, with the blossom out on the hills all around."

He broke off and gazed at Francesca in concern. With her face buried in her handkerchief, she was suffering from a distressing bout of sneezing.

"Oh dear," murmured Francesca, her eyes streaming, "I am so sorry. I am always affected thus at this time of year. Oh — a-a- tishoo! A-a-a — *tishoo*!"

Such was the violence of the last sneeze, that Francesca's head jerked sharply forward and her riding hat fell off. Dabbing her eyes, she watched it roll back down the path, and under a flowering broom bush.

"Allow me," said the Duke, dismounting. He threw his reins round a thorn tree and strode down the path to retrieve the riding hat.

Calmly, Francesca trotted her chestnut forward, untied the Duke's horse from the thorn tree and with a tight hold on the reins, slapped the grey hard on the rump. "Come on boy. Come on!"

And with that she was gone, flying across the top of the Down, her dark hair streaming out behind her, and the Duke's grey galloping neck and neck with her chestnut. She dared not look back. Even now, with a full mile between herself and the Duke, Francesca could feel the stinging fury of the fair-haired man's wrath as he watched her galloping his grey away across the Downland road.

After another mile, Francesca drew up, and released the grey's reins. "Home boy!" she instructed. Delighted to be free, the magnificent horse turned to the right and began picking his way down a chalky path. Francesca had no qualms about letting him go. He was clearly a well-trained animal with the intelligence and instinct to find his way back to the Wexford Hall stables.

As she cantered on along the Roman road, Francesca laughed out loud at the outstanding success of her plan. Whenever she travelled the countryside alone, she always took the precaution of tucking a small bag of pepper into her saddle. It was something her brother Edward had recommended to her.

"If you are attacked by a highwayman, Francesca, "he had said earnestly, "you can throw the pepper in his face and make a speedy escape."

"But Edward," she had laughed, "surely a highwayman would have no truck with me? Why, the only jewellery I own is Mama's wedding ring and one simple gold chain."

Edward's round blue eyes had widened. "All the more reason for you to take care, sister. If the highwayman decides you have wasted his time, he might take revenge by treating you dishonourably. Please carry the pepper, Francesca. Otherwise all the time I am away at Eton, I shall worry about you."

Touched by her brother's concern, Francesca had promised never to travel alone without the pepper.

"My, how Edward will laugh when I write and tell him to what excellent use I put the pepper," smiled Francesca. "Oh, I should imagine that odious Duke is jumping up and down with rage at this moment!"

Francesca felt quite unrepentant. The trouble with Dukes, she decided is that they are far too accustomed to having their own way. All their whims, however fanciful, must instantly be obeyed. Well it is good that he realised that I am no petticoated lackey to whom his ducal word is law. How dare he attempt to escort me off his estate, and then deliver me up to my aunt, no doubt with a final lecture on my impertinence in trespassing on his land!

Yet despite her defiant air, Francesca could not resist turning round once or twice and casting nervous glances back along the straight Roman road. What if the Duke had rushed into a nearby hamlet, borrowed a horse and set off after her in hot pursuit? Francesca's blood ran cold at the thought. No man ever relished the prospect of being bested by a woman. But the Duke, Francesca realised, would be so livid that he would probably set her down from her horse and make her walk into Winchester, with him lashing at her with his whip every inch of the way. Yes, thought Francesca, if he catches me now, whilst he is still in a white heat of rage, he will be merciless!

Francesca leaned forward in the saddle and goaded on the chestnut. Below her lay the red roofs of the city which was once the capital of England. She was, however, oblivious to the breathtaking view of the city, to the smell of the May blossom, and to the sweet song of the skylark in the blue sky overhead.

As she thundered down into Winchester, she had but one frantic thought in her head: to reach the safety of her aunt's house before the wrathful Duke caught up with her! As she rode through the cobbled streets, Francesca received the impression of an elegant, friendly city with red brick buildings, patterned with green from the plentiful trees.

A cheerful errand boy directed her to Upper Brook which Francesca soon realised was a street in the most fashionable part of the city. She found to her delight that number 11, her aunt's house, was an impressive Jacobean-styled residence, with dark oak beams forming a pleasing contrast to the gleaming white plaster work. As she entered the house, and gave her name to the footman, she cast one last apprehensive glance down the street. But it was empty, apart from a flower seller pushing a cart laden with pink and white cherry blossom.

With a sigh of relief, Francesca heard the front door of the house close behind her. She smiled as she considered her achievement. She had outwitted the arrogant Duke of Wexford, and evaded his retribution! A satisfactory morning's work indeed.

Still smiling Francesca, with a light step and a happy heart, entered her Aunt Cecilia's drawing room.

★　　★　　★

"This is outrageous!" screamed Lady Rothersay, aiming a punch at the beige velvet cushion on the sofa. "She has stepped beyond the bounds of civilised behaviour, Aithne! Why, if I were a man, I'd lose no time in taking a horsewhip to her!"

The fair-haired Aithne laid down the newspaper and rushed to her mother's side. "There must be some mistake, Mama! I am sure it was not meant. Lady Sombourne could not have intended to use you so shamefully!"

"Fiddle faddle!" snapped the greying woman, clawing in her fury at the brown tassels on the sofa, "This is all quite deliberate, Aithne! She means to humiliate me in front of all

Winchester. Well she shall not succeed. It is she who has thrown down the gauntlet. Very well, if it is a fight she desires, then a fight she shall have. And Aithne, I, Lady Rothersay, intend to win!"

"Oh well said!" cried Francesca impulsively from the door. The footman had, of course, announced her, but the two ladies in the brown and beige Drawing Room were so immersed in their own affairs that they had not noticed her entrance.

As Francesca spoke, Lady Rothersay straightened her back and demanded imperiously, "And just who might you be? Do you usually enter other people's drawing rooms, uninvited, and immediatley take part in a conversation that does not concern you?"

Francesca hastily dipped a curtsey. "I — I beg your pardon, Madam. But I assure you, although my face is unknown to you, my name is familiar. I am Francesca. Your sister's daughter."

Lady Rothersay said nothing. Slowly, her flinty eyes examined every inch of Francesca, missing nothing from the scuff on her left boot to the loose thread hanging from the collar of her riding habit.

"I regret I must declare myself appalled," she said in ringing tones. "That the daughter of my dear departed sister should dare to present herself before me in such a disreputable state! Why, I consider myself gravely insulted!"

Lady Rothersay stood up and shook out the folds of her grey silk dress. Pausing only to pick up a silver-topped cane from the sidetable, she advanced across the room towards her niece. Francesca, although understandably alarmed at her frosty welcome, boldly stood her ground as the gaunt, reed-thin woman descended on her. In fact, of the two young girls in the room, it was the golden-haired Aithne who looked the most alarmed as she cowered by the oak fire screen.

Lady Rothersay glided to a halt one foot from Francesca and, with a swift action of her wrist smacked the cane smartly against Francesca's left boot. Francesca winced. But, though her grey-green eyes blazed, pride forbade her to utter a sound.

"Your boots," snapped Lady Rothersay, "are covered in mud. Your skirt is torn. The front of your riding habit is unfastened. And the ends of your disgracefully unkempt hair are wet. In short, Francesca, you look as if you should be placed in a field and put to good use scaring the crows away!"

Francesca swallowed. She knew she had no defence. Oh dear, she thought, if only I had stopped for a few minutes to tidy myself before I entered the rarified atmosphere of this Drawing Room! But I was so relieved to have escaped the vengeful Duke that I did not give a thought to my disreputable appearance. If ever there was a case of jumping straight from the frying pan into the fire, then this is it!

"Well?" rapped Lady Rothersay. "Has the cat got your tongue, girl?"

Francesca rallied. "I . . . I am afraid I encountered somewhat difficult climatic conditions during the latter part of my ride here, Aunt. A . . . a sudden downpour on the Downs drenched my hair, and caused a great deal of mud."

"Rain?" enquired Lady Rothersay icily, with a lift of her sparse eyebrows.

"Yes, rain, Aunt," said Francesca desperately, paling at the thought of Lady Rothersay's reaction if she knew her niece had that morning been bathing totally unclothed in the waters of the Duke of Wexford's river.

Lady Rothersay said nothing, but turned dramatically to the window and gazed out at the bright sun shining in a cloudless blue sky. Aithne began to giggle, but hastily smothered her laughter with a cough as her mother rapped the silver-topped cane on the window seat.

"And would you be so good as to tell me, Francesca, how this mysterious rain came to drench you, and how your boots became so disgustingly muddied, when you were sitting within the confines of your father's coach?"

Francesca clenched her hands behind her back. She was caught, she knew it. Oh, she could invent a tale about the coach overturning and tipping her out into the rain-soaked road, but Lady Rothersay would be sure to check on her story. Francesca could see that one stammered prevarication would lead to another, with the result that her aunt would finally succeed in dragging onto the elegant drawing room carpet the shameful details of her niece's bathe in the Duke's river.

Far better, Francesca realised, thinking quickly, to admit to riding alone from Salisbury to Winchester. Once her aunt had vented her wrath over that episode, with luck Francesca would not be forced into admitting anything about her more watery adventures that morning.

Taking a deep breath, Francesca said bravely, "It was such a beautiful day, Aunt, I forsook the carriage, and rode on horseback along the Roman road from Salisbury."

As she made her confession, Francesca kept a careful eye on the silver-topped cane. But Lady Rothersay was so amazed and outraged that her entire body began to tremble.

"Aithne!" she cried. "Kindly help me to the sofa, and ring the bell for some brandy."

The terrified Aithne rushed to do her mother's bidding, settling cushions behind her back and sending a footman scurrying for the brandy. Francesca watched, fascinated. She had never before seen anyone speechless with rage but this was, quite clearly, what now afflicted Lady Rothersay.

However, a few sips of brandy were enough to restore the lady's powers of locution. "I blame myself," she murmured wearily, holding a hand to her head. "I should never have allowed my sister to marry the Earl of Marlow. I knew no good would come of it. After all, what is one to expect, with such bad blood in the family? The old Earl drank too much, gambled to excess and indulged in . . . "

She glanced guardedly at her daughter and murmured. "Well, let's just say he was completely lacking in decency and self discipline. And now, it seems his granddaughter has inherited all his worst qualities!"

Francesca bit back the laughter bubbling up inside her, and said meekly, "But Aunt, I assure you I never gamble, I take only one glass of wine at dinner and . . . "

"Be silent!" ordered Lady Rothersay. "It is obvious to me that he has left you a legacy of all his wild, wilful ways. Why, you even have the same appearance as his side of the family. They are all tall and dark with strong-boned faces. Admirable enough in a man, of course — your father is an exceedingly handsome man — but when it comes to the female side, these characteristics put you at a distinct disadvantage."

She held out her hand to her daughter, who came and sat on a velvet stool at her side. "Now Aithne resembles my side of the family. Such golden hair, such delicate features — oh, you are indeed as pretty as a picture my dear!"

As she smiled indulgently at the simpering Aithne, Francesca regarded her Dresden cousin with loathing. It had not escaped Francesca that, during the twenty minutes they had been together in this Drawing Room, Aithne had failed to say one word of greeting or welcome to her cousin and guest. In fact, Francesca realised, apart from a whispered, "Yes Mama" and "No Mama," Aithne had said precisely nothing at all.

Characteristically, Francesca decided to take the initiative in extending the hand of friendship to her cousin. "What a very pretty and unusual name you have," she smiled. "I have never before been acquainted with anyone called Aithne."

Aithne opened her rosebud mouth to speak, but Lady Rothersay was there before her. "Yes, isn't it charming?" she enthused. "It means *little fire*, you know. An apt choice of name, for dear Aithne has brought such warmth and light into our lives."

"Yes indeed, Aunt, I can well imagine," murmured Francesca, the merest glimmer of a smile dancing in her eyes as she regarded the milky-skinned, pale-haired, limp figure of the family's *little fire*.

Realising that by encouraging Lady Rothersay to talk about her family, she had successfully diverted the lady's attention from her own exploits on the road from Salisbury, Francesca pressed home her advantage:

"And Lord Rothersay. Am I fortunate enough to find him at home?"

"Oh, indeed not. He takes his responsibilities at the House of Lords extremely seriously. And then there are his other London duties also." Lady Rothersay's voice assumed a reverential note as she went on, "Lord Rothersay, you know, is one of the Prince Regent's most trusted advisers."

Lady Rothersay arose and assumed a bravely weary stance by the mantel. "It means, of course, that as my husband is so much in London I do not see as much of him as I would wish. But *sacrifice* and *duty* are burdens which all of Winchester knows I am proud to bear."

Francesca longed to break into wild applause at this splendidly melodramatic speech. But from Aithne's gravely admiring expression it was clear that Lady Rothersay was determined at all times to be taken seriously. Which was a pity, mused Francesca. For if she would just unbend a little and learn to laugh at herself, she would be a most interesting and entertaining personality.

The Drawing Room doors opened, and a footman entered to inform Lady Rothersay that Lord Compton had arrived.

"Kindly show him into the library," instructed Lady Rothersay, murmuring at Aithne, "Heavens, we cannot allow Lord Compton to see Francesca in such a disreputable state. Quickly, take her upstairs and show your cousin her bedchamber. She is in the Blue Room, is she not, next to yours?"

"Yes, Mama."

"Hurry both of you," cried Lady Rothersay, waving her hands and shoo-ing them from the room. "No, don't *run* Aithne! How many times must I tell you? Ladies never run. Just walk very fast!"

Feeling rather like a badly wrapped package marked *Not Wanted on Voyage*, Francesca allowed herself to be rushed upstairs.

"Would you care to see my room?" asked Aithne, ushering Francesca into a bedchamber decorated entirely in pink and white.

"Isn't it enchanting?" smiled Aithne, settling herself prettily on a rose velvet stool at her dressing table. "Mama says that pink is the most charming colour for ladies of all ages."

Francesca gazed at the deep rose bedcurtains, the pale pink carpet and the blush pink window-hangings, tasselled with white, and felt as if she had wandered into a nightmare wedding cake, decorated with over-sweet pink icing.

"Your bedchamber is not at all as pretty," Aithne went on in a smug tone. "It is blue, which Mama feels is a cold colour for furnishings, but as it is Papa's favourite she indulged him by having one room in the house decorated in that shade."

Smothering a yawn, Francesca remarked, "I was most impressed to hear that your father is an adviser to the Prince Regent. On what aspect of the country's affairs does the Prince consult Lord Rothersay?"

"Why, I have not the faintest notion," said Aithne indifferently. "I have never enquired."

"But are you not curious?" asked Francesca in surprise.

"Indeed not," said a shocked Aithne, twisting a golden curl round her finger. "Mama says it is most unfeminine for young ladies to ask questions of a political nature. Lady Sombourne, of course, disagrees. But then Lady Sombourne disagrees with everything Mama says, simply to be perverse."

"Ah yes, I seem to recall my aunt mentioning Lady Sombourne's name as I entered the Drawing Room," said Francesca. "I fear I made my entrance at an inconvenient time, as Lady Rothersay seemed greatly incensed by something."

Aithne's blue eyes widened. 'Mama was so enraged one could practically see the sparks shooting from her eyes! It is all because she has learned that Lady Sombourne is holding a charity ball for the Orphans of St Anne's in two weeks time."

Francesca nodded. "That sounds very admirable."

"Oh it is. Except for the fact that Lady Sombourne knew perfectly well that Mama has for months been planning her own charity ball for the Hospital of St. Cross on exactly the same date!"

"I am beginning to understand why she was so furious," said Francesca to her cousin's reflection in the glass as Aithne splashed rosewater onto her face. "The two ladies will now be in fierce competition to see who can persuade the most influential people of Winchester to attend her ball."

"Just so," said Aithne, patting a pretty rose blush onto her cheeks. "And to make matters worse from Mama's point of view, she opened the *Winchester Courier* today and found they had devoted a whole half page to Lady Sombourne's forthcoming ball. So the Winchester elite will now be convinced that it is Lady Sombourne's ball, and not Mama's, which will be *the* fashionable event of this Spring."

"Oh dear. So what is to be done?" wondered Francesca.

Aithne giggled. "Fear not, Cousin. Mama will think of something. She always does. What would be perfect is if she could let it be known that the Duke of Wexford had accepted for her ball. He alone in Winchester has the presence to draw the rest of the elite after him." She sighed. "But of course he will not come. He never accepts any invitations to balls."

Francesca was vastly relieved to hear it. The Duke of Wexford was one person whose presence she was anxious to avoid — unlike the rest of Winchester, who if Aithne was to be believed regarded him as second only in importance to the Prince Regent himself.

Nevertheless that night, as she lay in the coolly attractive Blue Bedchamber, her thoughts strayed back to the tall, fair-haired man whom she had first seen standing so angrily on the river bank. She understood now why he had been so anxious to accompany her into Winchester.

He knew, Francesca realised, exactly what my reception would be if I arrived at my aunt's house in my dishevelled, muddied state. By contrast, had I been covered from head to foot in mud and walked into the Drawing Room on the arm of the Duke of Wexford, I should have received the warmest welcome. The Duke understands what manner of woman my aunt is, and was trying to help me.

Francesca's cheeks burned with guilt as she recalled her high-handed dismissal of his gallantry. But it was partly his own fault, she argued. Had he told me exactly why he desired to escort me to my aunt's, then of course I should have been reasonable, and grateful too. But he, of course, would not condescend to explain his behaviour to a mere female like me. Oh no. Dukes are not accustomed to offering explanations, they simply announce their intentions and expect us lesser mortals to thank them humbly.

After half an hour of such thoughts, Francesca managed to convince herself that she was perfectly justified in behaving as she had towards the Duke. His attitude was arrogant and cavalier. Francesca was glad to hear that he rarely accepted invitations, for she had no desire for their paths to cross again.

And yet, despite these defiant thoughts, as she drifted into sleep Francesca's last vision was of a bowl of anemones — a mysteriously feminine touch in an uncompromisingly masculine domain.

2

Francesca's peaceful slumber was rudely disturbed the following morning by an insistent hammering and banging. Hastily she arose and dressed, and realised that the dreadful noise was coming from outside the house.

In the apricot Breakfast Parlour she found Aithne wincing at the sound of every hammer blow whilst Lady Rothersay was gazing stoically into the middle distance, her countenance set in a "'We Shall Overcome" expression.

"Ah, good morning Niece," she said, as Francesca bent to kiss her dry cheek. "I trust you slept well? That is a charming dress you are wearing. Green becomes you well."

Francesca's murmured thanks for the compliment were interrupted by a long groan from Aithne.

"Aithne *please*," said Lady Rothersay in a long-suffering tone. "Will you kindly refrain from behaving as if each strike of the workman's hammer is being directed straight at your head."

"But Mama," wailed *little fire*, "the noise is hurting my head excessively!"

Francesca was in sympathy with her. The crashing, sawing and banging were indeed reaching deafening proportions, and the crystal chandelier above Aithne's golden head was beginning to shake in the most alarming fashion.

"To be sure, Aithne, we all find the noise somewhat irritating, but it simply cannot be helped," said Lady Rothersay firmly. "It is vital that I have the work on the house done now, before your father returns in the summer."

"What is being done to the house, Aunt?" enquired Francesca, remembering just in time the strictures of her old Nanny, and taking the smallest piece of cold meat from the silver dish.

"I am having the house brought up to date," Lady Rothersay informed her niece. "All those beams were so dreadfully old-fashioned, I could not bear them a moment longer. So the workmen are covering them up, and putting in a raised parapet to conceal the roof line, and I am toying with the notion of having pretty bow windows as well."

Francesca was appalled. She had noticed on her arrival in Upper Brook that the house was one of the finest Jacobean buildings she had ever seen. Now, merely for the sake of a fashionable facade, her aunt was set on destroying the whole character of the house.

"Lord Rothersay will not, I admit, be pleased," went on Lady Rothersay, "but if I present him with a *fait accompli* he will shout and rage for a day but there will be nothing he can do about it."

"Oh Mama," said Aithne fearfully, "you know he expressly forbade you to change anything about this house."

"Only because King Charles II himself gave it to our family," said Lady Rothersay, raising an eyebrow as Francesca unthinkingly took a third piece of toast. "But King Charles has been dead for over one hundred years, King George III is now our monarch and I desire a residence that suits the age in which I live, rather than a shrine to days gone by."

"Why did King Charles give the Rothersays this house?" enquired Francesca with interest. She had read a great deal about this most dashing of English monarchs and was always eager to learn new facts about him.

"Winchester has strong connections with King Charles," smiled Lady Rothersay. "He ordered a palace to be built here, though unfortunately it was never finished. But during the regime of that vulgar Cromwell individual, six of Winchester's families were instrumental in giving refuge and help to the ousted King. And when he was restored to the throne, he did not forget those who had remained loyal to him. He held a magnificent banquet and each of the six families was presented with a magnificent golden goblet, each encrusted with a different jewel."

"Ours is encrusted with diamonds," said Aithne proudly. "I will show it to you later, Francesca."

"In addition," said Lady Rothersay, raising her voice over the deafening hammering, "the Earl of Rothersay was given this house, as his own residence had been razed to the ground by the rebels."

"What a romantic tale," breathed Francesca, quite entranced. "The golden goblets must by now be quite priceless."

"Indeed yes," agreed Lady Rothersay. "Ours is certainly one of the family's most treasured possessions. Poor Lady Sombourne turns green with envy whenever she sets eyes on it." Lady Rothersay gave a little sigh of satisfaction at the thought of her rival's discomfiture.

Then she rose to her feet and said briskly, "Come. We shall call on the dressmaker, Aithne, and inspect her progress on our dresses for the charity ball. And of course it will be necessary to have Francesca fitted for a new gown."

"That is extremely kind of you, aunt," said Francesca, "but I have brought with me a very pretty blue ballgown."

Lady Rothersay raised an eyebrow. "And how long, may I ask, have you owned this pretty blue gown?"

Francesca blushed. "For . . . for three seasons, Aunt."

Aithne tittered. "Heavens, Francesca, everyone in Dorset must be overly familiar with each worn thread of that dress by now."

"I am extremely fond of this particular gown," Francesca declared stoutly.

"You shall have something new and that's an end to it," said Lady Rothersay in a voice which brooked no argument. "I have no intention of allowing any niece of mine to appear before the Winchester elite at my ball wearing a tattered three-year-old dress."

"But will the *ton* be present at your ball, Mama?" quavered Aithne, smoothing the lace on her pink muslin dress. "Lady Som — "

"No more!" commanded Lady Rothersay, raising a dramatic hand. "I have never yet been bested by Lady Sombourne, and I do not propose to start now. Mercy me, Aithne remember we can trace our family right back to the Norman Conquest. Lady Sombourne goes no further back than the Plantagenets. Do you seriously imagine that someone with my antecedents could possibly be outmanoeuvered by an upstart like her?"

"No Mama," murmured a quenched *little fire.*

★　　★　　★

The main thoroughfare was, of course, the High Street, which ascended gently through the entire length of the city, presenting a pleasing array of gabled houses and low arcades. But it was the solemn grandeur of the celebrated Cathedral which most delighted Francesca, with its low Norman tower and perpendicular nave, silver-grey against the cloudless blue sky. She would have liked to linger awhile on the strikingly beautiful avenue of limes leading to the West Front, but Lady Rothersay hurried her away, asserting that there was much to be done that morning.

At the modiste's in Hyde Street, Lady Rothersay immediately took charge. When she had inspected her own half-finished peach silk gown, and her daughter's inevitable pale pink creation, she turned her attention to Francesca. With the dressmaker in meek attendance, she patrolled up and down the bales of material, fingering each piece of fabric for its quality, weight and tendency to crease.

"I do believe this lavender satin would look fine on you, Francesca," she declared at last, tapping the bale with her parasol.

Francesca recoiled in horror as she regarded the fabric. Lavender, she knew, was the least becoming colour for someone with her healthily clear skin and dark hair. Lavender was for pale complexioned blondes of the English rose type. But how was she to express these feelings to her aunt? Francesca was only too aware by now that once Lady Rothersay had made up her mind on an issue, she was not easily dissuaded.

Francesca, however, possessed a will just as strong as her aunt's — and quick wits too. "The lavender is quite exquisite, aunt," she enthused. "But do you think it would be a wise choice in view of the fact that you are wearing peach and Aithne will be gowned in that pale rosy pink? Would it not be more graceful for us to wear colours complimentary to each other?"

Lady Rothersay frowned. "Mmm. Yes, that lavender would make you stand out rather. Well, we shall have to find something else for you Francesca."

She glanced round, and noticed that Francesca was standing with her hand resting casually on a bale of deep cream satin into which was woven a fine gold thread.

"Ah, move aside now Francesca, I do believe I've found just the fabric. You will tone in very nicely in that cream. You will do respectable credit to the family, but there will be no suggestion that you are putting yourself forward."

"But Mama," protested Aithne, "that satin has a lovely gold thread in it, whereas my pink crêpe is boringly plain!"

Seeing Lady Rothersay beginning to waver, Francesca said quickly, "But Aithne, you have the advantage that you will be wearing those beautiful diamonds you showed me yesterday. Such an exquisite necklace needs no competition from an overadorned dress. And I have no jewellery to wear, apart from my simple gold chain."

"Heavens!" exclaimed Aithne, "You must be dreadfully poor, Francesca."

"Aithne!" rapped Lady Rothersay sharply with a glance at the interested dressmaker. "That is settled, then. The cream satin it is. The modiste will take your measurements now, Francesca, and you will meet us in twenty minutes at the goldsmiths in the High Street."

Francesca joined the ladies as arranged, and endured a tedious half hour whilst Lady Rothersay interrogated the goldsmith on the merits of the setting for the sapphire brooch she had decided her husband was to give her for her birthday. It was as they were leaving the goldsmith's that Aithne uttered a little cry of alarm:

"Oh Mama. See, there is Lady Sombourne coming towards us!"

"Compose yourself, Aithne!" ordered Lady Rothersay, straightening her back and squaring her thin shoulders.

Francesca followed Aithne's wide-eyed gaze, and took stock of Lady Rothersay's arch rival. Lady Sombourne was a short, well-upholstered woman in her middle years, dressed in a high-waisted blue silk gown.

"That waist line is one inch too high for this year's fashion," hissed Lady Rothersay in a low voice. "And what an absurd choice of bonnet for Clorinda. Those double yellow ribbons only serve to emphasise all her chins."

This last barb was directed against the bun-faced girl accompanying Lady Sombourne. Francesca brightened as the two ladies advanced at a stately pace towards one another. My, now the fur would fly! Francesca couldn't wait to see who would come off best in the confrontation. She held her breath in delighted anticipation as the rivals halted a foot away from one another.

Lady Rothersay was the first to speak. "My dear Lady Sombourne!" she trilled. "How delightful to see you. And your charming niece, too. That is a most attractive bonnet you are wearing, Clorinda!"

Lady Sombourne gave a sweet smile, "Indeed, Clorinda has such exquisite taste. But how well you are looking, Lady Rothersay. And dearest Aithne too. This gracefully tall young lady must be your niece from Dorsetshire about whom I've heard so many good things."

Francesca dipped a curtsey and stood demurely side by side with Aithne whilst the two older ladies exchanged pleasantries about the temperate spring day. As she listened, Francesca was consumed with disappointment. She had expected, if not physical blows in the Winchester thoroughfare, at least an entertaining verbal tussle. But instead, Lady Rothersay and Lady Sombourne were behaving for all the world as if they were the dearest, most intimate friends.

Francesca was grateful for the diversion when a dark-haired man in a dashing wine-red coat paused to raise his hat to Lady Sombourne as he rode past. Lady Sombourne favoured him with a gracious smile, and a slight bow.

"That was Sir Peter Jamieson," she said, waving a plump hand in his direction. "He is the new proprietor of the *Winchester Courier*. A charming individual."

"Indeed?" replied Lady Rothersay with smiling disdain. "I never cease to envy your wide circle of acquaintances Lady Sombourne. It is a matter of great regret to me that my husband will only allow me to associate with those on the same social level as ourselves."

"Ah yes, how is dear Lord Rothersay?" enquired Lady Sombourne smoothly. "Lord Sombourne and I often say, as we sit peacefully together in the evenings, how brave it is of you to continue your life here on your own. We both admire enormously the manner in which never a word of complaint passes your lips about the increasingly long absences of your husband."

Francesca was bored no longer. Ah, this was better! Now the two ladies were beginning to release their ammunition.

Lady Rothersay gazed vaguely London-wards over the head of her rival. "Since Norman times Duty has been the watchword in our family. It has been our fate to be called to the service of Kings — and whether it be Charles II or as now, the Prince Regent to whom my lord is an adviser, we Rothersays have never shirked our loyal task. If the Prince Regent requires my husband in London then it is a sacrifice I am happy and proud to make."

Amused, Francesca watched Lady Sombourne's brown eyes narrow, "And is it likely, do you imagine, that the Prince will relinquish the services of his valuable adviser for a day to permit him to honour your charity ball?"

So, thought Francesca, the preliminaries were over! Now the battle would really commence!

"Oh, it is all extremely complicated," said Lady Rothersay airily, "I am afraid I am not permitted to say too much, because delicate affairs of State are involved. I'm sure you understand, my dear."

From Lady Sombourne's triumphant smile, it was clear that she did understand only too well. Lord Rothersay would attend the ball, or not, just as the whim took him. She pressed home her advantage. "I am only sorry that I and Lord Sombourne will be unable to attend your ball, Lady Rothersay. But, as you may have read in the *Winchester Courier*, my own charity ball for the Orphans of St Anne's falls on the same day as yours!"

"Yes, it is most distressing for you," said Lady Rothersay with concern. "It worries me that you may not find enough people to attend, for naturally the elite of Winchester will be patronising *my* ball for the Hospital of St Cross."

Lady Sombourne was not at all put out. "I fear you have been misinformed, Lady Rothersay. I am confident of an excellent attendance, especially when people hear whispers of the important announcement which will be made that night."

Francesca sensed a stiffening in Lady Rothersay. "Announcement, Lady Sombourne?"

Lady Sombourne laid a gloved hand on the arm of her niece. "Ah, the child is blushing!"

"But Aunt," whispered Clorinda, "It is supposed to be a secret!"

"Oh come now," protested Lady Sombourne. "Surely you can have no objection to such a dear and trusted friend as Lady Rothersay hearing your good news?" She beamed at the taller woman. "I want you to be the very first to know, Lady Rothersay. On the night of my charity ball, the engagement will be announced between Clorinda here and Viscount Polesdon."

The ladies standing blocking the pavement in the High Street were instantly aflutter with cries of surprise and delight.

"A betrothal! Oh my dear Clorinda I am so happy for you! Aithne, is that not wonderful news?"

"Indeed yes! How exciting, Clorinda. Oh, you must

come riding with me some day soon and tell me all! I am in a fever of impatience to hear every detail of the romance!"

But Francesca's sharp eyes had noticed that Lady Rothersay's parasol was being ground hard round and round on the cobbled road. And Aithne's hands, behind her back, were clamped hard together, her nails tearing ruthlessly into her gloved palms.

"The Viscount is a charming man," declared Lady Sombourne. "It is an excellent match to be sure."

Lady Rothersay nodded. "To be sure, I am confident you will find his maturity a great asset, Clorinda. How wise of you to choose a man who has travelled beyond the follies of youth."

"He is only just in his fortieth year," said Clorinda, clearly stung. "I do not consider that old at all."

"But of course not!" exclaimed Lady Roterhsay soothingly, "And in any event, I have always considered you an extremely mature girl, Clorinda, for your eighteen years. The difference of twenty-one years between you does not signify at all."

Francesca hid a smile as Lady Sombourne charged to the rescue. "It will be sad for Aithne losing the friend she grew up with. But marriage, and all its responsibilities, claims us all in the end. I'm sure it will soon be your turn, Aithne dear."

Lady Rothersay was equal to the occasion. "Oh, Aithne has so many beaux I am quite dizzied by them all."

"I am delighted to hear it," smiled Lady Sombourne. "No doubt you will be passing on your spares to your cousin Francesca. What a gay time you two girls will have!" She reached forward and gave Lady Rothersay a sympathetic glance. "And what a time ahead for you, my dear, with two unmarried girls on your hands!" She started as the High Street clock stuck twelve. "Oh, is that the hour!

Come Clorinda, we have your trousseau to arrange, the guest list to think about, oh so much to do!"

And with much bowing, expressions of affection and promises to meet again very soon, the ladies parted company.

It was but a short step back to the Rothersay house in Upper Brook. Lady Rothersay and Aithne said not a word on the journey. But, as she swept through her front hall, Lady Rothersay snapped her fingers at a footman and told him to dismiss the hammering workmen for the day.

"My head," she moaned as she collapsed onto the Drawing Room sofa, "feels ready to split asunder."

Aithne was in such an agitated state she could not remain still. "Oh Mama!" she wailed, "what are we to do? Clorinda is six months younger than I, and she is fat and stupid, and she is already betrothed! It isn't fair!" She stood at the window, tore off her gloves and bonnet and threw them down furiously on the window seat.

"Come away from the window," ordered Lady Rothersay. "Do you want everyone who passes to see your face contorted in such rage?"

"But Clorinda — "

"She is engaged to a portly, forty-year-old Viscount with bad breath and no great fortune. We can do better than that for you, Aithne!"

Aithne stamped her foot. "But I have not received a single proposal! And I am far prettier than Clorinda."

In an attempt to ease the tension in the Drawing Room, Francesca suggested, "Would you care for me to ring the bell for some refreshments, Aunt? After a glass of wine and something to eat, I'm sure all our spirits will be revived."

"That is a sensible notion, Francesca," agreed Lady Rothersay. And as Aithne opened her mouth to bewail her plight once more, she said, "Now please be quiet for a while, Aithne, and let me think. This has been a disastrous week. First the business of our two charity balls being held on the same day, and now Clorinda is to have the glory of an engagement. It is all quite dreadful. But a solution must and will be found.''

As the wine and sweet biscuits were brought in, Francesca settled herself quietly on the window seat and smiled wryly to herself. She felt a sense of bitter amusement at her aunt's use of the terms disastrous and dreadful. She knew that back in Dorsetshire, her father would be worrying about Edward's school fees, whether the servants' wages could be met and how he was to raise the funds to deal with the hole in the west wing roof. Yet here were Lady Rothersay and Aithne, working themselves into a suicidal state over the matter of a ball and an engagement!

The morning had, she reflected, been most revealing in its exposure of the artificiality of life here in Winchester. First there had been the matter of Lady Rothersay's insistence on destroying a beautiful Jacobean house in favour of a fashionable contemporary facade. Francesca's heart cried out at such wanton destruction of England's heritage.

But to Lady Rothersay, she mused, appearances are paramount. Witness her behaviour with Lady Sombourne this morning. Instead of confronting her rival and expressing herself plainly and forcibly, there had been the farce of pretended friendship, charitable feelings and good will. What nonsense it all is, thought Francesca hotly. What unbearable, constricting, time wasting, dishonest nonsense! More than ever, Francesca appreciated the honest simplicity of the life she led at home at Marlow Manor. They were far from rich, it was true, and because of the family's difficult financial situation they entertained only rarely.

But although our social circle is small, it is one rich in

genuine warmth and friendship, she thought. When the fire broke out in our stables last year, everyone from the surrounding houses rushed immediately to our aid. Even Lady Bentworth who is in her eightieth year, came rushing over in a carriage filled with buckets of water! And when Lord Stimpson was stricken with gout, we all took turn and turn about to visit him and allow him to beat us at backgammon. Yes, in Marlow there is a wonderful sense of good neighbourliness, of community spirit. And when feuds erupt, as they inevitably do, there is no coy pretence of sweeping the matter under the social carpet. There's a blazing row. Blows may be exchanged. But the matter is settled, to everyone's satisfaction. Which to my mind is far healthier than smiling, and simpering and pretending all is well, whilst underneath both parties are festering with undeclared resentment.

Glancing round the elegant brown and beige Drawing Room it was apparent to Francesca that Aithne was smouldering with resentment. Her wine was untouched and she was sitting with her mouth downcast, sulkily unravelling the pink threads of her girdle.

Lady Rothersay sat with closed eyes, her face drawn, her long fingers beating a tattoo on the rim of her Wedgwood plate. After some time, she crumpled her napkin, smoothed her skirt and announced:

"Very well. Let us deal sensibly and calmly with each problem in turn."

Aithne brightened and, with her blue eyes full of hope, rushed to sit on the stool at her mother's feet. "Oh Mama, what have you decided? What is to be done?"

"Short of shooting Viscount Polesdon, there appears to be no way in which we can prevent Clorinda and Lady Sombourne from glorying in the announcement of the engagement," said Lady Rothersay thoughtfully. "The ideal solution, of course, would be for us to be able to announce your betrothal, Aithne, to a gentleman of higher rank than the Viscount. But with our ball less than two weeks away, the prospects of a suitable beau appearing out of the blue are somewhat dim."

"It's so beastly of Clorinda to have become engaged to a Viscount," pouted Aithne. "Now it is absolutely imperative that I marry someone of higher rank. But who?"

Lady Rothersay arose, and crossed to the walnut bureau in the alcove. Taking a silver key from her reticule, she opened a drawer and took out a sheet of paper. Returning to the sofa, she settled a cushion behind her and said with a sigh, "What we have here, Aithne, is a list of gentlemen who would make suitable escorts for you at the ball. If we can find someone celebrated enough, although it won't be the same as an engagement announcement of course, it will detract somewhat from the impact of Clorinda's betrothal."

Francesca sipped her wine. From her short acquaintanceship with Aithne, she could summon little liking for her cousin. Yet at this turn of events, she could not but feel sorry for her. How terrible to be so spineless that she was not capable of attracting and choosing her own beaux! Francesca found it impossible to imagine a situation whereby someone else sat with list in hand, deciding who was to be pressganged into escorting her to a ball.

"I agree, it is extremely aggravating of Clorinda to have captured a Viscount," murmured Lady Rothersay, "for I had in mind Viscount Medway for you, Aithne."

"Viscount Medway!" screamed Aithne, her pink and white face contorted. "But Mama, he is even older than Clorinda's fiance! He has grey hair, and in his breeches, his legs are all knotted with horrid veins!"

Lady Rothersay gazed at her severely. "Aithne, never again let me hear you mention the subject of a gentleman's legs! Well bred young ladies do not notice such things. Is that clearly understood?"

"Yes Mama," Her eyes filled with tears. "It is so vexing! All the young, eligible men are away in London, enjoying the Season. There is no one of any substance left in Hampshire . . . apart from the Duke of Wexford of course."

"Aithne!" said Lady Rothersay in an exasperated tone, "you must appreciate that it is beyond even my considerable influence and powers of persuasion to make the Duke of Wexford escort you to the ball. You know perfectly well he never shows his face at such events."

And, thought Francesca, her eyes dancing with laughter, I cannot imagine a man of the Duke's stature taking kindly to the idea that he should escort a girl who begins every other sentence with the chilling words, *Mama says* . . .

"No," said Lady Rothersay firmly, "I have decided to approach the Earl of Featherstone on your behalf Aithne."

"Oh Mama," groaned Aithne. "He has been married before. He has four dreadful children and he smells of manure."

"I am sure you will grow to like him on better acquaintance. You must trust in me, Aithne. Have I not always know what is best for you?"

"Yes Mama." Aithne's shoulders drooped disconsolately. "I must find someone to marry me! In six months time I shall be eighteen! Oh the shame of being unwed at such an age, especially with Clorinda showing off her new wedding band."

Francesca laughed. "Oh Aithne, I assure you it is not such a tragedy to be unwed! Why, I am twenty-one years of age and I am happy to be free."

Aithne dismissed her with a scornful glance. "It isn't the same for you, Francesca. You can go back to your rural life in Dorset and die a happy old maid. Everyone knows how poor you are, and what with that and your forthright manner no man would want to marry you. But I belong to one of the first families in Winchester. My marriage, *when* it happens, will be the social event of the year. I simply cannot be seen to be sitting on the shelf gathering dust as each birthday looms.''

Aithne sank back against the arm of the sofa, exhausted with the effort of making such a long speech without the benefit of any prompting from her mother.

Lady Rothersay frowned. ''You are partly right and partly wrong, Aithne. I agree absolutely with your view of your position in Winchester society. But you are wrong in your remarks about Francesca. Of course it is important that she marries. And soon. Why do you think I wrote to her father and suggested that she come to reside with us here?''

Francesca coloured. ''I assure you, Aunt, I have no wish to marry. Apart from the fact that I am perfectly content as I am, I have yet to meet a man to whom I could give my heart and my love.''

''Love?'' snapped Lady Rothersay. ''What nonsense is this? Your father is practically destitute. You arrive in my house looking like a walking scarecrow with a three year old ballgown in your box, and you dare to talk to me about finding a man to love? Surely you realise it is your duty to your family to find yourself a rich husband who will salvage the de Lisle fortunes?''

Francesca stood up and faced her aunt boldly. ''Two years ago, the Earl of Stimpson offered for my hand. Although I did not love him, I told my father I was willing to marry him for the exact reasons you mentioned. My father was horrified at the suggestion and made it clear to me that on no account would he allow me to marry without love in my heart. We discussed the matter long into the night, and he made me promise that, however much financial hardship we suffered, I would never wed purely for money."

Francesca turned away, her lovely eyes stinging with tears as she remembered that night, sitting at her father's feet in the Marlow Manor library. In the peaceful room, the light from the log fire flickering on the leather bound books, the Earl had talked of his great love for Francesca's dead mother. Holding Francesca's hands in his, he had told his daughter gruffly.

"Have the patience to wait, Francesca. Wait for love to enter your life. For when it does, it will bring you greater and more long-lasting joy than any vast fortune. The capacity to love is not given to everyone on this earth, but I sense it in you, my daughter. Like your mother before you, there is fire and passion within you. One day, you will meet a man who will kindle that fire and make it blaze into a great and enduring love. You are very precious to me, Francesca, and I will not see you squandered. Take my advice and wait, and I promise you will not be disappointed."

"Your father is a romantic fool," declared Lady Rothersay harshly. "I shall listen to no more of your soft-headed ramblings. As your aunt, I consider it my duty to find you a reasonably wealthy husband. Now," frowning, she perused her list of candidates. "Well, it seems to me that as Viscount Medway is no longer suitable for Aithne, he had best become your beau, Francesca. Who knows, if you behave towards him in a proper, ladylike manner, within a month or so you could return to Marlow Manor as Viscountess Medway!"

Francesca's eyes blazed with fury. I don't care, she thought, if I am sent home in disgrace on the next stage. I will not be treated thus! I will not allow my aunt to sit here with her wretched list, graciously handing out men like alms to the grateful poor. I shall speak my mind, and make my position clear to my aunt once and for all!

But as she drew breath to launch into a stream of vitriolic invective, the doors opened and a footman advanced into the room bearing a package on a silver salver. "This has just been delivered for the Lady Francesca, my lady," he informed Lady Rothersay.

"Oh yes, it is probably a selection of ribbon trimmings for your ballgown, Francesca," said Lady Rothersay, blissfully unaware of how the package's arrival had rescued her from a verbal whipping at the hands of her niece. "Kindly open it immediately, Francesca, and I will tell you which of the ribbons will be most suitable."

Francesca was so angry she could scarcely control her trembling hands long enough to tear open the box. As she began to wrench off the lid, it crossed her mind that the package felt rather too heavy to contain ribbons. Reaching into the box, she realised she was right. It contained a dome-shaped object, wrapped in a length of dark blue velvet.

Curiously, she cast aside the velvet to reveal a riding hat. As she did so her nose began to prickle, her throat constricted and she found herself convulsed with a violent fit of sneezing. The riding hat fell to the floor as she blindly reached for her handkerchief, her eyes streaming, her sneezing continuing unabated.

Lady Rothersay recoiled in horror. "What absurdity is this, Francesca?" she demanded. "Kindly leave the room until you have gained control of yourself."

Francesca was only too glad to make an escape. Pausing only to scoop up the riding hat and the velvet, she rushed up to her bedchamber. There she flung the offending objects into her water pitcher, and collapsed onto the bed with her handkerchief over her face.

Gradually, the sneezing fit subsided, and Francesca mopped the tears from her face. But by now they were tears of laughter.

That incorrigible Duke, she laughed, has paid me back in my own coin! Oh yes, I must hand it to him. It was a masterly jest and timed to perfection to cause me the utmost discomfiture before my aunt and cousin!

I should have known that he would not just sit back and meekly accept the manner in which I bested him on the Roman road when I was on my way to Winchester. He must have realised that I utilised pepper that day, and determined to turn the tables on me.

Still laughing, Francesca crossed to her toilette table where she splashed rosewater on her face and tidied her hair. Her grey-green eyes were sparkling, and she felt suddenly restored to good humour. Somehow, the arrival of the package had succeeded in putting all the events of the morning into perspective.

How foolish of me to be on the verge of losing my temper with my aunt at her suggestion that I should charm Viscount Medway into marrying me, mused Francesca. The notion is absurd, of course. It is simply not in my nature to simper, and flutter my eyelashes, and employ feminine wiles to snare a man. But my aunt belongs to a society, and a generation which believes that this is the right and proper thing to do. I am a guest under her roof, and it would distress my father if family relations were put under strain by my being sent home in disgrace because I was rude to my aunt.

What I must do, then, is humour Aunt Cecilia. When in her presence I must present the appearance of a docile, grateful niece. But even if she does succeed in throwing Viscount Medway and me together, she will be far too occupied with Aithne to have the time to supervise my behaviour with my beau. So when my aunt is out of earshot, I shall have plenty of opportunity to deter the Viscount. And when my three months in Hampshire are over, I shall return to my beloved home in exactly the same state that I left it, lighthearted, free and blissfully unmarried!

3

Lady Rothersay eyed Francesca with disfavour as the dark-haired girl returned to the Drawing Room.

"Now, Francesca. Perhaps you would be so good as to explain your extraordinary behaviour. Who sent you that riding hat? And why was it covered in pepper?"

Francesca repressed a gurgle of mirth at the thought of her aunt's reaction if she told her the truth. That the highly respected Duke of Wexford had . . . oh no! Her aunt's interrogation, Francesca realised, would continue for hours, probably days. Clearly, evasive measures were called for — and swiftly!

"I beg your pardon for causing such a commotion in your Drawing Room, Aunt Cecilia," said Francesca demurely. "I regret to say that the entire episode was a foolish prank of my young brother Edward's. I fear he has yet to outgrow his love of practical jokes."

Lady Rothersay sighed. "Obviously, the standard of discipline of Eton is going rapidly downhill. I shall ask Lord Rothersay to speak to the Prince Regent on the matter."

"Yes, Aunt," murmured Francesca, in what she considered to be a creditable imitation of Aithne's *Yes, Mama.*

"We must now concentrate our minds on the matter of

the charity ball," said Lady Rothersay. "It is of course essential that my ball for the Hospital of St Cross attracts more attention and raises more money than Lady Sombourne's for the Orphans of St. Anne."

Aithne toyed with the petals of the white lilac on the sidetable. "But Lady Sombourne already has the advantage, Mama, after that half page was devoted to her in the *Winchester Courirer*.

"Yes, well I shall expect the newspaper to have the decency to give me the same coverage for my ball," snapped Lady Rothersay.

"If I might make a suggestion, Aunt," ventured Francesca, who was seated on a straight-backed chair near the bureau. "Would it not be a sensible notion to ensure that the newspaper looks favourably on your ball by quietly becoming acquainted with the proprietor. I seem to recall that Lady Sombourne this morning pointed him out as he rode past us in the town."

Lady Rothersay sniffed. "Indeed so, Francesca. She was smiling and waving at the man for all the world as if he were the Prince Regent himself. What was the man's name, now? Jenson . . . Jarmi — "

"Jamieson," said Aithne, "Sir Peter Jamieson."

"Why do we not try to beat Lady Sombourne at her own game," said Francesca, taking a leaf out of the Duke of Wexford's book. "Clearly, she has devoted a considerable amount of time to cultivating Sir Peter. And the results, it has to be faced, have been excellent. Could you not call on Sir Peter, Aunt? I am sure he would be so honoured that he would be most obliging in the matter of spreading the word, in print, about your ball."

Lady Rothersay sat straight up on the brown velvet sofa. "Are you in your right mind, Francesca? Are you seriously suggesting that I, Lady Cecilia Rothersay, a member of one of the most important families in Winchester, should call on a common trader?"

Francesca repressed a sigh of exasperation. "I don't believe Sir Peter actually gets ink on his hands, Aunt. He is the proprietor not the printer. And ultimately it is he who decides what shall be included in the newspaper."

She waited as Lady Rothersay struggled with herself. The only sounds in the room were the ticking of the carriage clock on the mantel, and the nervous tap of Aithne's foot on the brass fender.

"It is no good," Lady Rothersay burst out at last, "I have my position in society to think of, Francesca. Not for all the newspaper coverage in the world could I allow myself to be seen calling on anyone who is involved in trade."

Thoroughly annoyed at her aunt's snobbish attitude, Francesca resolved to have nothing further to do with the planning of the charity ball. As far as I am concerned, thought Francesca, I don't give a bean if no one attends and Aunt Cecilia is the laughing stock of the whole city. It will all be her own silly fault.

Then she heard Aithne's piping voice: "Why cannot Francesca make contact with Sir Peter? Francesca has no social standing in Winchester, apart from the fact that she is related to us. Surely it would not be amiss for her to be seen in the company of a tradesman?"

Lady Rothersay's brown eyes narrowed. "Mmm. Yes, I think you have something there. We shall send Francesca to see Sir Peter and persuade him, in the most tactful manner of course, to have one of his minions write in glowing terms about my ball. What a capital notion, Aithne!"

"Would you care for me to call on Sir Peter this very afternoon, Aunt?" asked Francesca, delighted at the prospect of escaping from the house.

Lady Rothersay shook her head. "Certainly not. Remember we saw him in town only this morning. We do not wish him to think we are chasing after him. And besides, we have yet to think up a convincing reason for your visit."

Francesca was confused. "But Aunt, I thought I was to call on Sir Peter to persuade him — "

A weary sigh escaped from Lady Rothersay. "Heavens, Francesca, have you no sense of propriety at all? Clearly, at your home in rural Dorsetshire, it is quite accepted practice for unmarried girls to go calling on unmarried gentlemen. But here in Winchester such behaviour is quite unthinkable."

"I beg your pardon, Aunt," said a perplexed Francesca. "I was under the impression that you yourself agreed with Aithne that I should visit Sir Peter."

"Quite so," continued Lady Rothersay, in a slow, patient tone, "But we must think of a way to make it look as if you are not calling on him. Do you understand?"

No, Francesca did not understand. She felt as if she had been led into the middle of a maze and left there, alone in the dark.

But gradually all was revealed to her. Aithne was sent to fetch the previous week's edition of the *Winchester Courier* from the Morning Room. Lady Rothersay riffled through the pages, and at last jabbed triumphantly at a small item.

"Ah! I knew I'd seen the name Jamieson somewhere recently. Listen to this: *The Honourable Mrs Elizabeth Jamieson of Penn House, Dorset is visiting Winchester for a week before she travels north to join the Duke of Devonshire's party at Chatsworth. In Winchester, she is residing with her nephew, Sir Peter Jamieson at Chilcombe Lodge.*"

Lady Rothersay went on, directing her remarks to Francesca, "Mrs Jamieson is from Dorsetshire. You are acquainted with her of course?"

"No, in truth I have never heard of the lady," admitted

Francesca. "Dorsetshire is a large county, Aunt, and we have but a small social circle."

Lady Rothersay held a weary hand to her head. "Really, Francesca, you can be so trying at times! Please do endeavour to be more co-operative!"

"But Aunt," Francesca protested reasonably, "it is not my fault that I have never been introduced to the lady you speak of."

"Francesca," intoned Lady Rothersay chillingly, "You will knock on the front door of Sir Peter's residence, and you will announce to the footman that you have come to call on the Honourable Mrs Elizabeth Jamieson."

"But she won't be there," exclaimed Aithne. "It says here in the newspaper that she was residing in Winchester for only seven days. She will have departed yesterday."

"Precisely," said Lady Rothersay heavily. "Sir Peter, who will have peered out of an upstairs window and observed the Rothersay coat of arms on the carriage, will hasten down to greet you, Francesca. You will express dismay and regret that Mrs Jamieson has departed because as an acquaintance of long standing you had hoped to enjoy a long talk with her about the delights of Dorsetshire. Sir Peter will in his turn express dismay and regret that you have travelled to the house to no avail, and gallantly he will usher you into his Drawing Room and offer you refreshment. Which you, my dear Niece, will prettily accept."

Francesca was seized with an overpowering urge to burst into wild, hysterical laughter. Quickly, she dropped to the floor and occupied herself gathering together the pages of the *Winchester Courier* which Aithne had scattered so carelessly over the carpet.

Really, she thought, my aunt is quite priceless! I can't help thinking that it is wrong that it should be Lord Rothersay who is adviser to the Prince Regent. For with my aunt's quick wits and devious mind, it is surely she who would make the most able politician!

For the life of her, Francesca could still not understand why it was socially impossible for her simply to mount the steps of Chilcombe Lodge, and ask to see Sir Peter Jamieson. The charade involving Mrs Elizabeth Jamieson struck Francesca as not just absurd, but totally unecessary. However, she had resolved to humour her aunt, so she listened carefully to her instructions, and made no more protests even when Lady Rothersay said archly.

"And when you enter Sir Peter's Drawing Room do try, Francesca, to take small, neat little steps. I have noticed you have a distressing tendency to stride. Remember, the entire reputation of the family rests on your shoulders. Which reminds me. Are you aware that the shoulder seam on your dress has split? Is this bad workmanship, Niece, or are you wearing yet another antediluvian gown?"

★   ★   ★

What am I going to do, wondered Francesca as the luxuriously appointed Rothersay carriage traversed the cobbled streets of Winchester, if Mrs Elizabeth Jamieson has decided to extend her stay? Oh what fun that would be.

Smiling, Francesca leaned back against the chocolate brown velvet seat and regarded with interest the views from the carriage window. She was so elated to be away from the constricting presence of her aunt, that she was sure nothing could go wrong today. Even the weather smiled kindly upon her. This morning the Spring rain had teemed down. But now the clouds were swept away and the rinsed grey stone of the beautiful cathedral glistened in the sunlight.

Francesca's appearance had, naturally, been carefully supervised by Lady Rothersay. The blue muslin had been rejected as the neckline was half an inch too immodestly low. The yellow muslin was deemed too frivolous. Finally a brown and white sprigged gown had found favour, accessoried by a brown straw bonnet, brown gloves, brown boots and a white parasol. The gown was the least favourite of Francesca's dresses. She thought it dull. But it was the bonnet she loathed most.

She tore it off and flung it onto the opposite seat. Brown straw! Why, she thought, it makes me look at least fifty years old! For two pins I would not wear a bonnet at all, but someone would be bound to see me and tittle tattle the facts back to my Aunt.

Then, as the carriage began its laborious ascent up St Giles Hill, Francesca's eye fell on a cluster of marguerites growing at the roadside. The coach was travelling so slowly it was not necessary for her to pull the cord and order the driver to stop. She opened the door and jumped nimbly out. A few moments later, she had run up the hill, caught the coach and was back in her seat, happily threading the lovely white flowers through the straw on her bonnet.

A Winchester lady, mused Francesca, would have just one or two flowers. For in Winchester, I have learned, we do nothing to excess. But I am not Winchester born and bred. I hail from Dorsetshire, which is a county in full glorious bloom, and proud to be so.

Accordingly, Francesca decorated her bonnet with a splendid array of twelve marguerites, piled prettily round the brim. She had only just completed her task when the carriage rolled into the neat drive of Chilcombe Lodge.

The house was larger than she had expected, a square, white residence made all the more imposing by the magnificent elms on either side. Hastily tying the ribbons of her gay bonnet, Francesca descended, and approached the front door.

At first, everything went according to Lady Rothersay's carefully devised plan. No sooner had the footman informed Francesca that Mrs Jamieson had departed for Derbyshire than Sir Peter himself strolled into the hall. Francesca's grey-green eyes appraised him thoughtfully.

He was in his late twenties, she surmised, of average height and somewhat on the thin side. His hair and eyes were dark and his clothes impeccably cut, although Francesca felt that his peacock-blue watered-silk waistcoat would be considered rather flamboyant by Winchester's conservative standards.

She was ushered into an attractive green Drawing Room which overlooked an expanse of sweeping lawn. The bell was rung for tea.

But then, as Francesca relaxed against the jade green cushions of the comfortable sofa, Sir Peter Jamieson turned to her and said with a pleasant smile. "You have come, I take it, to talk to me about Lady Rothersay's forthcoming charity ball."

"Oh! How did you know?" blurted Francesca, taken completely off guard.

Sir Peter laughed, and seated himself at the table near the window. "My dear Lady Francesca, all Winchester is aware of the rivalry between Lady Rothersay and Lady Sombourne. And when I saw you all conversing together yesterday morning I could well imagine Lady Rothersay's train of thought when Lady Sombourne greeted me with such warming civility."

Francesca found his frankness disarming. It was impossible for her to maintain any further pretence in the face of his roguish smile.

"I am a stranger to Winchester," she confessed, spreading her hands. "All the rivalries and the subtle nuances of social competition between this lady and that are a total mystery to me."

"Fear not," said Sir Peter. "I understand it all only too well. Lady Rothersay, of course, could not demean herself by calling on me in person. So you have been appointed as her envoy. She desires, I take it, that my newspaper should print news about her ball, in order to entice as many patrons as possible away from Lady Sombourne's rival affair?"

Francesca nodded. Tea was brought in and, at Sir Peter's invitation, she arose to pour. "I realise," she said politely, "that we are verging on the impertinent in requesting such a thing. You must have far more important matters deserving of inclusion in the *Winchester Courier*,"

"Indeed I do," agreed the dark-haired man, brushing a speck of dust from his waistcoat. "However, I shall be delighted to accede to Lady Rothersay's request — "

"Oh, how kind!" exclaimed Francesca.

"On one condition," continued Sir Peter. "I shall, of course, purchase a ticket for her charity ball. And my newspaper will be most generous in its coverage of the event. But in return, I should like Lady Rothersay to invite me as a regular guest to her Thursday Afternoons."

"Thursday Afternoons? Whatever are they?" enquired Francesca, sipping her tea.

"Lady Rothersay is *At Home* every other Thursday afternoon," said Sir Peter, "and the elite of Winchester are encouraged to call on her. The word salon, with its Parisian overtones, is never employed in such a refined environ as Winchester, but that in effect is what Lady Rothersay conducts on her Thursdays."

Francesca found it impossible to understand why Sir Peter should be so eager to cross the threshold of the Rothersay residence. She herself, ironically, spent every spare minute conspiring to escape from the house! However, she could well appreciate why Sir Peter had never been invited to any gathering at the house. He had muddied his hands in the sewers of Trade and that, in Lady Rothersay's book, was quite beyond the social pale.

"You know that I cannot make any promises on behalf of my aunt," Francesca told Sir Peter frankly. "But I will do my best."

"I'm sure you will," he grinned. "After all, it will be in your interests as well as mine. Those Thursday Afternoons are I hear insufferably boring events and you will be glad of my presence to provide a little light relief."

"If the Thursdays are so tedious, why are you so anxious to be invited," asked Francesca with a cool smile.

"For private reasons of my own," replied Sir Peter shortly. "Now, to work. Tell me all you know about Lady Rothersay's ball."

"It is to be held at Lord Compton's house," said Francesca, setting down her cup, "because of course the Rothersay house is not large enough to contain a ballroom."

Sir Peter scribbled this down. "Do you know what the important ladies of your party will be wearing? Could you draw their gowns for me?"

Francesca shook her head. "I have seen the gowns, but I fear I am totally unartistic Sir Peter."

He beckoned her across to the table. "Sit yourself down, then, and write me a description of Lady Rothersay's gown. And yours, and your cousin's. All the fashionable ladies of the city will be agog for news such as this."

When she had finished, Sir Peter said, "Now if you learn of any more interesting details about the forthcoming ball, you must let me know at once, so I can mention it in the next edition."

Glancing over her shoulder he perused what Francesca had written in her bold, sloping hand, and remarked, "Lady Aithne! That is an uncommonly pretty name."

"Yes. It means *little fire*," said Francesca gloomily.

"Charming," he murmured, "Quite charming. Now," he said briskly. "Do you happen to know if the ladies Southport, Featherstone and Sutton have accepted for your aunt's ball. Or are they waiting to see if Lady Sombourne's event promises to be more socially important?"

"I have not the faintest notion," murmured Francesca. "Who are these ladies?"

Sir Peter recoiled against the green damask window hangings, his dark eyes wide in mock horror. Who are they? My dear Lady Francesca, surely you have been told about the celebrated golden goblets given to six Winchester families by King Charles?"

"Yes of course," smiled Francesca. "My cousin very proudly showed me the goblet owned by the Rothersays. It is encrusted with diamonds and is absolutely exquisite."

"Well you should know that the six families who own these goblets are considered the elite of Winchester," said Sir Peter. "And because Winchester is very much a matriachal society, in effect it means it is dominated by six very formidable ladies. Plus Lady Sombourne, of course, who is by no means to be trifled with. But she, to her eternal chagrin, lacks the cachet of a royal golden goblet."

"Heavens," breathed Francesca, "I had no idea when I rode down the Roman Road into Winchester that I was to become enmeshed in such a tangle of social tripwires."

Sir Peter grinned. "Fortunately, the situation has eased somewhat, as two of our elite ladies have recently departed from the city. Lady Beddows has gone to Westmorland for her health, and Lady Montfort has been called suddenly to her estates in Norfolk. The oldest of the celebrated six is the Dowager Lady Featherstone. You must have noticed her incredibly ugly house as you rode down the Roman road."

"The marguerites on Francesca's bonnet trembled as she shook her head. "No, I er . . . I was so eager to reach my aunt's house that I galloped in at a somewhat excessive speed. I fear I noticed very little." As I recall, mused Francesca, I was too intent on listening for the Duke of Wexford chasing after me!

"This is a truly shocking state of affairs," Sir Peter declared. "Winchester is justly celebrated for its surrounding views. Come," he took her arm and hustled her towards the door, "it will be my pleasure to escort you round the outskirts of my city."

"But . . . but Sir Peter," Francesca protested breathlessly as he swept her towards the front door. "My aunt is expecting me home. She will be extremely worried if I am late."

Sir Peter paused on the front steps. "Yes, you are right. How thoughtless of me. Very well, I shall just show you a few carefully selected views. It will take no more than an hour of your time and I promise you, you will consider it as sixty minutes very well invested."

Laughing, Francesca capitulated. "You are extremely persuasive, Sir Peter." And of course, in truth, Francesca was in no hurry to return to the stifling confines of her aunt's house.

"Would it inconvenience you if we travelled in your carriage?" enquired Sir Peter, his hair glinting reddish brown in the sunlight. "My best horse is being shoed up at one of the villages. It would suit me very well to arrange our excursion so that I may call at the blacksmith and ride the horse home."

Francesca could see nothing amiss with this arrangement, and accordingly they set off sitting opposite one another in the splendid Rothersay carriage. At the top of St Giles Hill the carriage was halted to afford Francesca a splendid view of the city.

It was the Cathedral which immediately dominated the scene, so tranquilly situated amidst soaring trees, with clusters of red and grey houses spread around and beyond. The glint of the River Itchen caught Francesca's eye, meandering out through lush water meadows towards what Sir Peter informed her was Winchester College, one of the finest educational establishments in England.

Winchester, Francesca realised as they drove on, was a city surrounded by lovely green hills, its houses adorned by pretty gardens and neat allotments. Leaving the town behind, they rode through villages dotted with thatched cottages and bright houses, smothered in roses and climbing ivy. And through the magnificent beeches and elms, was spread a vista of cornfields, meadows and the gently rising Downs.

In one of the villages, Sir Peter ordered the carriage to halt outside a blacksmiths. Whilst he went in to enquire if his horse was shod, Francesca wandered down the sleepy road and seated herself under a spreading oak tree which sheltered the village green. Drowsily, she closed her eyes in the warm afternoon sun, and nibbled on a juicy piece of long fresh grass.

"Dear me," said a mocking voice, "Can it be that you are not being properly fed at the Rothersay establishment?"

Francesca's eyes flew open and she found herself staring into the amused, handsome face of the Duke of Wexford. "No doubt," said Francesca, rallying quickly, "it would please you to imagine that my aunt was so infuriated by your foolish prank with my peppered riding hat, that she sent me to bed without any supper."

He towered over her, splendidly attired in beige breeches and dark green riding coat.

"I confess myself flattered, Lady Francesca," he said, "that after all your protestations to the contrary, you should find yourself drawn back, so speedily, to the lands of my estate."

Francesca raised a delicate eyebrow. "Your estate? But I imagined myself to be miles from Wexford Hall." They had taken such a circuitous route that afternoon, that in truth Francesca was not sure where she was.

"You are in the village of King's Langley," the Duke informed her with a smile. "It has belonged to my family for centuries."

Francesca sighed, "If I had known that, I assure you I should not have come." She glanced away, seeking for a way to rid herself of the Duke. His presence disturbed her greatly — though why, she could not imagine. *It is probably because of the unfortunate circumstances under which we first met* Francesca reasoned. *Whenever I encounter the Duke, I cannot rid myself of the suspicion that he is recalling the memory of me bathing in his river. Oh, how I wish I had not so impetuously cast off my clothes and plunged into the water that day! For now, the episode puts me at such a disadvantage with this mocking man!*

She noticed the Duke's phaeton further down the road, and caught a glimpse of a fair-haired girl sitting within. "Pray do not allow me, Your Grace, to detain you," Francesca said coolly, "your companion in the phaeton will be growing restive."

The Duke waved a careless hand. "Oh, Evelina is perfectly content. She knows me well enough by now."

Evelina is clearly a doormat, thought Francesca scornfully, *to allow herself to be treated in such a cavalier fashion by the Duke. It is typical of the man, of course, that he would leave one lady sitting twiddling her thumbs in the carriage whilst he crosses the road to converse with another. Such arrogance! If I were Evelina, I should seize the reins and leave the Duke staring into a cloud of dust!*

The Duke leaned against the great oak, and said thoughtfully, "I am extremely attached to this village. Whenever I return from my travels abroad, and ride over the Down to catch the first sight of the old Norman tower on the church, then I know I am truly come home. I often think, you know, that many of my ancestors must have experienced that some emotion . . . as they returned, tired and battle weary from the Crusades, or Agincourt."

Francesca had a great love of the heritage of her country, and her imagination was fired by his words. "And whilst they were away in foreign lands, they must have dreamed of King's Langley," she breathed. "After the heat, dust, noise and brutal turmoil of battle, the thought of this tranquil English village must have brought balm to their souls."

"I like to imagine so," said the Duke quietly. "Though of course, in ancient times the village was named simply Langley. It was King Charles II who designated it King's Langley in recognition of my family's loyalty to him."

"King Charles again!" exclaimed Francesca. "My, is there anything in this part of the world untouched by his royal hand?"

The Duke laughed. "Ah. I see your aunt has lost no time in regaling you with the saga of the six golden goblets! If only the King had known what friction he would cause in Winchester when he presented those goblets to the six families of the town."

"From what I have read of King Charles, he would have been most amused by the jealousies aroused by the goblets," smiled Francesca, reflecting that it was far more impressive to have the King confer his name on your family village, than to receive a single goblet, even if it was made of gold and encrusted with jewels.

She stood up and brushed the grass from her skirt as she saw Sir Peter emerging from the blacksmiths. The Duke followed her gaze. "Well, well," he murmured. "You have wasted no time, I see, in finding yourself an escort. Good-day to you, Lady Francesca."

And with a curt bow, he strode off up the road to the gleaming phaeton, where the fair-haired girl greeted him with a smile which for some reason made Francesca feel suddenly quite out of temper.

★　　★　　★

"There you are at last, Francesca!" beamed Lady Rothersay from the Drawing Room sofa. "Come along in, child, and sit by me. My, what pretty flowers in your bonnet! So delightful to have living proof that Spring has arrived, is it not?"

Francesca, who had expected a scolding for her late return, sat gingerly down on the edge of the velvet sofa. She could not believe that this smiling, sparkling-eyed lady was the same person as the gaunt, formidable aunt who had rapped strict last minute instructions to her only three hours ago.

But no doubt, mused Francesca, Aunt Cecilia is in good humour because she is anticipating a favourable account of my encounter with Sir Peter. And she will not be disappointed. My mission was successfully accomplished, and I must delay no longer in informing my aunt of Sir Peter's plans to print extensive details of her charity ball in his newspaper.

"I am pleased to tell you that I did indeed find Sir Peter at home, Aunt," she began, "and he very kindly — "

Lady Rothersay waved her hands impatiently. "Yes, yes. You shall tell me all about that later. But first I must give you *my* news! Oh Francesca, you see before you an extremely happy woman! I am simply so delighted! Aithne, in fact, is in such a state of excitement that I have been compelled to send her to bed to rest."

Francesca could not imagine what dramatic event had

befallen the house during her absence. Had Viscount Polesdon reneged on his engagement to Lady Clorinda, and
eloped with the laundry maid? Had Lady Sombourne's
house burnt down? Had England finally won the war
against the French?

Lady Rothersay took a deep, shuddering breath and
announced in tones of reverential awe, "We had a visitor
this afternoon. It was . . . it was none other than the Duke
of Wexford himself! And he has accepted, Francesca, for
my charity ball!"

Francesca said nothing, but listened politely for her aunt
to proceed and reveal details of this exciting event.

Lady Rothersay seized her hands. "Oh, you dear girl,
you are quite stunned with surprise! Well, so were we all at
first. As you know, the Duke has never before been known
to honour any of our charity balls with his presence. And to
call here personally to tell me that he would be attending,
well! Oh, I can't wait to spread the word to Lady Sombourne! She will be speechless with rage! In fact, I shouldn't
be surprised if she cancels her ball. For when it becomes
known that the Duke is attending mine, I shall be assured of
all the elite of Winchester!"

Hastily, Francesca summoned the congratulatory words
her aunt was longing to hear. But in her heart, Francesca felt
a stab of anger. Everywhere I go, everything I do in
Winchester seems to be under the sardonic eye of the Duke
of Wexford, she thought. And now he is to be the most
important person at the ball, deciding with a snap of his
arrogant fingers which ladies to honour with a lordly
request to stand up with him for the minuet. Well, if he asks
me I shall refuse, Francesca resolved. Let all the other girls
go scrambling for his favours. I shall make it plain that
rather than take the floor with him, I would rather sit
against the wall with the chaperones all evening.

Besides, she reasoned, he has such an unsettling effect on me, if I did allow him to partner me I should be sure to stumble, and miss a step — and how that would amuse him!

Lady Rothersay was still discoursing in a vivacious manner: " . . . wondered what caused him suddenly to look so favourably on my charity ball. And then I realised! The other day, when Aithne and I were walking towards the goldsmiths, the Duke rode past. As always, he most courteously raised his hat, bowed and continued on his way. But I recall musing at the time, that his eye did seem to linger for a second or two more than was necessary on Aithne. She was looking particularly pretty that day, you know. Oh", sighed Lady Rothersay rapturously, "what a feather in the family cap if I were in a position to announce Aithne's betrothal to the Duke of Wexford. Why, Lady Sombourne would jump off her roof with rage!"

"Is Aithne excited at the prospect?" enquired Francesca carefully. She knew better than to enquire if Aithne liked the Duke or admired his character and disposition.

"Poor child, she was so overcome during the Duke's call that she could hardly utter a word!" laughed Lady Rothersay. "And now she is resting after all the excitement. Do go up and see your cousin, Francesca. I am sure she will have much to tell you."

As Francesca entered the pink and white bedchamber, she found Aithne huddled on her bed, her face awash with tears.

"Come now, Cousin, what is this?" enquired Francesca gently, seating herself beside the weeping girl. "I was given to understand that this was a day of rejoicing."

"I wish the Duke hadn't come," sobbed Aithne. "I shall have a miserable time now at the ball. Mama will be on the other side of the room, organising everyone, and meanwhile I shall have to talk to the Duke, all on my own. I shan't be able to think of anything to say and he will think me stupid. He won't ask me to marry him and Mama will be furious!"

Francesca struggled for words. In her own way, she realised, Aithne had given a very accurate forecast of what was likely to happen!

"Er . . . what is your opinion of the Duke, Cousin? Do you find him attractive?"

Aithne blinked away the tears. "He is a Duke. Mama says that all Dukes are attractive. And of course, he is a far better catch than Clorinda's geriatric Viscount." She sighed. "Perhaps he will talk all the time to me, and I shall just be required to say yes and no. Do you imagine that is likely?"

Francesca was on the point of expressing her true opinion, based on her own experience of the gentleman, when she remembered that as far as the Rothersays were concerned, she had not yet been formally introduced to the Duke. Francesca fetched Aithne a fresh, dry handkerchief and said:

"You are probably worrying unnecessarily, Aithne. After all, the purpose of a ball is to dance, and no one can expect you to make witty conversation whilst you are concentrating on the steps. All you need do is move well and smile a great deal."

"You do not understand about Mama's charity balls," said Aithne, blowing her nose. "The purpose, as far as we are concerned, is most certainly not to dance and enjoy ourselves. Mama is determined to raise more money for her charity than Lady Sombourne. So you and I, Francesca, will be required to move amongst the revellers, selling tombola tickets, flower buttonholes, gold pins, silver combs and the like. I assure you. Mama will not be at all pleased if she observes us neglecting our duties and dancing."

Casually, Francesca turned her back on Aithne and

moved across to close the window a fraction. Her shoulders were shaking with suppressed laughter. Oh dear, she thought biting her lip, the pity of it is that I have no one to share all this with. I am sure that by the time the fateful ball is over, I shall have disgraced myself by bursting into unseemly, uncontrollable laughter at my aunt's strange ways!

4

Just imagine! There were Aithne and I, wrote Francesca to her brother Edward, *working as hard as any shopgirls, selling flowers, tokens, dance cards and tombola tickets, whilst on the other side of the ballroom Aunt Cecilia was practically apoplectic in her attempts to avoid acknowledging the newspaper proprietor Sir Peter Jamieson — because, my dear, he is in trade!*

Francesca carefully shook sand over the finished page, and reached for a fresh sheet. The house was blessedly quiet, as Lady Rothersay and Aithne were out riding. Francesca had no doubt that their route would take them through the village of King's Langley in the hope of a chance encounter with the Duke of Wexford.

Taking up her pen once more, she continued. *Lord Compton's ballroom was a riot of flowers, garlands, music, light and perfume. He himself is a dapper gentleman in his middle years and much favoured by the Winchester ladies because of his extremely fastidious nature. When a footman spilt claret on his lordship's white gloves one would have imagined, from the commotion, that it was a disaster of national proportions. Fresh gloves were brought, scrutinised, rejected, as were a second pair, and a third. It was whispered in my ear, meanwhile, that Lord Compton is so terrified of eating contaminated food, that he employs a valet specially for the purpose of tasting every morsel. Recently, the valet sufferd from a bad tooth, and Lord Compton almost starved for three days until the unfortunate food taster was fit once more to resume his duties!*

The person who had whispered this intelligence into Francesca's ear was a golden-haired girl with laughing blue eyes. Francesca recalled noticing her at once as she entered the ballroom on the arm of the Duke of Wexford. His arrival, of course, caused a *frisson* of excitement amongst the bejewelled ladies in the ballroom, and Aithne was immediately instructed by her mother to approach the Duke and offer him a flower for his buttonhole.

Aithne had paled, and hidden behind a cascade of roses, causing the exasperated Lady Rothersay to push Francesca forward towards the distinguished arrival. Lord Compton was at the door, receiving, and it was at this point that the mishap with the claret occurred. Thus it was that Francesca was allowed a few minutes quiet conversation with the Duke, and his female companion.

Gazing into the girl's open, amiable face, Francesca had known instinctively that hers were the hands which had placed the anemonies in the Duke's hall. This must be Evelina, Francesca had realised, wondering if Lady Rothersay was aware that the Duke's companion clearly felt very much at home at Wexford Hall.

Francesca's surmise over the girl's identity had proved correct as the Duke, splendidly dressed in a dark blue velvet frock coat, said with a smile, "May I present the Lady Evelina Penshurst."

The girl laughed. "How formal you are, Aidan! I think you should know Lady Francesca, that as a child, my dear brother here dubbed me Evelina the Screamer, because I was such a noisy wretch."

Francesca had experienced an unaccountable surge of

relief at these words. "Oh, I beg your pardon. I did not realise you were related."

"Francesca, you are my friend for life!" Evelina exclaimed gaily. "I am delighted that you see no resemblance between my charming self and my brute of a brother. Come, let us sit in the window arbour and talk for a while."

"I should like that very much, but I am supposed to be circulating amongst the guests, selling flowers," Francesca had confessed. At this Evelina had groaned. "Oh, Lady Rothersay never eases up for a moment, does she!"

The Duke having gallantly thrown a guinea into the basket, had taken a white carnation.

"Fear not, Francesca, I will do my duty by conversing with Lady Rothersay, whilst you two ladies become better acquainted. But after ten minutes, Evelina you are to come and rescue me!"

Francesca smiled now as she recalled the delighted expression on the face of Lady Rothersay as the Duke, ignoring all the other ladies in the ballroom, strode across and, with a flourish, pressed the white carnation into Aithne's trembling hand.

I conversed for some considerable time with the Lady Evelina Penshurst, Francesca continued. *You would like her, Edward. She has a wonderful sense of fun, and is refreshingly unconventional. She told me that the reason Lady Southport (a woman with the permanent look of one who has just stepped onto a garden rake) was giving her such arctic glances was that Lady Southport knew Lady Evelina to be enceinte. "But I see no reason why I should hide myself away from society, as if I have done something to be ashamed of," Lady Evelina asserted. I agreed with her wholeheartedly, for did not our own dear Mama hold the same views, Edward? Do you remember when Cousin Mary was with child, and Mama insisted on taking her to dine at Lady Bentworth's. "There is no cause to scatter to the four corners of the room* in such cowardly fashion," Mama declared imperiously to the company at large as she and Cousin Mary entered the crowded Drawing Room. "Mary is not a plague-ridden cannonball. She will neither infect you, nor explode!"

Talking in the window arbour with the radiant Lady Evelina, Francesca had smiled to herself as it became clear to her why the Duke of Wexford had unexpectedly agreed to attend the ball. It was his sister who persuaded him, Francesca realised. She was restless at home at Penshurst Lodge, and sought a diversion. Her husband, Lord Penshurst, had broken a leg in a hunting accident, so Lady Evelina had prevailed upon her brother to escort her to the ball.

What else can I tell you about the event, Francesca went on. *Lady Featherstone's ostrich plumes became gloriously entangled with a hanging garland of roses. All would have been well had she remained quietly still until Lord Compton hastened to the rescue. But instead she began flailing her arms in windmill fashion, hooting and screeching way over the strains of the orchestra, with the result that she wrenched the garland from the wall and smashed a priceless Sevres flower urn in the process! A furious Lady Rothersay informed Lady Featherstone that she possessed all the grace and delicacy of a carthorse. Lady Featherstone riposted tartly that Lady Rothersay was merely revealing her own crass ignorance of horse-flesh as carthorses in fact were much admired for their natural controlled strength . . .*

Francesca shook with laughter as she recalled the incident. Dutifully circulating round the ballroom offering her posies for sale, Francesca had been in an ideal position to hear every scandalous conversation and cutting remark. She had enjoyed herself immeasurably, and was delighted now to have a quiet hour or two in which to share her experience with her brother.

The Duke of Wexford stayed but an hour and a half at the ball, Francesca wrote, *because he did not wish his sister to become overtired. I danced only twice, towards midnight, partnered by Lord Sutton and then by Sir Peter Jamieson. Since he printed so many favourable advance details of the ball in his newspaper, my aunt could not openly protest at our dancing together — but she made her feelings known by turning her back and engaging Lord Compton in animated conversation. Thus she was able to pretend, for the duration of the quadrille, that neither Sir Peter nor I existed at all!*

Francesca laid down her pen and gazed out onto the garden. The day had started misty, but now the sun had broken through and was drying the tiny drops of moisture on the May blossom. Swiftly, Francesca gathered up the pages of her letter and folded them into her reticule.

I'll finish the letter later, she decided. It is too lovely a day to remain shut up in the house.

Within fifteen minutes she was strolling happily through the flowery meads bordering the tranquil River Itchen, taking the path which led to St Cross, the Hospital which was to benefit from the funds raised at Lady Rothersay's ball.

Francesca had no notion of the time, but sudden pangs of hunger warned her that she had walked further and for longer than she intended. But so much was she enjoying her solitary walk that she was reluctant to turn back and enter once more the claustrophobic atmosphere of her aunt's house.

I'll just go as far as the bend in the river. Francesca resolved, to take a peek at the vista beyond. Then I shall adopt the face of Duty once more, and return to Upper Brook.

It was as she approached the river bend that she heard the first alarmed shouts:

"Gently, man! She's not a sack of coal. Try and position your arms under her shoulders."

"It's difficult in all this mud. And the weight of her clothes is dragging us both under!"

Francesca began to run. Breathlessly rounding the corner, she gasped with horror at what she saw. Two fisherman stood thigh deep in the water, heaving towards the bank the wet, mud-splattered body of a large woman. By the time Francesca had rushed to the scene the two men, perspiration pebbling their brows, had dragged the lady onto the soft moss of the bank.

Francesca cried out in alarm as she bent over the bedraggled figure. "Merciful heavens! It is Lady Sutton!"

One of the men wiped his forehead with the sleeve of his shirt. "We noticed her walking along the bank. But then she must have tripped over a fallen branch. Next thing we knew, there was an almighty splash and she was floundering in the river."

"Hysterical she was," put in the second man, emptying water from his boots. "Fought us like a wild cat when we tried to rescue her. Then she seemed to swoon, and went all heavy on us, which was even worse. She's a large lady, and — "

"One of you must run immediately to the Hospital at St Cross," Francesca instructed. "The nurses there will know what to do. Thanks to your prompt action she is not unconscious through drowning, but more out of shock I believe."

The larger man ran off at once towards the Hospital. Meanwhile Francesca tore off her light pelisse. After mopping as much water as she could from Lady Sutton, she covered her with the pelisse and began rubbing her chilled hands. After a while, a faint tinge of colour returned to the prone woman's face and her eyes fluttered open.

"Do not be alarmed, Lady Sutton," Francesca murmured reassuringly. "You took a tumble into the water, but you are safe. Quite safe. Two kindly fishermen rescued you."

Lady Sutton began to shiver, as she tried to speak. "Fools", she said, in a stuttering whisper. "Stupid fools."

"Poor Lady Sutton is delirious," Francesca said hastily to the exhausted fisherman who was understandably looking extremely indignant at this ingratitude from the lady he had saved.

Glancing up, she was relieved to see three nurses running down the path, their capes swirling behind them in the breeze. With the fishermen's assistance, Lady Sutton was speedily removed into a coolly serene room within the Hospital. Her husband had already been sent a message about her mishap, and Francesca stayed with her until he arrived.

Lady Sutton, watching his approach through the luxuriant fig trees of the Hospital grounds, suddenly covered her face with her hands and burst into tears. A natural reaction, thought a deeply sympathetic Francesca as she tactfully took her leave. After her dreadful ordeal, Lady Sutton is naturally in a state of complete emotional exhaustion.

Francesca walked at a fast pace back along the river path, conscious that only if she put her best foot forward would she arrive back at Upper Brook before her aunt. Consequently, she was not at all pleased when Sir Peter Jamieson came riding up beside her and called, in an urgent tone.

"Lady Francesca! Kindly pause a moment. There is something I must say to you."

Francesca strode on. "Then you must say it to the top of my head, Sir Peter. I must warn you that I am in a tearing hurry!"

He laughed, and trotted his grey alongside her. It was then that Francesca observed a familiar object being dangled in front of her face.

"Oh!" she cried, stopping short. "My reticule! Why how careless of me. I did not even realise I had lost it. Thank you so much, Sir Peter." She must, Francesca realised, have thrown it down when she rushed to Lady Sutton's aid.

She stretched out a hand but, infuriatingly, Sir Peter hoisted the reticule out of her reach.

Francesca glared up at him. "Sir Peter I am in no mood for foolish pranks. I am late for luncheon, and my aunt will be furious."

"Come and have luncheon with me," the dark-haired man suggested. "I feel it is the least you can do after I have raced all along the river bank in the hope of catching you up. Besides, there is something most particular I wish to discuss with you. And, if you are late already, what difference will another hour make?"

"You know perfectly well that my aunt would not look favourably on the notion of me lunching *à deux* with you," Francesca informed him tartly.

He grinned. "Ah. But I happen to know, Lady Francesca, that you are an independent-minded young lady who cares not a fig for your aunt's opinions. And I assure you, the matter I wish to discuss is very much in your best interests."

Francesca sighed. "And no doubt unless I agree to lunch with you, you will continue to make difficulties about the return of my reticule. How gallant!" she said scornfully.

Sir Peter was not at all put out. "Now you cannot expect we vulgar tradespeople to possess the flowery manners of gentlemen, Lady Francesca!"

Francesca stared up at him, a chilling suspicion forming in her mind. "You scoundrel! You — you've read my letter to Edward!" she blazed. "The letter was in my reticule. You've read every word of my private correspondence haven't you!"

"You hold your horses," exclaimed Sir Peter, backing

his grey down the path as Francesca flew at him, her grey-green eyes stormy with anger.

"Did your nanny never tell you that reading other people's correspondence is the most despicable thing to do!" flared Francesca. "I am beginning to think that my aunt was right about you, Sir Peter. You are indeed a snake, through and through!"

Sir Peter swore under his breath. "Dash it all, Lady Francesca, calm yourself for a moment. Else we'll both end up in the river. And I should warn you that I do not number swimming amongst my accomplishments."

"Capital! A watery grave is just what you deserve," snapped Francesca.

"If you will calm yourself for just one moment," said Sir Peter, turning his horse broadside on to the furious girl, "you will divine that it was necessary for me to peruse your letter, in order that I might discover to whom the reticule belonged. Fortunately, I recognised your handwriting. If you recall, you wrote down for me some details of Lady Rothersay's charity ball, and I remember at the time admiring your bold, stylish hand."

Francesca stood hands on hips, glaring up at him. "Indeed? And no doubt I would be right in further divining that instead of reading just the first paragraph of my letter, you perused every line, right through to the last page."

He grinned. "But my dear, it was all so fascinating! I especially adored your aunt's contretemps with Lady Carthorse. And I had never before heard that anecdote about Lord Compton and his food taster. I assure you I sat by the river and positively howled with laughter!"

Observing with relief that Francesca had now simmered down a little, he ventured to repeat his invitation to luncheon.

"Thank you, no," said Francesca with icy disdain. "I

should be glad if you would hand me my reticule, and then depart from my sight."

But instead of complying with her request, Sir Peter swung himself down from the grey, commenting in a resigned tone, "My, but you can be a difficult person at times, Lady Francesca. I will strike a bargain with you. If I hand you back your reticule, here and now, will you spare me five minutes of your time whilst I put a certain proposal before you."

"Proposal?" echoed Francesca. She laughed. "I trust you are not seriously intending to ask for my hand in marriage, Sir Peter?"

Sir Peter tethered his horse, and replied over his shoulder, "Pray do not allow me to raise your hopes, Lady Francesca. I was talking of a business proposal, not one of marriage."

"Indeed," murmured Francesca wryly. "I was under the impression that in Winchester the two were one and the same. However, yes, Sir Peter, I agree to your bargain. My reticule, if you please, in return for which I give you my undivided attention for five minutes." And then, she thought I must race home to face the wrath of my aunt.

Sir Peter led her to an elm bench shaded by a young alder tree. There he gravely handed Francesca her reticule.

"Thank you," she said quietly, laying it on the bench beside her.

"Are you not going to open it, to check that all the pages of your letter are there?" he enquired.

"I should not stoop to such behaviour," said Francesca with dignity. "I make it a rule, Sir Peter, always to show good manners myself, even when I am in the presence of one who's behaviour is at times beyond the pale."

The thin man at her side roared with laughter. "That is what I so admire about you, Lady Francesca. In truth, you don't give a damn for society — but you are mistress of the art of turning a pretty phrase to make it appear that you are a model of propriety." He leaned forward and went on eagerly. "And that is what I wanted to discuss with you. For I feel strongly that your gift of words — and gift it is, make no mistake — should be put to good use."

Francesca raised an amused eyebrow. "Indeed? And in what manner, pray?" Her observant eye noticed that for all his confident airs, Sir Peter's bony hands were drumming nervously on the knees of his riding breeches.

"How would you feel," he said slowly, "if I suggested that you wrote a regular column for my newspaper? Not under your own name of course," he added hastily, seeing her start of alarm. "We would invent a pseudonym."

For once in her twenty-one years, Francesca found herself bereft of words. "What . . . what sort of column do you have in mind?" she stammered at last. "I fear I should die of boredom writing a series of 'A Lady's Fashion Notes' or 'Scenes of Winchester Life as Viewed by a Visitor from Dorsetshire'."

He smiled. "I see I did not underestimate you, Lady Francesca. I find it interesting that you have expressed no shock, no horrified dismay, that I should suggest that a lady like yourself should turn your hand to writing for my newspaper."

"The notion is clearly preposterous," replied Francesca with a dismissive wave of her hand. "One could not for a moment seriously entertain the idea."

Sir Peter's brown eyes regarded her steadily. "Let us remain, then, for the moment, in the realms of fantasy. Let us imagine, just imagine, that you are not unreceptive to my suggestion. Now of course it would be absurd for you to attempt flowery prose on fashion, or the delightful kingcups blooming by the river. That would not be your style at all."

"I am relieved to hear it," said Francesca, watching an exotically plumed kingfisher dart up the river.

"What I had in mind," said Sir Peter, watching her closely, "was something on the lines of a Journal. We could call it 'Lady Selina's Journal'. And what it would contain would be exactly the kind of information that is contained in your letter to your brother Edward."

Francesca's eyes widened in surprise. "Oh but Sir Peter! It is one thing to write in such a full and frank manner to one's brother, but quite another to publish such spicey intelligence. Why, the notion is quite scandalous!"

"But how readable," murmured the dark haired man. "Imagine the scenes over the fashionable breakfast tables of Winchester as Lady X gasps over the account of what Lord Y said to Lady Z that made her colour to the roots of her dyed hair! I assure you, after a few weeks, *Lady Selina's Journal* will be the item turned to first in the *Winchester Courier*. You will be read before the news of the war, before even the details of the Prince Regent's receptions in London. All Winchester will be agog for fresh scandal about their favourite enemies, and tremble with trepidation for fear that Lady Selina had barbed intelligence of them in her column that week!"

Francesca sat for a minute, looking at the quiet waters of the river. Then she suddenly burst into laughter. "Sir Peter, you are a wicked man! I do not for a moment believe it would be right for me to pose as your Lady Selina, but the idea is wonderful! And you are right, of course. Before long all Winchester would be talking about Lady Selina, wondering who she is and whom she will next expose in her column."

"You are the ideal person to write as Lady Selina," Sir Peter said persuasively, "As a guest of Lady Rothersay's, you will be invited to all the best houses. You will mingle with the elite of the city. But, because Lady Rothersay is determined that her daughter Aithne should be the centre of attention — "

"I shall be pushed somewhat into the background," Francesca finished for him. "You need not mince words, Sir Peter. I am only too well aware that I am a poor relation, tolerated only because of my aunt's sense of duty towards my late mother."

Sir Peter gazed up the river. "I trust it will not offend you if I mention this, Lady Francesca. But of course, it goes without saying that I should not expect you to devote your time and energies to the Journal without some form of remuneration. As I said earlier, I do believe your gift for words should be put to good use. *Profitable* use."

A blush tinged Francesca's cheek. "No, you have not offended me, Sir Peter. When your family is in such financial distress as mine, you soon learn not to see anything shameful in earning an honest penny or two. But out of respect for my aunt, I feel I cannot accept your proposition. It would not be proper for me, as a guest under her roof, to take advantage of her hospitality and that of her friends and acquaintances by spying on them."

"Do you not feel," replied Sir Peter, "that by exposing in my newspaper their feuds, their foibles, their artificial way of life, you might make them realise the folly of their ways. *Lady Selina's Journal* would be like a breath of fresh air through Winchester, blowing away the cobwebs of etiquette, and heralding a new, more healthily open way of life."

Francesca smiled, and picked in her reticule. "You speak most persuasively, Sir Peter. But I fear my answer must be no. Now if you will excuse me, I must hurry home or my aunt will be sending out a search party."

He placed a light hand on her arm, detaining her. "Don't give me a definite answer today. Just promise me you will think the matter over."

"Very well," Francesca agreed. "I will give it my consideration. But you must not be disappointed if the answer is still no!"

And with that, Sir Peter had to be content, for Francesca walked briskly away down the riverside path, her reticule swinging gracefully on her arm. He watched the tall, willowy girl until she was out of sight, and then he mounted his horse and rode towards the highway, well pleased with his morning's work.

Francesca had much to ponder over as she hurried back to Upper Brook. Of course, had she been at home at Marlow, she would have picked up her skirts and run all the way. But this, she appreciated, was traditionalist Winchester and the cobbled streets were teeming with sharp eyes ready to report her behaviour back to her aunt.

Francesca could not make up her mind whether or not she totally approved of Sir Peter Jamieson. On the one hand, he possessed an engaging manner and the ability always to surprise her. Francesca admitted that this aspect of his character pleased her a great deal. A free spirit herself, she was always ready to smile on anyone who had the courage to flout convention.

But on the debit side, Francesca could not avoid the suspicion that Sir Peter was something of an opportunist. Just consider the smooth manner in which he persuaded me to put to my aunt the notion that he should be invited to her exclusive Thursday Afternoons. Although I made it clear that I could make no promises on my aunt's behalf, it would now be distinctly bad-mannered of my aunt *not* to invite him. For whatever may happen behind the closed doors of number 11 Upper Brook, my aunt Cecilia would never allow herself publicly to exhibit a lapse of civility.

Invigorated by her walk, the fresh air and the events of the morning, Francesca felt, as she entered her aunt's Drawing Room, as if a thick sooty blanket had suddenly been thrown over her. Lady Rothersay, seated on the sofa with Aithne, went immediately into the attack:

"Francesca! What is this I hear about you and that newspaper proprietor individual?"

The dark-haired girl paled. Was her aunt clairvoyant? Why, she had only left Sir Peter fifteen minutes ago. Surely news did not travel that fast in Winchester?

"How could you be so gullible!" Lady Rothersay raged. "I admit that it was with my permission that you called on him, in order to obtain favourable coverage of my ball in his wretched newspaper, but now I hear that he was seen that afternoon, riding with my niece, in my carriage, with my family crest on the door!"

Oh dear, thought Francesca, recalling her first meeting with Sir Peter. It had sounded so innocent coming from Sir Peter's lips. How sensible that we should travel in my, that is the Rothersay, carriage to collect his horse which was being shoed.

She cleared her throat. "Seen, Aunt? May I ask by whom?"

"By *whom*?" Lady Rothersay's gaunt face was contorted with indignation. "Why, by half of fashionable Winchester, that's who. Already six ladies, including Lady Featherstone, have reported to me that they observed you and Sir Peter riding together. Lady Featherstone said you were *laughing*, Francesca!"

"I beg your pardon, Aunt," murmured Francesca.

"I won't have it, do you hear? I will not tolerate any member of my family riding in public with a common tradesman. I am only sorry that I shall now be obliged to invite him to my Thursday Afternoons. But that is the price of doing one's duty, and ensuring that one's charity ball is a success, and raises a heart-warming amount of funds for the Hospital of St. Cross."

With relief, Francesca seized on this reference to the Hospital to recount the watery mishap which had befallen Lady Sutton. With a cry of alarm, Lady Rothersay went immediately to her bureau and wrote a note of sympathy to Lady Sutton, which was despatched forthwith by a footman.

When the Drawing Room doors had closed behind the servant, Lady Rothersay returned to the sofa and smiled at the pale-haired Aithne.

"Well, my dear, have you informed your Cousin of the surprising intelligence which has so delighted us today?"

"No, Mama."

Aithne, dressed in palest lavender, held in her white hands a book which Francesca noticed was entitled *Christian Names and Their Meanings*. Lady Rothersay took the volume from her daughter and opened it under the letter A.

"You are probably unaware, Francesca, that the Duke of Wexford's Christian name is Aidan. And according to this book, the name Aidan means *Great Fire*. Now does that not strike you as a charming omen? Aidan and Aithne. *Great Fire* and *Little Fire*!"

"Enchanting," murmured Francesca, imagining her aunt's reaction if, in the end, her hopes were not fulfilled.

She sat beside her aunt and examined the book as she enquired, "Did you by any chance encounter the Duke on your ride this morning?"

"By a happy coincidence, yes," beamed Lady Rothersay, her hands fluttering to the pearl choker at her throat. "We met in his village of King's Langley and he has graciously agreed to honour us with his presence at my next Thursday. The only drawback is that I was of course compelled to invite Lady Evelina also."

"I am glad," said Aithne. "I like Lady Evelina."

Lady Rothersay smiled indulgently at her daughter.

"Naturally, my dear. It is only prudent to establish an excellent rapport with the lady who is destined to become your sister in marriage. No, the only reason I have reservations about entertaining her in my home is that with her confinement only five months away, I believe it would be more discreet for her not to be seen in public until after the happy event. Lady Southport was aghast, you know, when Lady Evelina made her entrance at my ball."

"It was a wonderful success, was it not Mama," said Aithne, her blue eyes shining. "Over the week before and after, there were pages and pages about it all in the *Winchester Courier*. Did you see the illustration of my dress, Francesca? Sir Peter certainly kept his word, did he not? He promised he would print columns and columns about our ball, and he did just that. There was hardly a word about Lady Sombourne's rival event."

"Our ball was a success, Aithne, because of the presence of the Duke of Wexford. Sir Peter's efforts were all very fine in their way, but to be frank I regret now agreeing to Francesca's suggestion that we should patronise him in return for the use of his newspaper," she sighed, and settled back against the cushion. "I have heard not a word from Lady Sombourne since the ball! But she will be obliged to come on Thursday, of course. If she does not show her face all Winchester will know that her nose has been put severely out of joint. And I expect she will bring Clorinda and her fiancé also. Ah, now that reminds me . . . "

Francesca looked up and found her aunt's birdlike eyes fixed upon her. "Yes Aunt?" she asked, with a sudden chill of foreboding.

"It was most unfortunate that Viscount Medway took a chill and so was prevented from attending my ball as your escort, Francesca." She brushed down her skirt and remarked briskly, "I understand that he is somewhat prone to sudden chills. It will be something you will have to watch most carefully when you are wed. You must keep him out of all draughts, and make sure at night — "

"But Aunt," Francesca laughed nervously, "how can you talk thus? Why I have not yet been introduced to the Viscount. Yet you speak as if the wedding is a foregone conclusion!"

"Why, so it is," smiled Lady Rothersay. "I have spoken to his mother, the Viscountess, on the subject and she has given her consent to the union. Ideally, I should like you to be wed with the minimum delay, but of course it would not be proper for you to wed ahead of Aithne. Now as I see it, the Duke will desire to delay his wedding plans until after the birth of his sister's child. I am sure he would consider it most indecorous for Lady Evelina to appear at the Cathedral in a state of expectancy . . . " Her gaunt face paled. "At least, I *hope* he would consider it indecorous! One can never tell with the Duke, of course, he appears to be a law unto himself!"

Normally, Francesca would have sighed silent agreement to this remark about the Duke. But she was in such a state of shock at her aunt's galloping conclusions that for the moment her characteristically wry sense of humour had completely deserted her.

Lady Rothersay's long fingers drummed on the velvet sofa arm as she continued, "So it will be a November wedding for you, Aithne, whilst you Francesca, will be a Christmas bride! How enchanting!"

Utterly appalled, Francesca sat dumbstruck, quite incapable of moving a single horrified muscle. Then her grey-green eyes met those of Aithne, seated beside her mother on the sofa. And Aithne's eyes, Francesca noted, were filled with frozen despair.

Francesca gazed long and hard at her cousin. What she saw there gave her the courage to speak.

It was one thing, she realised, for her to take an amused

view of her aunt's matchmaking activities, and hence plan to thwart them by seeking in private moments to deter Viscount Medway from desiring to marry her. But for her aunt formally to have approached the Viscount's mother, and for the two formidable ladies to have raised their glasses to toast the happy pair — well, thought Francesca hotly, that is another matter altogether. I must speak now, or condemn myself to a married life spent smothering the weakling Viscount with rugs, draught screens and comforters.

"I do not wish to seem ungrateful, Aunt," she began, "But I do believe my father would prefer it if I were left to make my own choice of husband."

Lady Rothersay closed her eyes and declared, in a long suffering tone, "Please, Francesca! Do not subject us to yet another tedious conversation about the foolishly romantic nature of your father!"

"I happen to believe," said Francesca firmly, "that his views on love and on life are just, and wise and true. And I must make it clear to you once and for all that I have no intention of agreeing to marriage with a man I have not yet even been introduced to!"

Aithne gasped. Lady Rothersay rounded on her and said quietly. "Kindly go to your room, Aithne. I wish to talk to your Cousin in private."

"Yes, Mama." Aithne, clearly regretting that gasp of horror which deprived her of witnessing what promised to be a rare scene, obediently left the Drawing Room. Soberly, Lady Rothersay regarded her niece. "I requested Aithne to withdraw, Francesca, because I fear I have some harsh things to say to you, and I did not wish to cause you embarrassment in front of your Cousin."

Francesca sat straight-backed on her chair and waited for the storm to break.

"I have been observing you closely, Francesca," said

Lady Rothersay crisply, "and it is my regretful duty to inform you that I have been sorely disappointed in my sister's child. Your unfortunate appearance, of course, cannot be helped. Regrettably, you inherit your tallness, your fresh complexion and your strong bone structure from your father. But your walk, Francesca! There are times, you know, when I have watched you positively stride into a room!"

Francesca said nothing. She was well aware that her aunt was merely warming to her theme, and had yet to reach the heart of the matter.

"We have already touched," Lady Rothersay went on disdainfully, "on the matter of your flagrant disregard for the social proprieties. But what distresses me above all else is your total arrogance over the matter of your family fortunes. You must be aware that you are offering yourself up for marriage without the benefit of a dowry. Worse, your father urgently requires you to make a successful marriage in order that the de Lisle family fortunes may be salvaged."

She held up an imperious hand as Francesca attempted to interrupt. "Kindly allow me to finish, Francesca. When you arrived in my house I decided that it was my duty to find you a husband in possession of reasonable wealth and position in the world. But you yourself make my task extremely difficult. Quite apart from your most singular appearance, you appear to have no accomplishments at all. Not once have I seen you engaged in embroidery, or watercolours, or practising upon the piano forte. And when you were dancing with Lord Sutton at my ball, Lady Southport mentioned to me that at times *you* appeared to be leading *him*! Surely you appreciate, Francesca that a marriageable girl must have accomplishments. What, pray, are yours?"

Francesca gazed helplessly at her aunt. What can I say, she wondered frantically. It is true that I cannot draw, or sing, or embroider or play on the instrument. I have received instruction in all these arts, to be sure, but I have no aptitude for them. And at home, after my dear mother died, most of my time has been taken up in running a household and entertaining my brother Edward.

What are my accomplishments? Well, I have taught myself a little Latin and Greek to the great pleasure of my father, and he says I mix his snuff to perfection. Also he will eat no other redcurrant jelly than that made by my own hand.

I can ride a horse bareback (oh what fun Edward and I had riding across the Dorsetshire meadows!) and I am remarkably skilled at fencing. Embroidery is too finicky an occupation for me, but I have been obliged to learn how to sew curtains and even make my own dresses. I can run like the wind, and I am a strong swimmer and when Edward challenges me to a tree climbing race, then it is always I who wins!

But of course, Francesca realised, none of this would carry any weight at all with Lady Rothersay. In her eyes, I am a complete social failure. Someone to be married off and hidden away without delay.

"From your silence I take it that you see my point," Lady Rothersay said, pacing the room in an agitated manner. "To all intents and purposes you are totally unmarriageable material. Why, then, are you not properly grateful when I arrange a marriage for you with an eminently suitable gentleman. And a titled one at that!"

Francesca could contain herself no longer. Rising angrily to her feet she stormed at her aunt. "Grateful? You expect me to curtsey my thanks at the proposal that I should wed a semi-invalid whom I do not know and whom I most certainly do not love? No, Aunt Cecilia, no, no, *no!*"

Two bright red spots appeared on Lady Rothersay's cheeks as she regarded the blazing eyes of her niece. With one swift, sure movement she picked up the silver-topped cane from the sidetable and smashed it down on Francesca's hands.

"You wicked, impertinent girl! Take that! And that! How dare you speak to me in such a brazen manner. Go to your room this instant, and do not return until you are ready to apologise."

Gritting her teeth against the searing pain from her hands, the livid Francesca reached forward and seized the cane from her aunt's grasp. Furiously, she flung it on the fire, and as the flames licked up she stormed from the room, banging the double doors in her aunt's outraged face.

Up in her bedchamber, Francesca plunged her aching hands into a jug of cool water. She was trembling with rage.

How dare she, Francesca whispered. How dare she treat me like this. Even my own mother never raised a hand in anger against me. And I most certainly shall not tolerate such disgusting treatment from my aunt.

Crossing to her toilette table, she wrapped two handkerchiefs round the broken skin across her throbbing knuckles. But the pain in her hands was as nothing compared with the searing fury in her heart.

For two pins I would pack my box and leave this house within the hour, she thought. But the resulting family feud would cause endless distress to my father. No, for his sake I must endure the remaining two months of my time in Winchester. But suffer in silence I will not! My aunt has humiliated me. Therefore I feel no further obligation to her.

With a determined gleam in her eye, Francesca crossed to her writing table. Putting pen to paper with her aching, bandaged hands was no easy matter, but Francesca's message was brief and to the point. In fact, it contained, just two words, *Yes*, followed by her signature.

She sealed the letter and handed it to a footman to deliver. Then she hurried purposefully down the corridor and swept without knocking into her cousin Aithne's bedchamber.

5

She found Aithne sitting at her toilette table, anxiously examining her complexion for freckles.

"Aithne," said Francesca without preamble, "do you really want to marry the Duke of Wexford?"

"Why, if Mama says I want to wed him, then I suppose I do," Aithne replied, dabbing cucumber juice over the bridge of her nose.

Francesca stood by the draped and tasselled pink window curtains. "But, what about *you*, Aithne! Have you no views of your own on the matter?"

Aithne replied in a shocked whisper, "In this house, Francesca, the only views that count are Mama's. Be warned, Cousin. If you dare to express an opinion which is contrary to her own, she is apt to let fly with that horrid silver-topped cane."

"She won't do that any more," Francesca informed her. "For I have just thrown it on the fire!"

The golden-haired girl whirled round on her stool and gazed dumbstruck at Francesca. Then her childish face dissolved into laughter. "Oh, Francesca, how brave of you! I have wanted to do that for years, but I have never had the courage." She noticed Francesca's bandaged hands, and exclaimed, "Oh, you poor thing. I remember the last time Mama did that to me — it was when I refused to go to my room the instant I was ordered to — it took over two weeks for the scars to heal."

"It is of no consequence," said Francesca with a dismissive shrug. "I am convinced that by tomorrow my aunt will sorely regret her hasty action."

"That she will not," Aithne contradicted her. "You will find that Mama will ignore the matter completely. But if your hands hurt, and she sees you wincing, she will seize on the opportunity to remind you that it is all your own fault, and how you brought your punishment upon yourself."

Francesca watched her cousin as the girl twisted her ringleted hair into a knot on top of her head. "Oh, Francesca, I do wish I had naturally curly hair like yours. I am compelled to go to bed every night in rags, and it hurts so!"

Francesca felt like slapping her. Here was a situation where Lady Rothersay was sitting downstairs, plotting the weddings of her daughter and niece, probably at this very moment drawing up guests lists — and all Aithne could find to worry about was her lank hair!

"Cousin," said Francesca urgently, "to return to the subject of the Duke of Wexford. What is your opinion of him? Do you believe you would be happy as his wife?"

"I do not know. I cannot tell," sighed Aithne. "Whenever we meet I find him so overwhelming I can never think of a word to say, and I spend my time staring at his boots, whilst Mama engages him in conversation." Her eyes narrowed as she regarded Francesca. "Why are you so interested, Cousin? Do you wish to marry him yourself? If so, you are doomed to disappointment. The only way Mama would allow you to marry a Duke is if I were swept off my feet by no less than a Prince!"

Francesca laughed. "Fear not, I have no matrimonial

designs on the Duke, or Viscount Medway or any other gentleman for that matter."

Aithne's blue eyes regarded her with suspicion. "Oh come now, Francesca! I admit I am not very bright, but I am not that much of a goose. Why, every girl wants to marry."

"Not I!" declared Francesca with a toss of her dark head. "I have no desire to become any man's chattel. I treasure my freedom far too much to allow any man to dominate me."

"That is all very fine, Cousin, but it is not as if you are a wealthy woman with the financial means to indulge in such eccentric attitudes," Aithne pointed out. "You talk of freedom. But without a man to support you and provide for you, how are you to live?"

"I have no intention of giving myself body and soul to a man in return for clothes, board and lodging," said Francesca in a spirited tone. "No, I intend to support myself in life by finding employment."

Aithne choked in horror. "But Francesca! That is unthinkable! Mama would go up in a cloud of blue smoke! And in any event, what saleable skills have you? Most ladies of good families who find themselves in financial distress turn to millinery. But I cannot imagine you sitting in a dreary workroom sewing ostrich plumes onto bonnets."

"I agree, a lifetime of bonnet-making would be a dreary prospect indeed," smiled Francesca. "Well, never fear Aithne, I shall think of something. Anything will be better than marriage to a man I have no love for."

"I do want to get married," said Aithne slowly, tucking her lavender satin shod feet under her. "And of course I do most urgently want to be wed before Clorinda. But it is what comes after the wedding that I dread."

"Ah. You are referring to the Wedding Tour?" asked Francesca delicately.

"No, no. I do believe I should enjoy that," smiled Aithne shyly. "I mean when one is settled in one's house and all the grand Winchester ladies come to call. They are pretending to be most civil, of course, but in reality they are watching to see if you control your servants properly, and if you understand the order of precedence which dictates that Lady Featherstone must be served with her tea before Lady Southport, but Lady Southport has hers ahead of Lady Sombourne. It would defeat me, Francesca, I know it would. I should do it all wrong, and Mama would scold me, and tell me how perfectly Clorinda performs as a hostess . . . " She took out a lace-edged handkerchief and wiped away a self-pitying tear.

"Heavens! It all sounds most alarming," remarked Francesca dryly.

"You don't believe me," pouted Aithne, "but when they all arrive at Mama's Afternoon on Thursday you will see then that I speak the truth. All the elite of Winchester will be in our Drawing Room, standing elegantly on their dignity. And heaven help anyone who utters an unconsidered remark, or who's social etiquette is at fault — for it will never be forgotten or forgiven."

Francesca smiled to herself. Excellent, she thought. Lady Rothersay's celebrated Thursday Afternoon will suit my purposes admirably. Contrary to my earlier expectations, it promises to be a most rewarding afternoon!

*   *   *

"A thousand apologies for keeping you waiting," said a breathless Sir Peter Jamieson as he seated himself beside Francesca on the riverside bench the following afternoon. "I was delayed by the latest alarming news about Lady Sutton. You have heard about the accident of course?"

Francesca nodded. A messenger had arrived in Upper Brook the previous evening with intelligence from Lord Sutton that his wife, whilst under the influence of a sleeping draught, had attempted to jump from the third floor window of Sutton Hall. Fortunately, a maid had happened upon the scene and dragged her distraught mistress to safety.

Whilst wishing no ill towards the unhappy Lady Sutton, Francesca had been grateful for the incident, for it had swept from Lady Rothersay's mind the tense relations between herself and her niece.

"My aunt went immediately to Sutton Hall," Francesca told Sir Peter. "And has remained with Lady Sutton all day. Which was fortunate, in its way, for it meant she was not at home to intercept your message requesting that we meet here by the river."

He smiled. "I am delighted that you have decided to accept my little business proposition, Lady Francesca. May I enquire what caused your change of heart?"

"No you may not," Francesca replied coolly. "I asked you to meet me in order that we may finalise matters in a formal manner."

"I admire your professional approach," he said promptly. "Now, as you know, the *Winchester Courier* is published every Friday. But in order that the printers have sufficient time to set *Lady Selina's Journal* in type, I need to receive your material by Tuesday evening at the latest."

"That is easily arranged," said Francesca pushing aside the overhanging branch of alder to allow the warm sun to play on her face. "But I have decided not to style myself Lady Selina. I do believe that Lady Alethia would be more appropriate. I was leafing through a book of names and their meanings recently, and I discovered that the name Alethia means *truth*."

Sir Peter's brown eyes gleamed with laughter. "Yes, that is most admirable! *Lady Alethia's Journal.* I like the sound of that very much. Now, we must be extremely frank and discuss the matter of your financial remuneration. I had in mind to pay you half a guinea for each of *Lady Alethia's Journals.*"

Francesca twirled her pale green parasol and replied sweetly, "Indeed? Then I regret that our thoughts in no way coincide. It had occurred to me that one guinea would be far more appropriate."

"A guinea a week!" exclaimed the outraged newspaper proprietor. "Why, that is quite extortionate!"

"I think not," said Francesca calmly. "After all, there is no one else in Winchester whom you dare approach to write such a Journal. And you have said yourself that I am extremely gifted, and deserve to be properly rewarded."

"Yes, I did say that," Sir Peter agreed, choking over the memory. "But a guinea, Lady Francesca! I must ask you to re-consider."

Gracefully, Francesca rose to her feet. "I fear there is nothing more to be said, Sir Peter. Good day to you, and goodbye!"

As she swept away up the river path, Sir Peter remained on the bench, his head in his hands, thinking furiously. The lady in green, her head held high, did not look back.

But she had not progressed more than a hundred yards before the dark-haired man went rushing after her crying, "Lady Francesca wait! You will bankrupt me! You will send me to the debtors prison! But I agree to your terms. Do you hear? I agree!"

★   ★   ★

Lady Sombourne, dutifully attended by the plump Clorinda and Viscount Polesden, were the first to arrive on Thursday. From her first words, it was evident that Lady Sombourne had decided to wipe from her mind all recollection of her disastrous charity ball, and concentrate instead on the glorious triumph of her niece's engagement.

"Such a well-matched pair," she sighed, watching the newly betrothed couple sit down with Aithne on the window seat. "They are to be married in January, you know, when Clorinda has completed a year of mourning for her mother."

Lady Rothersay brightened considerably at this intelligence. "I do so admire Clorinda's respect for her poor, departed Mama . . . Er, you have heard, of course that the Duke of Wexford has been paying considerable attention to Aithne?"

To Francesca's eternal regret, Lady Sombourne's astringent reply was drowned by the arrival of Lady Featherstone and Lady Southport, who hastened towards their hostess shrilly demanding news of the unfortunate Lady Sutton.

"She is resting comfortably," Lady Rothersay assured them as they sank down like anchors, one on either side of her on the sofa. Lady Sombourne, considerably peeved at being elbowed out of the most comfortable seat, swept to the far side of the room and was soon engaged in animated conversation with Lord Compton.

"Whatever is it that ails Lady Sutton?" Francesca heard Lady Sombourne enquire of Lord Compton. "First she takes a tumble into the river, and then we hear that she is attempting to hurl herself out of the window. Do you imagine that she has heard the rumours about Lord Sutton and the laundry maid, or that actress creature from Salisbury?"

The fastidious Lord Compton shuddered with distaste. "Dashed bad do. Even the fellows at my Club raised an eyebrow or two at Sutton's latest escapades. However, I cannot believe that a whisper of the scandal could possibly have reached Lady Sutton's ears. It is more likely that the incompetent physician gave the lady an overstrong dose of the sleeping draught, which induced in her severe nightmares, of a sleepwalking variety."

He glanced up and observing that the Duke of Wexford had just made his entrance with Lady Evelina, excused himself with the remark, "Ah, Wexford. Pray excuse me, Lady Sombourne. I want to have a word with him about my trout . . ."

Lady Sombourne was immediately joined by Lady Southport, who gushed, to Francesca's delight, "My dear Lady Sombourne, what a delightful gown! That particular shade of grey is so becoming in my opinion, to a more mature complexion!"

Lady Sombourne drew herself up and replied frostily, "I will be glad to give you the name of my dressmaker. Clearly you are astute enough to appreciate her valuable advice on styles which flatter ladies in the prime of life."

Francesca moved away to greet Sir Peter Jamieson, who was being pointedly ignored by his hostess.

"I shall invite him, and I shall acknowledge him with a nod when he arrives," Lady Rothersay had declared, "but I shall not be seen conversing with him."

Francesca was wryly surprised that her aunt's formal invitation to Sir Peter had not included the scribbled instruction, "Tradesmen's entrance at rear of premises."

As she conversed in a lighthearted manner with Sir Peter, Francesca realised what it was she had found lacking at Number 11 Upper Brook. It was, quite simply, the broadening effect of male company. Shut up for these past weeks in a house dominated by women, no wonder I have felt so caged mused Francesca. Especially as both Lady

Rothersay and Aithne are for the majority of the time concerned solely with such trivial matters — should Aithne wear the blue bonnet or the yellow? Are waists half an inch higher or lower this Spring? Was Lady Sombourne being deliberately offensive when she rode past the house with her carriage blinds drawn?

"You are looking particularly enchanting this afternoon," Sir Peter complimented her, his dark eyes admiring her brilliant eyes, and her glowing complexion so perfectly complimented by her deep apricot gown "I trust that you are hearing much that entertains and amuses you?"

"I am indeed," murmured Francesca. "But I feel if my identity as Lady Alethia is to remain a secret, it would be best if we were not seen conversing too long together."

He sighed. "Who, then, do you recommend that I captivate with my sparkling repartee?"

"Go and talk to my cousin Aithne," Francesca recommended. "She is extremely shy and would welcome someone who could make her laugh."

"It shall be my pleasure," he said, strolling to the windowseat where Aithne sat staring miserably at the handkerchief twisted in her hands.

Francesca circulated round the crowded Drawing Room, exchanging a pleasant word here, a smile there, and to all outward appearances acting the dutifully sociable niece of the hostess. But her sharp eyes and ears missed nothing — from Lady Southport's lecture to Lady Evelina on the impropriety of appearing in public in her condition — to Lord Sutton's hand resting briefly, but unmistakeably on the *derrière* of Lady Rothersay's maid as she entered with a cologne-soaked handkerchief to cool her mistress's wrists.

At last however, as the tea was poured, Francesca came face to face with the one person whose company she wished to avoid.

"I have been observing you observing the assembled company," remarked the Duke of Wexford. "Tell me, Lady Francesca, are you fascinated or repelled at what you see?"

"I am surprised that you should honour my aunt's Drawing Room with your presence," replied Francesca, unsettled as always by the amusement in his deep blue eyes. "Will not your precious fish become restive in your absence, my lord?"

"The reason," he said levelly, "that I was so annoyed with you for plunging into my river that morning, was that I have just stocked it with some rather rare Samlet trout. This is one of the few places in England where they breed successfully. But, understandably, the sight of an unclothed, beautiful woman swimming amongst them is liable to render them positively dizzy with excitement."

"All the more reason, I should have thought," said Francesca guilelessly, "for you to stay at home by your river and sing a lullaby to them, instead of exposing yourself to this perfumed jungle."

He laughed, and said lightly, "My sister Evelina was in favour of a diversion this afternoon," He gazed round the Drawing Room at the cream of Winchester Society graciously smiling their way through a social quadrille, and murmured in a politely conversational tone to the girl in the apricot dress, "Tell me, Lady Francesca, have you ever been kissed?"

Francesca was so startled that she all but spat out her mouthful of tea. Then, realising that he was taking a perverse delight in unnerving her, she replied in an offhand manner, "But of course."

"Ah," said the Duke, raising a courteous hand in greeting as the Earl of Featherstone lumbered into the room, "From your reaction am I to infer that the experience was somewhat lacklustre?"

"I have no intention of discussing my private life with you," said Francesca tartly, nettled that he had hit precisely upon the truth.

"I would guess," the Duke went on, quite unperturbed by her frosty demeanour, "that your kisses have been furtive, muddled efforts, bestowed on you by green youths in dark corners as they claimed from you the supper dance!"

Francesca could not meet his eyes. Gazing wildly across the room, she bestowed a brilliant smile on Sir Peter Jamieson, willing him to hasten to her rescue. But he, interpreting her smile as one of thanks for the fulfilment of his promise to entertain the shy Aithne, turned back in animated conversation to the golden-haired girl at his side.

The Duke, utterly at ease, rested an elbow on the bureau and continued in a low voice, "You should be kissed, Francesca, out in the open, on the flower-scented Downs, with a carpet of grass at your feet, and sunlight in your hair."

Francesca was infuriated to find herself blushing. Frantically, she searched her mind for a cutting retort but could think of nothing that was effectively cool and disdainful.

"Francesca dear," cooed her aunt's voice in her ear, "perhaps you would be good enough to offer Sir Peter some tea. He has been talking so long to Aithne that his throat must be fair parched by now."

As Francesca, highly relieved at her aunt's intervention, moved out of the Duke's hearing, Lady Rothersay hissed at her in a low tone, "Really, Niece, whatever are you thinking of, to monopolize the Duke in such a brazen fashion! To be sure, his intention in honouring our gathering this afternoon was not to be bored with your ignorant chatter!"

"No, Aunt," Francesca replied meekly, hastening across the Drawing Room with tea for Sir Peter. She was furious with the Duke. Every time we meet, she raged, he is not content until he has either displayed ducal arrogance, or tried in some manner to put me to the blush. And today he was in priceless form! For in the impertinent remark he has just made to me, he contrived both to exasperate and embarrass me!

No doubt if my aunt had not happened so fortuitously by, the Duke would have gone on to suggest, in that maddeningly mocking tone of his, that he should be the one to bestow on me this scented, sunlit kiss. My, what an honour! Why, I am surprised I am not already swooning at the very thought.

"My dear Lady Francesca," murmured Sir Peter, as Aithne was whirled away towards the Duke by her mother, "your beautiful eyes are positively ablaze! Do tell. Have you heard something utterly scandalous which will appear next week in *Lady Alethia's Journal*?"

Francesca had not realised that her eyes were such a mirror of her inward turmoil. Composing herself, she replied lightly, "I have no intention of informing you in advance of the nature of my Journal. You will just have to wait and see, like everyone else!" She glanced round the room, and went on, "Now, your next duty is to go and practise your charm on Dowager Lady Featherstone."

Sir Peter groaned. "Oh no. She and her son, the Earl, can talk of nothing but farming and horses. In fact, I've heard it said that the loose boxes at Featherstone Court are far more luxuriously appointed than the bedchamber."

Sir Peter ambled off in the direction of the formidable Dowager, who was holding court on the sofa. Francesca was hoping for the opportunity to converse with the lively Lady Evelina, but she was forstalled once more by her aunt, who trilled.

"Francesca, may I present to you Viscount Medway? Viscount, I have the honour to present my niece, the Lady Francesca de Lisle."

The Viscount, a pasty-faced man in his early forties, bowed over Francesca's gloved hand. Francesca regarded him with distaste. This, then was her suitor — the man her aunt and Lady Medway had decreed should be her companion for life. In December, if these ladies had their way, she would walk up the aisle of Winchester Cathedral and promise herself to this goose-fleshed Viscount.

Absurd. Quite impossible, Francesca decided. She mused that the only good thing about the alliance would be that the Viscount was clearly not much longer for this world. Even the mere act of bowing over her hand had caused him to puff.

"How sensible of you to wear gloves indoors, Lady Francesca," he said, his bulging pale blue eyes regarding her soberly. "One should at all times protect one's wrists from draughts, you know. Wrists and necks, Lady Francesca, they are the real danger points of the human physique."

Francesca, who was wearing the gloves to conceal the broken skin on her knuckles, wondered how much Viscount Medway knew of his mother's plans for his nuptuals.

"I trust I find you in good health Viscount," she murmured sweetly.

He shook his greying head. "I have been suffering with the most dreadful chill, but Mama has taken care of me wonderfully. Really, without her, life would be unbearable."

No, thought Francesca, it is life *with* Lady Medway which would be unbearable. Marry the son and, clearly, you will find yourself wed to the mother too.

Lady Rothersay bustled up, "Did I hear dear Lady Medway's name mentioned? Do present her with my compliments, Viscount, and inform her that I shall be bringing Aithne and *Francesca* to call on you both very soon."

Francesca's spirits plummeted at the notion of being

looked over, and given the red rosette of approval by Lady Medway. "She . . . she is not here this afternoon?" enquired Francesca apprehensively.

"Indeed no," replied the Viscount, "my mother has not left the house for over fifteen years — since my father died."

"Lady Medway is so devoted to Medway Grange that she will not leave it for even so much as a short breath of sea air at Lyme Regis," Lady Rothersay informed Francesca, poking her sharply in the back as a reminder to smile at the Viscount.

Francesca's smile was in the nature of a grimace. The prospect of marriage to the Viscount became grimmer by the minute. Not only was he a sickly creature with a domineering mother — but the mother was an ever present fixture in the house! The new Viscountess Medway would not be free of her presence for a single second of any day of the year.

Lady Rothersay's attention was distracted by her realisation that the Duke of Wexford was about to take his leave of the gathering. As Lady Evelina passed by, she smiled at Francesca and remarked.

"It would please me greatly if you would ride out one day and visit me at Penshurst Lodge, Lady Francesca. My husband's broken leg is well on the mend now but he is still unable to move far, so a lively-minded caller would prove a most welcome diversion for him."

"Thank you," smiled Francesca, "I should like that very much." She stiffened as she sensed the Duke's presence beside her.

"I would recommend that you take the path up over the Downs, Lady Francesca. On a sunny Summer's day, I do believe you would find the experience most rewarding!"

Boldly, Francesca faced the challenge in his laughing blue eyes. He is daring me to ride out over the Downs, and run the risk of him waylaying me and honouring me with his ducal kiss in the sunlight.

Well, we shall see about that, my arrogant Duke, Francesca resolved. I am growing a little tired of the manner in which you choose to amuse yourself at my expense. The time has come, I feel, for me to seize the initiative, and turn the tables smartly on you!

★   ★   ★

On Friday morning the Duke of Wexford rode over to visit his sister at Penshurst Lodge. He was surprised to find her, at eleven o'clock, still seated at the breakfast table, wearing a loose wrap over her beribboned night shift. Her husband, Lord Penshurst, sat with his injured leg up on a stool, wincing at the shrieks of laughter emitting from the mother-to-be as she perused the *Winchester Courier*.

"Ah, Wexford, thank God you are come. I think you should be the first to know that I am demanding a divorce from your sister. I have been grievously deceived. Had I known she possessed a voice with the carrying power of a coaching horn I should never have married her."

He winked at the Duke, who replied in the same vein, "I am in total sympathy. It was not for nought that I dubbed her Evelina the Screamer you know."

Evelina pushed back her thick fair hair which waved, undressed, to her shoulders.

"Oh do stop carping, you two! Aha! Here is something to wipe that smug smile from your face, Aidan. Listen to this:

"*I have been charmed to see the Duke of Wexford so much in society of late. Indeed a little bird has whispered in my ear that since the marriage of his sister Lady Evelina, Hampshire's most eligible bachelor has found Wexford Hall a cold and solitary place.*

But which of our winsome Winchester damsels is soon to be honoured with the glittering Wexford tiara? I have my suspicions, dear readers! Rest assured, when an engagement is imminent you shall hear about it first in my journal!

Stony-faced, the Duke snatched the newspaper from his sister. "What impertinent nonsense is this!" he roared. "Who has dared to write about me in such terms?"

"Why Aidan, it is a new column in the newspaper, penned by someone called Lady Alethia," his sister replied sweetly. "See, there is a charming drawing of her at the top of the page. If you would just stop striding up and down and breathing fire and brimstone for a moment, you'll see what I mean."

The furious Duke flung himself into a chair and spread the *Winchester Courier* over the mahogany table. "Huh! Most of her face is concealed by that ridiculous fan she's holding," he exploded. "All one can see is a pair of laughing eyes topped by a ridiculous hat."

"I rather admire the hat," said Evelina thoughtfully. "Ostrich plumes are quite the thing this season, you know."

Lord Penshurst, enjoying the scene enormously, took a delicate sniff of snuff, as the Duke raged on.

"Evelina, you will kindly stop talking trivialities? Don't you realise that because of this absurd intelligence from the so-called Lady Alethia, every household within a hundred miles containing an unmarried daughter will now be on full red alert? Don't you recall what happened when the Duke of Pirbright returned from Italy and rashly announced that he was looking for a bride? Why, the Mamas of the town were so desperate to oblige they were practically pushing their daughters out of upstairs windows into his path."

Evelina giggled. "But Aidan, be practical! You cannot remain a bachelor for ever."

"Quite. But when I wed, Evelina, I wish it to be to a lady and at a time of my own choosing. I have no intention of being goaded up the aisle by a lady in an absurd feathered hat!" His blue eyes scanned the rest of the column. "Ah ha, Penshurst! No doubt you were vastly entertained by Lady Alethia's paragraph pertaining to you."

Lord Penshurst groaned. "Oh God. Tell me the worst, Wexford. Are the names of my eight mistresses in four counties printed there for all to see?"

"*I was most distressed,*" read the Duke in a falsetto voice that sent Evelina into paroxysm of mirth, "*to hear of the injury to the Earl of Penshurst's leg. I wish him a speedy recovery, and control once more of the marital reins. Lady Evelina has, I fear, been causing more than a frisson of disapproval in fashionable Winchester Drawing Rooms. Take my advice, Lord Penshurst, and confine your high-spirited wife to the home until after the happy event.*"

"Marital reins!" squeaked Evelina indignantly. "Why—"

"Calm yourself, sister, dear," smiled the Duke. "Remember your condition."

"Clever pun on *confine* by Lady Alethia," commented Lord Penshurst equably.

'Really, Charles, how can you sit there sniffing snuff and making admiring remarks about her literary style! I am simply livid at the suggestion that you should put a curbing bit on my freedom!"

Lord Penshurst reached across and massaged her shoulder. "I know better than to try, my dear. I love you as you are, headstrong, free-thinking, warm-hearted and gay. If I ordered you to stay at home until our child is born, you would be intensely miserable and thus you would make my life insufferable as well."

Evelina looked tenderly into his eyes. "Oh Charles, how well you understand me! I do love to go out into society, and you know I am perfectly safe with Aidan as my escort."

"It occurs to me," remarked the Earl dryly, "That in future, Evelina, it will be Wexford who will require *your* protection, against the legion of damsels throwing themselves at his eligible feet!"

Evelina glanced across at her brother. "You're very quiet, suddenly, Aidan?"

When the Duke looked up from the newspaper his eyes were agleam with laughter. "I have just been reading the rest of *Lady Alethia's Journal*. And I would give anything to be a fly on the wall of certain Winchester Breakfast Rooms at this very moment!"

★   ★   ★

In the Breakfast Parlour at Number 11 Upper Brook, the servants had been dismissed. Lady Rothersay sat at the head of the table, reading aloud in tones of horrified disbelief.

"*After an enchanting morning strolling under the limes in the Cathedral grounds, I returned home to change, and then took my carriage to the quaintly restyled home of Lady Rothersay in Upper Brook.*"

"Quaintly restyled?" shouted Lady Rothersay. "Why, the woman is obviously a complete ignorant. Now we have done away with those mouldering oak beams, the facade of this house is utterly contemporary. There is nothing quaint about it."

"No Mama," agreed Aithne, holding her breath as Lady Rothersay continued.

"*Lady Rothersay, bravely holding the fort in her husband's continued absence, was ably supported by her daughter and niece.* Supported? It makes me sound like a crumbling monument! *Lady Aithne was looking particularly charming again in* the pretty pink shade we have all grown so fondly familiar with this season."

Lady Rothersay gulped for breath. "Aithne! You will give all your pink gowns to your maid, this very morning, without delay."

"But Mama," pouted Aithne. "You yourself told me how well I looked in pink."

"I did not intend you to wear it day in and day out to the point of making yourself a laughing stock in the city. Oh heavens! This dreadful Lady Alethia creature then proceeds to make remarks about you, Francesca! Really, is there no end to her insolence?"

Francesca could not remember when she had enjoyed a morning more. Toying with her napkin in what she hoped was a suitably agitated manner, she listened as her aunt read aloud Lady Alethia's observation that Lady Francesca had poured tea for her aunt without removing her gloves. "*Is this the latest fashion in Lady Francesca's charmingly rural native Dorsetshire, or can it be that Lady Francesca is ashamed to reveal her washerwoman's hands to the world?*"

When she had penned this line, Francesca had wondered if she had gone too far. Would Lady Rothersay realise that the barb was intended directly against herself, for causing the damage to her niece's hands? And if so, would she then suspect that she was harbouring the mysterious Lady Alethia under her own roof?

But as Aithne had predicted, Lady Rothersay felt no sense of shame over the incident. And her attention was soon distracted as she read on, "*And mention of the sociable world brings to mind the mysterious behaviour of Lady Medway. It is now fifteen years since she honoured any public gathering with her presence. Speculation, naturally, is rife as to the reason why. But let it be known that I myself hold no brief with the shocking rumours that Lady Medway is a deranged recluse, stalking the stark salons of Medway Grange in a vain search for her long departed youth.*

"Youth! Ah, what a precious gift it is. Regrettably, all too soon our maidenly forms begin to thicken, and it is so easy to fall prey to the danger of over-eating, in order to compensate for the girlish charms so cruelly snatched away from us.

"It grieves me to learn that Lady Sombourne is at this moment in the grip of such an affliction. On dit —"

Lady Rothersay paused. "*On dit?* What does that mean, Aithne?"

From Aithne's helpless stammers it was evident that she had paid scant attention to her French tutor, and it was left to Francesca to murmur.

"I believe it means *they are saying*, Aunt."

"Indeed?" sniffed Lady Rothersay. "Well why can't the woman say so then, in plain English? Now where was I. Ah, *on dit that at Lady Sombourne's ill-starred charity ball she puffed her way through the minuet with all the finesse of an overstuffed turkey.*"

Solidarity with the Winchester elite would not permit Lady Rothersay to give way to mirth at this, but the gleeful twitch of her lips was not lost on Francesca.

"*No doubt this affinity with the farm yard explains her attachment to dear Lady Featherstone, whose loose boxes, I hear, are far more luxuriously appointed than the Featherstone Court bedchambers.*"

"Oh," gasped Lady Rothersay, "I can read no more of this filth! I shall summon Sir Peter Jamieson here forthwith, and demand an immediate explanation of this outrage!"

"But Mama," protested Aithne, "Sir Peter is not a servant! Surely it is not within your power to *summon* him to the house?"

This was so patently true that Lady Rothersay did not waste breath on reprimanding her daughter for contradicting her. Seizing one of the silver knives from the table, she slashed viciously at the open newspaper before her.

"Nevertheless, action is called for!" she declared in menacing tones. "If I die in the attempt I shall expose this Lady Alethia creature, and call her publicly to account!"

6

The first day of Summer dawned disappointingly wet and windy. But at midday, a break appeared in the clouds and by three o'clock the sun was so bright and warm that Francesca was able to enjoy a stroll with Lady Evelina around the Penshurst gardens.

Penshurst Lodge was a rambling, two-hundred-year-old mansion onto which most of Lord Penshurt's ancestors had added at whim a wing, a storey or a conservatory. Yet despite the lack of unity, Francesca found the ivy-covered house extremely pleasing to the eye. She certainly felt more relaxed here than at any time in the formal confines of her aunt's house in Winchester.

Lady Evelina was justly proud of her garden and took a great delight in pointing out her special favourites to her guest. "I am so glad you were able to come up today, Francesca. Look at those roses! They are always at their best, I think, just before they reach full bloom."

"They are especially delightful with the raindrops still glistening on them", remarked Francesca, reaching out to touch a damp, velvety rose petal.

"Oh yes, do be careful not to muddy your pretty blue dress," cautioned Lady Evelina. "Lady Sutton was here yesterday, and a crow settled on a low branch of one of the walnut trees, and sprayed the lady with rain from the leaves. Oh, the commotion was endless! Just a few drops of water were enough to send her into total hysterics."

"Perhaps it in some way brought to mind her dreadful accident when she fell in the river," suggested Francesca.

Lady Evelina sighed. "In normal circumstances no doubt I too would have had the same charitable thought, and not been so irritated by the incident. But circumstances yesterday were far from normal. I was obliged to entertain, you see, all the ladies of the elite of Winchester. Poor Charles was quite terrified at the prospect, and hid in the gun room all afternoon!"

Francesca smiled, "Ah yes. I heard from my aunt that there was to be a meeting of the ladies to discuss this matter of *Lady Alethia's Journal*. But she has said not a word about what transpired.'

Laughing, Lady Evelina led Francesca across the lawn to a rustic garden seat. They waited whilst a gardener wiped off the moisture, and brought dry cushions for the ladies to sit on. Lady Evelina settled one of the cushions comfortably in the small of her back and continued.

"Well, of course, they were all arguing so much amongst themselves, it was impossible for anything to be decided!"

"I thought it was remarkably brave of you to invite them all in the first place," commented Francesca.

Lady Evelina spread her hands in a helpless gesture. "But my dear, I did nothing of the sort! They invited themselves. I received a message from Lady Southport saying that it had been decided that a meeting was necessary, and that it would be politic for all the ladies to gather here at Penshurst because of course it was felt that I should not care to travel far *in my condition*."

Francesca smiled. It was not often, she suspected, that the

Duke of Wexford's sister found herself so smartly outman-oeuvered!

"I had made ready my gold Drawing Room for the occasion," said Lady Evelina, "but Lady Featherstone declared the room to be unsuitable. She marched round peering behind the screens, and whipping back the window hangings, convinced that Lady Alethia herself was lurking there with her pen at the ready. At one point she even stared very hard at the fireplace, as if challenging Lady Alethia to jump down the chimney."

Francesca shook with laughter, alarming a young blackbird which hopped back across the lawn to the safety of the rosebed.

Lady Evelina went on in a mocking, long suffering tone, "So finally, Lady Featherstone led us all out onto the terrace, and there was a further delay whilst chairs were brought and everyone jockeyed for a position out of the sun, and with the best views across the lawn. Then they began."

Francesca found it impossible to contain her mirth as Lady Evelina described this historic meeting of the Winchester ladies. True to form, they had each found it impossible to state honestly that what *most* aggrieved them were the remarks Lady Alethia had made about them personally.

"Oh no," said Lady Evelina, "Lady Rothersay professed herself outraged by Lady Alethia's unkind and unjust remark comparing Lady Sombourne to an overstuffed turkey. And Lady Sombourne, in turn, was distressed beyond measure by Lady Alethia's sly hints about Lord Rothersay's continued absence."

"How touching," murmured Francesca, "that they should each be so concerned about the reputation of the others. There is true friendship indeed."

"Lady Southport," gurgled Lady Evelina, "was so incensed by the paragraph which insulted Lady Featherstone that she recommended that they draft a strong letter of protest to Sir Peter Jamieson, threatening to have their husbands blackball him from all Winchester clubs and societies unless he agreed to banish Lady Alethia from the pages of his newspaper."

This did not surprise Francesca. In London society, such a notion would be laughable. But Francesca knew enough by now of the ladies of Winchester to realise that it would be child's play for them to influence their husbands to blackball Sir Peter from their gentlemen's clubs.

Lady Evelina crossed her trim ankles and continued, "But I pointed out that such a public display of their displeasure would only be playing into Sir Peter's hands. Everyone in Winchester would be vastly amused by the ladies' wrath, and henceforth every copy of the *Winchester Courier* would be snapped up like hot cakes. Lady Sutton agreed with me, and recommended a public show of icy disdain towards Lady Alethia's scurrilous Journal."

"But were they not at all concerned to discover the identity of the mysterious Lady Alethia?" enquired Francesca, watching a lemon brimstone butterfly dancing along the fragrant lavender border.

"Indeed yes! That was the next topic of discussion. Would you believe it, Francesca, because I had been the one to recommend that no action be taken against Sir Peter, Lady Southport had the impertinence to suggest that *Lady Alethia's Journal* had in fact been penned by me!"

Francesca sat transfixed at the indignation in Lady Evelina's blue eyes. The fair-haired girl went on, "The trouble is, of course, that I am well known for my independent ways, and Lady Southport indicated she knew I would gain considerable private amusement from making such mischief."

Lady Evelina gave Francesca an impish smile. "And so I would too, had it occurred to me first to masquerade as Lady Alethia. However, it was your aunt who came to my rescue, pointing out somewhat waspishly to the others that I am expecting a child in the autumn and would therefore have neither the time nor the energy to go galloping abroad, collecting scandal for a weekly journal."

How typical of my aunt to rush to Lady Evelina's defence, thought Francesca. She would not be so foolish as to let an opportunity slip to ingratiate herself with the sister of the man she hopes to see wed Aithne. But hopefully, my Journal paragraph about the Duke will put a hefty spoke in my aunt's wheel. For now Lady Alethia has declared it to be common knowledge that the Duke is seeking a bride, he will be too terrified to set foot in Winchester city, for fear of being assailed by pretty young hopefuls and their aspiring Mamas! And that, in turn, will make life so much more comfortable. For with the Duke safely ensconsed within his estate. I shall be able to go about my business in Winchester without the fear of encountering his unsettling, arrogant presence.

"Then, with suspicion from me thankfully diverted," Lady Evelina went on, "all eyes turned to Lady Sutton. She, after all, had supported me in my remarks about Sir Peter and what's more, she was the only lady not mentioned in Lady Alethia's Journal!"

This had been deliberate on Francesca's part. She had felt that after her accident in the river and the near fall from a top floor window, Lady Sutton should be spared unkind barbs from the pen of Lady Alethia.

"Lady Sutton was livid!" exclaimed Lady Evelina, her eyes sparkling at the memory. "She is an excessively large woman, you know, and she leaped from her chair, pounded across the terrace and almost garrotted Lady Featherstone with her pearls. She then reminded the company, in what I can only describe as most unladylike terms, that she had been half-drowned, and then had been within an ace of falling to her death. *In the midst of all this,* she screamed, *do you imagine me capable of sitting calmly at my writing tabe, penning artful paragraphs on such earth-shattering topics as how often Lady Aithne has worn that particular pink sprigged muslin dress?*"

Lady Evelina, it transpired, had hastily called for tea to be brought and the soothing brew had succeeded in lowering temperatures on the terrace.

"But the best was yet to come," said Lady Evelina, her eyes dancing mischievously as she regarded Francesca. "For Lady Sombourne then remarked, in her sweetest voice, that there was of course a newcomer to Winchester society who, as a stranger from Dorsetshire, would not have the same high standards of loyalty as those who had been born and bred here."

Francesca's gloved hand grasped the edge of the wooden seat. Surely she had not been exposed so soon, and so easily? She forced a laugh. "Me! Why, the notion is absurd!"

Lady Evelina nodded, intent on retying the ribbons of her flowered bonnet. "Lady Rothersay was swift to dismiss the notion as totally fanciful. She explained that you had fallen from your horse into a thorn bush and scratched your hands so badly that it was painful for you even to pat rosewater on your face, let alone spend hours wielding a pen."

Francesca smothered a sigh of relief, and Lady Evelina declared, "So as you see, Francesca, nothing whatsoever was resolved by the ladies. But of course, they are all secretly highly suspicious of one another, and they will be on tenterhooks until the next edition of the *Winchester Courier* appears on their breakfast tables." She hugged herself with delight. "Oh, I cannot wait to see what Lady

Alethia will say next! As you know, Lady Sombourne is holding a ball next Friday to honour the engagement of her niece to Viscount Polesdon, so no doubt Sombourne Court will be buzzing with outrage at that morning's poison-tipped intelligence from Lady Alethia!"

I sincerely hope so, mused Francesca, as Lady Evelina stood up and shook out her skirt. The fair-haired girl took her arm, and together they wandered back to the rose garden.

"I must pick some of these blooms and take them across to Wexford Hall," commented Lady Evelina. "I noticed when I was there this morning that the flowers in the hall were looking somewhat sorry for themselves."

"Yes, I noticed straightaway the lovely anemonies you had placed there," said Francesca. Then she drew up short, and blushed. For apart from herself and the Duke, no one knew of the unorthodox breakfast at Wexford Hall which had delayed her initial arrival in Winchester.

Lady Evelina smiled. "Do not look so alarmed, Frances-ca. My brother told me about your morning swim in the river, and how you stood in the water, arguing with him! My, how I should love to have been there. It is not often that Aidan meets someone with a wit and brio to match his own. But fear not, I shall never breathe a word of the incident to anyone else. Even my own dear Charles remains in blissful ignorance."

Mention of the Duke brought to Francesca's mind the vexing question of which route she should take from Penshurst Lodge back to Winchester. On the journey out, the rain had just stopped and she had taken the main highway, reasoning that the country road would be water-logged and muddy. But now the sun was shining brilliantly and Francesca was confident that the water would have drained away from the path over the chalk downs.

As the groom assisted her into the saddle, and she waved farewell to Lady Evelina and Lord Charles, Francesca was still in two minds over her route. Her instinct was to take the Downs path. It was now a beautiful summer's afternoon and she relished the prospect of an invigorating gallop over the lush green turf. But she had not forgotten the Duke's words to her in her aunt's Drawing Room.

You should be kissed, Francesca, out in the open, on the flower-scented Downs, with a carpet of grass at your feet, and sunlight in your hair.

And then there was the challenge implicit in his final remark to her on that same afternoon!

I would recommend that you take the path up over the Downs, Lady Francesca. On a sunny Summer's day, I do believe you would find the experience most rewarding!

Francesca brought down her whip with a crack on her burnished boot. I will not allow that man to intimidate me, she thought defiantly. To take the main highway home would be an act of cowardice. I should be admitting defeat by allowing him to influence me in this way. It would please me greatly to gallop over the Downs and if the Duke is impertinent enough to waylay me I shall simply greet him with the most chillingly daunting *hauteur* at my command!

Up on the downs, the air was fresh with the sweet scents of summer. As Francesca rode past, the young lambs ran baa-ing to the protection of their mothers and the peewits circled and dived by the side of the chalky paths.

Francesca felt so exhilerated, she pulled off her bonnet and tied it to her saddle. Ah, that was better, with the wind in her hair and the sun on her face! Oh, wished Francesca fervently, if only I were a man and free to ride astride, unencumbered by skirts and petticoats.

She flew on across the springy turf, her eyes roaming the hills for a man on a large grey, her ears pricked for the sound of galloping hooves behind her. But there was no sight or sound of the Duke, and Francesca was beginning to feel that she had probably misinterpreted his remarks. After all, she reasoned, the Duke has many responsibilities pertaining to his estate. He is hardly likely to waste time loitering up here on the Downs simply to tease me with the threat of a kiss.

It was then that she sped past a shepherd's hut and, out of the corner of her eye, she glimpsed a figure resting his horse out of the wind. She raced on, but he was an expert horseman and overtook her within minutes, seizing her bridle and wheeling her chestnut round to a halt.

"Dear me," murmured the handsome Duke reprovingly, "how ill-mannered are you young ladies from Dorsetshire. You might at least have raised a hand in greeting as you roared by."

"Indeed," replied Francesca with disdain. "I fear your presence was so insignificant that I failed to notice you."

He laughed, his blue eyes roving freely over her glowing complextion, sparkling eyes and wind tossed hair. "You look enchanting after your ride," he said, "this is the environment that suits you best, Francesca. You are not a creature destined for cloistered Drawing Rooms. You thrive in the open air, racing the wind, with your face lifted to the sun." He smiled lazily. "But then, I do believe I have said something of the sort to you before."

Francesca looked steadfastly over his shoulders. "I really cannot recall," she said distantly, though her heart was hammering. "Now if you will release my bridle, I am expected shortly at my aunt's house."

"You shall ride on very shortly," he promised her, in a tone which made Francesca prickle with indignation, "But there is something else I have to do first."

Helpless, Francesca watched as he dismounted, and tethered both horses to a gorse bush. She glared down at him. "So you have been lying in wait for me, you scoundrel! I suppose you have been up here on the Downs every day, waiting for me to ride past so you may take advantage of me!"

He laughed. "You flatter yourself, my dear. I was waiting for you, yes. But I fear I have not been sitting here every day, anxiously scanning the horizon for a glimpse of your lovely black hair. In truth, Evelina happened to mention this morning that you were to call. So I decided to take the opportunity to have a few private moments with you!"

Francesca was seething with anger. Both at the Duke, for the manner in which he treated her like a high-spirited filly whom he would enjoy breaking in, and at herself, for allowing herself to fall into his hands. He knew, she thought furiously, that I would respond to his challenge and take the high road over the Downs. He was so certain of it, that he did not bother to take up a vantage point where he could see both the Downs road and the main highway. No, he had no need. Having thrown down the gauntlet in my aunt's Drawing Room, he had not a shred of doubt that I would not be able to resist snatching it up and waving it aloft.

The Duke stood by the chestnut and said courteously, "May I assist you to dismount?"

Viciously, she lashed at him with her boot. "No you may not! Kindly release my horse and permit me to proceed on my way!"

The Duke of Wexford was not just a tall, powerful man, he was also extremely agile. Sidestepping Francesca's angry kick, he reached up, placed a strong, firm arm around her waist and swung her easily down onto the grass.

"Take off your gloves," he ordered, still keeping a hard hold on her arms.

Francesca's eyes blazed with anger. "Oh, 'tis a bare fisted

fight you desire, is it? When will you learn, my lord Duke, that I am not a mindless heap of muslin, to be thrown from my horse and given orders as you think fit!"

By way of reply he whirled her round and pinioned her arms behind her back. She writhed, twisted and kicked but to no avail.

"By heavens, Francesca," he muttered, tearing off first one of her gloves and then the other, "you are one of the most hot-tempered women I have ever had the misfortune to encounter."

He spun her round then to face him, but the unexpected tenderness in his eyes suddenly dispersed her pent-up fury.

"Who did this to your hands?" the Duke enquired quietly. He held her hands in his, with the scars of her aunt's cane still visible in the sunlight.

Francesca shrugged and said carelessly. "Oh, it was nothing. I fell from my horse into a thorn bush — "

"Yes, and this morning I flew to the moon and back," the Duke interrupted grimly. "I heard that thorn bush invention this morning, from my sister when she was giving me her highly amusing account of the gathering of the Winchester ladies at Penshurst. I didn't believe the tale for a moment, and resolved to waylay you on the Downs and inspect your hands for myself."

Francesca flushed. "Well, really! What right have you to take it upon yourself to *inspect* my hands!"

"Because I am curious to know why you and your aunt are not telling the truth over the matter," he replied. "You seem to forget, Francesca, that I have had the opportunity of seeing you ride. And I will tell you frankly that you handle a horse better than any other woman in the county. Not only that, but you are a proud woman. In the unlikely event that you had taken a tumble, you would have gone to any lengths to conceal the fact. So I repeat, Francesca. Who was it who inflicted these wounds on your hands?"

It would have been churlish of her not to have recognised the genuine concern in his voice, "I appreciate your interest," Francesca said quietly, drawing on her gloves once more, "You are right. I did not fall into a thorn bush. But I assure you, the injuries to my hands are of no consequence and I would ask you not to question me further on the matter."

He stood looking down at her for a moment, watching her button her gloves. Then he said, in a low, commanding voice, "Come here, Francesca." As he spoke, his hands reached out and grasped her gently but firmly by the shoulders.

Her heart was racing as he pulled her to him. Suddenly, she found her thoughts in turmoil. Her mind and her common sense told her to draw away, to fight this man who sought to dominate her. But already her capricious heart was preparing to surrender, to yield to the kiss he had warned her he would give her, here on the Downs, in the sunlight.

The Duke was clearly in no mood to be rushed. Slowly, his arms encircled her, and she knew that in another moment his lips would be on hers, and she would be lost. Her precious freedom, so jealously guarded all these years, would be gone, swept away by a man she had allowed to master her.

In a last final moment of blind panic, Francesca's eyes flew open and she gazed wildly over his shoulder. What she saw there made her cry out in horror:

"Look! Oh my God! Quickly, we must act!"

The Duke laughed as she trembled in his arms. "Come now, Francesca. That is the oldest trick in the book. But I confess that I am flattered that the prospect of my kiss sets you atremble in such a delightful fashion."

He broke off as the struggling Francesca aimed a well-placed kick on his shin. "I am not shaking with desire, you arrogant beast! Look behind you, oh quickly!"

He saw then the terror in her eyes and spun round. A phaeton and pair, wildly out of control, had breasted the hill and was careering down the slope at breakneck speed towards them.

The Duke reacted with lightning speed. Flinging out an arm, he threw Francesca sideways to safety with bare seconds to spare before the pounding greys brought the phaeton crashing upon them. Scarcely pausing for breath, he dived for the dangling reins, miraculously caught hold of them, and hung grimly on.

Francesca, sprawled in the grass, cried out in alarm as the foaming horses dragged the Duke along with them for ten yards or so, until at last his strength and will brought them under control. She scrambled to her feet and ran towards the battered though miraculously unbroken phaeton, where a man and a woman sat dazed and shaken.

The man she recognised as Lord Compton, though at this moment he was far from his customary immaculate self. His neck cloth was awry, his gloves were soiled and he was sweating profusely. The matron beside him, however, though clearly stunned by her ordeal, was still in command of herself.

Imperiously, she stretched out a hand indicating that Francesca was to assist her down from the phaeton. Ignoring the quaking Lord Compton, she moved to the Duke's side, where he stood quietly calming the agitated horses.

"Well done, Aidan," she rasped. "Thank heavens you were at hand, and capable of thinking quickly." she turned back to the man in the phaeton, who was fussing with the arrangement of his neckcloth. "Nothing to reproach yourself for, Lord Compton. I can't imagine why the horses suddenly took it upon themselves to bolt in that alarming fashion."

The Duke mopped his brow. His eyes were dark with anger. "Good day to you, Lady Medway. I trust these are not your greys?"

"Indeed not. They are from Lord Compton's own stables. But why do you ask?" enquired Lady Medway brusquely. Francesca brushing the grass from her skirt, stood quietly to one side, regarding with dismay this woman who if Lady Rothersay had her way, was destined to become her mother in marriage. Dressed from head to foot in unrelieved dark blue, she was clearly one of the Winchester Old Guard. Nothing, not even a bolting phaeton, would cause her to lose either her self control or her sense of her own importance.

The Duke strode to the phaeton and stood hands on hips, glaring at Lord Compton. "You've been treating those horses like whipping boys," he snapped. "Their flanks are sticky with blood. No wonder they took fright and made a bid for freedom. If you can't be bothered to learn how to handle your horses properly, Compton, you should rely on your own two puny legs in future!"

Lord Compton shrank back in the seat, blustering feebly, "Well really, Wexford! How dare you insult me in such a manner before two ladies too. I've a mind to call you out!"

"Oh don't be absurd," sighed Lady Medway dismissively. "Can't you see that Aidan here is somewhat fussed after we almost rollered him and his companion to the ground. Rest assured, he will regret his harsh words once he has simmered down and had time to reflect on the situation."

Francesca winced as she observed the Duke's face tighten with anger. But before he could explode with the wrath he clearly felt, Lady Medway had turned her flinty eye on Francesca herself.

"And will you not now introduce me to your young companion, Aidan?"

The Duke, his mouth set in a hard line, icily effected the formalities. Francesca hastily dipped a curtsey, aware that Lady Medway's hard eyes were raking her from top to toe.

"So you are the Rothersay niece of whom I have heard so much," said Lady Medway in tones of amazement. "May I enquire what, exactly, you are doing here, out on the Downs, unchaperoned, and in what I can only describe as a considerable state of disarray?"

Francesca dared not look at the Duke. What was she to say? It seemed unlikely, in all the terrifying confusion attending the bolting phaeton, that Lady Medway would have had time to observe herself and the Duke on the verge of a passionate embrace. Even so, there was still their presence together, dismounted from their horses, to be explained.

Just when it seemed to Francesca that the silence was destined to endure forever, the Duke stepped forward and said lightly, "The Lady Francesca called on my sister this afternoon, and as I have affairs to attend to in Winchester, I offered to escort her home. Now, as your carriage is mercifully unharmed, Compton, I recommend that we all proceed upon our way."

"Just one moment!" rapped Lady Medway. "I am not satisfied! Why are you both dismounted from your horses? Why is this girl not wearing her bonnet?"

Lord Compton, scenting an opportunity to avenge himself on the Duke, nodded his agreement, "Something wrong, here, Wexford."

Lady Medway waved him to silence. "That girl looks mightily flushed to me, Aidan. Lady Rothersay would be most displeased if — "

"Lady Medway!" the Duke's voice cut like a whiplash

through the soft June air. "Point one. The person of whom you speak is titled the Lady Francesca de Lisle, and not *that girl*. Point two, *I* am titled the Duke of Wexford and I should be glad if you would address me as such in future. Point — "

"Oh really!" exclaimed Lady Medway, "I have known you since you were a boy, Aidan — "

"And I am now thirty years old, the eighth Duke of my line and master of one of the largest estates in Southern England," the Duke shouted her down, "and I will tolerate no interrogation of my actions."

Lady Medway paled. Lord Compton, however, was reluctant to relinquish the slim advantage he felt he held over the Duke. "Seems to me you're protesting over much, Wexford. I can understand your wish to protect Lady Francesca, but you must admit the circumstances look damned fishy!"

It was a statement he regretted as soon as it was uttered. The Duke took one menacing pace towards him and enquired in deadly tones, "Are you doubting my word in this matter, Compton? Because if so, I warn you, I intend to drag you from that phaeton and give you the milling of your life!"

Lady Medway hastily stepped between them. "No cause for that, Ai — Your Grace. Of course we accept your word on the matter. And we must thank you most sincerely for your prompt action with the horses this afternoon. Now, with your permission, we shall proceed on our way."

The Duke favoured her with a curt bow, and stood aside as the phaeton moved off. Only when it was out of sight did Francesca release a great sigh of relief. "My, what a dreadful woman! But I was given to believe that Lady Medway was something of a recluse, that in fact she had not left Medway Grange for over fifteen years?"

Untethering the horses, the Duke assisted Francesca into the saddle. "I suspect that Lady Alethia's remarks in her Journal have finally flushed the old bird out." He glanced across at the dark-haired girl and went on, "I owe you an apology, Francesca. I should not have allowed my feelings to run away with me, and taken advantage of you in such a manner. It occurs to me that had matters progressed a stage further between us, and we had been observed, then life at Upper Brook would have been extremely painful for you."

She knew then that he had guessed the truth about the injuries to her hands. About their embrace, and the kiss of which the runaway phaeton had robbed her, she could find no suitable words. She still could not decide whether she was relieved or disappointed that he had not swept her fully into his arms and kissed her.

She smiled, imagining her aunt's outraged reaction at the intelligence that Francesca had been discovered in an embrace with the man she had, hopefully, designated for Aithne! But the smile soon faded from her attractive face as she remarked:

"To speak plainly, Your Grace, I imagine my aunt will not be best pleased when Lady Medway informs her of my dishevelled state of dress, and your own contretemps with her."

The Duke glanced sideways at the straight-backed girl with her head held proudly high. "I am only too well aware of your reluctance to take my advice on any matter, Francesca. But if you could bring yourself to listen to me for a second, instead of flying into a rage, I will tell you how best to becalm your aunt . . . "

Half an hour later, Francesca stormed into the Drawing Room at Upper Brook. Before her aunt could draw an astonished breath, Francesca threw down her bonnet on the sidetable and declared angrily:

"Aunt Cecilia, I must protest to you in the strongest terms about the treatment I have received at the hands of Lady Medway this afternoon!"

Francesca refused to calm herself, as her aunt admonished. Instead, she paced up and down the carpet, complaining in tones of outraged indignation about the Duke's kindness in escorting her back from Penshurst Lodge . . . how the ribbon on her bonnet had snapped, and how for safety she had tied her bonnet to her saddle . . . how they had both dismounted to examine the Duke's horse, which they feared had been improperly shod . . . and how the runaway phaeton had come upon them, causing Francesca to be flung in the grass with much disarray to her appearance.

"But how brave of the Duke to hold the horses in such a fashion!" exclaimed Lady Rothersay. "Why, they could all have been killed."

"Exactly!" cried Francesca. "Yet a moment later, Lady Medway has the impertinence to allege that the Duke and I were engaged in some manner of improper conduct! I am deeply distressed about this matter, Aunt. In fact, I feel it my duty to write to my father without delay, and set the entire affair before him. He will of course insist on an immediate apology."

Lady Rothersay leaped up and seized Francesca's hands in hers. "Now Francesca, my dear, I am sure that will not be necessary!"

Trembling, Francesca permitted herself to be led to the sofa and soothed. Naturally, Lady Rothersay had no desire to have this feud dragged through the mud of two counties, with everyone's reputations becoming sullied in the process.

"You must understand," said Lady Rothersay, "that Lady Medway is something of a foolish recluse, who knows little about the subtleties of our society. She is so accustomed to having her own way at home, and being listened to, that it comes as a shock to her to enter the outside world and find herself contradicted by a man she has not seen since he was a young pupil at Winchester College!"

"Yes, with hindsight I can appreciate that Aunt," said Francesca. "But Lord Compton was equally disagreeable."

"Oh, like many small men Lord Compton often indulges in Napoleonic daydreams," replied Lady Rothersay dismissively. "He is quite harmless, I assure you. But I give you my word, Francesca, I shall speak most strongly to Lady Medway and Lord Compton on the subject and make it clear that they are to treat you with respect in future."

"Thank you, Aunt," smiled the demure Francesca, highly amused at the thought of the forthcoming interview between the Ladies Rothersay and Medway. Lady Rothersay, naturally, would be intent on upholding her family dignity, and good name. But on the other hand she would not dare to aggravate Lady Medway too much, for fear that the Viscountess withdrew her agreement to the suggested union between her son and Francesca.

I do believe Lady Medway's impetuous behaviour has served my cause well this afternoon, mused Francesca. She will not dare admit to Lady Rothersay that this afternoon's episode has caused her to regard me in an unfavourable light. No, she will wait, and find some other reason over the coming weeks to cast a blight over me as a prospective bride. I am confident that were I the most wealthy heiress in England, she would still not allow me to marry her son.

Highly relieved at the thought, Francesca informed her aunt, "This has been a most taxing day, Aunt Cecilia. If you will excuse me, I should like to retire to my room to rest before dinner."

With permission graciously granted, Francesca hurried

to her cool blue bedchamber and locked the door. Without delay, she seated herself at her table, bent over a fresh sheet of paper and wrote at the top *Lady Alethia's Journal* . . .

7

Summer is come at last, wrote Francesca, *but sad to relate, the clement June weather has done little to improve the tempers of our little social circle here in gracious Winchester. Whilst shopping recently, I observed a lady of high repute berate her haberdasher for the poor quality of his Mechlin lace. Yet not half an hour afterwards, I witnessed the same well bred lady urging another of her acquaintance to purchase the lace, attesting in the warmest tones to its fine quality. The incident brought strongly to my mind the tale of the lady so much moved by a charity sermon that she placed her neighbour's purse on the plate.*

Francesca laughed to herself as she recalled Aithne's description of the scene in the haberdasher's between Lady Southport and Lady Featherstone. The latter had in fact purchased the lace, much to the delight of the Lady Southport who would now waste no time in trumpeting abroad the inferior taste of her companion. Shaking the ink from her pen, Francesca continued:

Before we leave the environs of the charming High Street shops, I cannot resist passing on to my readers a comment made to me by one of the more affluent tradesmen. I had complimented him on his well-appointed establishment, and enquired of his secret in attracting more custom than did his competitors. "Why my lady, in

Winchester there is one golden rule," he replied artlessly, *"I always charge very high and bow very low!"*

I am delighted to hear that Lady Medway has surfaced again into the fashionable pool. How distressing that her first outing should have ended in such near disaster. Dear Lord Compton, clearly overcome with the honour of driving his celebrated companion, lost control of the horses which ran wild with the phaeton across the Downs. But the Duke of Wexford bravely dashed to the rescue, galloping across country to cut off the wayward phaeton and pair.

Francesca was not displeased with that final sentence. What could be more natural than that by the time the incident had been relayed through several versions to Lady Alethia, the facts would have become somewhat exaggerated? If I tell the precise truth in every paragraph of my Journal, mused Francesca, the finger of suspicion will soon be pointed with great accuracy at me!

The Duke himself has been much in the company of Lord and Lady Penshurst of late. Has he, perhaps, been seeking the guidance of his married sister in the intriguing matter of whose slender shoulders shall be adorned by the ermine robe worn by right by the Duchess of Wexford?

No doubt his decision will be hastened by the sight of the radiant newly-betrothed Lady Clorinda and Viscount Polesdon at Lady Sombourne's forthcoming ball in their honour. Any gentlemen contemplating a dance with Lady Rothersay's niece, the Lady Francesca de Lisle, would be well advised to engage the services of a dancing tutor for a few hours beforehand. Country-bred Lady Francesca has an eccentrically rustic tendency to take the lead if her partner has the misfortune to hesitate over his steps.

It is regrettable that Lord Rothersay will not be present at the ball to effect a restraining influence on his niece. But Lady Rothersay, enduring her husband's absence with admirable fortitude, informs me that Lord Rothersay is regarded by the Prince

Regent as a great pillar of strength to the nation. Doubtless, if Lord Rothersay quitted London for even an hour, England would surely collapse.

I am compelled now to lay down my pen and attend to my toilette for the ball. Did I mention that we are all to wear masks? I must confess, I thought it scandalous of Lady X to remark that Lady Sombourne favours masked balls as a manner of concealing her increasingly grotesque appearance . . .

"Oh, what a dreadfully cruel thing to say!" gloated Lady Rothersay as the carriage advanced up the drive of Sombourne Court on the night of the ball. "I must make haste to reassure poor Lady Sombourne that no one of quality in Winchester would ever dream of thinking such a thing, let alone giving voice to it."

Aithne sat happily playing with her fan in a corner of the carriage. "I am so relieved that Lady Alethia had nothing to say about me in her Journal this week. But she was horrid to you, Francesca!"

"All eyes will be upon you this evening, Francesca, so do please attempt to be ladylike when you are dancing," instructed Lady Rothersay. "I realise it is a masked ball, but because of your height you will be easily recognisable."

Francesca, having been obliged by financial circumstances to lead an extremely quiet life at home in Dorset, had never before attended a masked ball. But as she entered the ballroom — decorated in silver and white to honour the newly betrothed pair — she was intrigued to find that despite their masks, many of the revellers were still instantly recognisable.

Easiest of all was Lord Penshurst, distinguished by the stick which was enabling him to relieve the pressure on his almost healed leg. And that must be Lady Evelina at his side, mused Francesca. How pretty she looks in that flowing indigo gown.

Francesca smiled as she observed a masked man of small

stature ordering a footman to close a nearby window. That could only be Lord Compton, divined Francesca, protecting himself against the poisonous night air.

"Extraordinary behaviour," murmured a tall, fair-haired man at Francesca's side. "The evening air outside is deliciously perfumed with honeysuckle. To own the truth, I would rather be strolling out there than condemned to the stuffy confines of this ballroom."

Francesca smiled up at him. "I must thank you, my Lord Duke, for your excellent advice regarding my approach towards my Aunt. I followed your instructions to the letter, raged and shouted in highly melodramatic fashion about Lady Medway, and was rewarded by soothing words and kind attention from Aunt Cecilia."

"Great heavens, I never thought the day would come when you actually took my advice over something," he said mockingly, "And this is supposed to be a mystery ball, Francesca. I confess myself mortified that you recognised me so speedily."

Wild horses would not have made Francesca admit that such was the power of the Duke's presence, she would recognise him anywhere, any time. She fluttered a careless hand, "Oh, however much people may disguise their faces with masks, it is always their walk which reveals their true identity. Posture, gait and attitude are the hardest things to disguise. Why, just look at that lady talking to the leader of the orchestra. There is only one person in all Winchester who in conversation always gives the impression that she is about to inspect one's fetlocks and offer one a carrot."

The Duke rocked with laughter at her astringently accurate description of the horsey Lady Featherstone. "I am glad to find you in excellent spirits tonight, Francesca. No doubt it is maidenly modesty which prevents you asking how I came to recognise you with such ease."

"That is easily divined," said Francesca scornfully. "According to the oracle of Lady Alethia, my great height is as good as a named label round my neck."

"You are taller than most ladies of your age," he agreed, "but thank heavens I maintain a generous height advantage over you. It pleases me greatly, you know, to see you tilt your pretty head to look up to me!"

"Oh, but the entire world looks up to you, my Lord Duke," retorted Francesca sarcastically. He smiled, quite unmoved by her taunts.

"What fascinating eyes you have, Francesca. When they glaze with hauteur they take on the exact same colour as your ice-green dress."

"Then beware you do not catch frostbite, Your Grace," smiled Francesca sweetly as Lady Rothersay swept across to join them, accompanied by Aithne, Lady Evelina and Lord Penshurst.

It was soon evident that Lady Rothersay had also recognised the Duke, and was now dangling poor Aithne before him in the hope that he would take the bait and ask her for the first dance. Lord Penshurst heightened the tension by bowing over Francesca's hand and declaring.

"Lovely lady in green, I would ask you to stand up with me, but I fear the nagging pain in my leg dictates that I must consign myself to the window arbour and talk of my lost youth with the chaperones."

"Oh poor Charles!" exclaimed Lady Evelina anxiously. "I feel so guilty for my selfishness in persuading you to attend this ball."

Francesca observing Lady Evelina's dainty slippered foot beating in time to the music, said quickly, "I shall be delighted to sit down with you, Lord Penshurst! We shall put our heads together and award a wooden spoon to the lady or gentleman who dances the worst!"

Lady Rothersay, well pleased with this development, glanced expectantly at the Duke. But he, equal as ever to the occasion, extended his hand not to the quivering Aithne, but to his sister.

"Come, Evelina, let us take the floor. I feel that a gauntlet has been flung down and the Wexford honour is strongly in the balance in the dancing stakes."

Lady Evelina fluttered her fan and exclaimed in mock despair, "Oh, that all my girlish, romantic dreams should come to this. My husband crippled, and I reduced to the shame of dancing with my brother!"

Lord Penshurst playfully tweaked one of her golden curls. "Away with you, woman. Or broken leg or not, I'll sweep you off into the perfumed night and smother you with kisses."

Laughing, the brother and sister moved off to join the set. Lady Rothersay, ashen at this horrifying, brazen exchange between husband and wife, stared desperately round for another candidate for the honour of Aithne's hand in the first dance.

Francesca, observing the downcast mouth of her cousin, was beginning to feel sorry for the girl, dressed with such care in a new spangled white satin gown, yet left high and dry on the dance floor. But fortunately, all was soon happily resolved as a dark-haired gentleman bore down on them and murmured a request in Aithne's ear. All smiles, she glided away to join the nearest set.

Lord Penshurst, a popular and amusing man, was soon joined by the gentlemen from Buckhurst's, his Winchester Club, and Francesca found herself whirled off onto the dance floor by adventurous partners interested to see if Lady Alethia was right, and Francesca did take the lead if she was given the opportunity.

The Duke of Wexford, much to Lady Rothersay's relief

and triumph, asked Aithne for the honour of the supper dance, which placed him, accordingly, at Lady Rothersay's table for the dancing interval. Francesca, and Lord and Lady Penshurst were also seated at the table. Inevitably, conversation soon turned to the scandal of *Lady Alethia's Journal*.

"I simply cannot fathom who could be writing such a scurrilous column," said Lady Rothersay heatedly. "It is appalling to contemplate that we in Winchester harbour such a cuckoo in our nest." She consumed a mouthful of lemoned chicken and enquired of the Duke, "Your Grace, you are a man of the world. Who do you imagine in masquerading behind the name Lady Alethia?"

Francesca held her breath as the Duke regarded them all thoughtfully. She knew that of anyone in Winchester, the Duke was the person with the wit and intelligence to divine the truth.

"I confess myself baffled," he admitted at last. "But then, living outside the city as I do, my eye is not as atuned as yours to any clues the lady may leave to her identity within her column."

Lady Evelina leaned forward eagerly. "We know that she enjoys shopping expeditions in the High Street, and lives at a sufficient distance from Upper Brook to be obliged to take a carriage to Lady Rothersay's Thursday Afternoons."

"All of which could be a cunning ruse to deceive you," put in Lord Penshurst, to Francesca's dismay.

Lady Rothersay laid down her fork. "Rest assured, Lord Penshurst, she will not deceive us for ever. Sooner or later, Lady Alethia will make a fatal slip. And once her identity is discovered, I shall ensure that she is received nowhere, but *nowhere* in all Hampshire!"

"My, what a terrible fate," murmured the Duke, earning himself a discreet kick on the ankle from his sister.

Fortunately the incident passed unnoticed by Lady Rothersay, who was bending her jewelled ear to the earnest whisperings of a gentleman who had approached the table. "What is that you say Lord Compton? It *is* Lord Compton is it not? Heavens, these masked balls are enough to give one spots before the eyes. Lady Southport has what? Fainted on the terrace? Mercy me. Are you positive it is she, Lord Compton? Why, I have known Lady Southport since we came out together as young girls. But even as a flighty young thing, I never knew her to faint!"

Lord Compton was beginning to look aggrieved. "Indeed, Lady Rothersay, one of the maids came running and removed the lady's mask. I was in two minds over whether to approach you first, or whether as hostess it should be Lady Sombourne that I informed . . . "

Lady Rothersay rustled immediately to her feet, desperate that her rival Lady Sombourne should not be the first on the scene to learn what had caused Lady Southport's unprecedented loss of consciousness. She returned after a quarter of an hour, but to everyone's chargrin steadfastly refused to say another word on the subject, beyond the fact that Lord Southport had been routed out of the card room and was at this moment on his way home with his wife in the carriage.

Meanwhile the orchestra had struck up once more and the two Rothersay ladies were whirled away onto the floor, Lady Rothersay with Lord Compton, and Aithne with a red-haired man who danced as if he were treading on hot coals.

Francesca, glad to be relieved for a while of the watchful company of her aunt, relaxed in her chair, preparing to enjoy a few minutes pleasurable conversation with Lady Evelina and her husband. But this was not to be. To her surprise, the Duke rose to his feet and requested that she join him in the quadrille.

As she took his hand, she remarked coolly. "How brave of you, Your Grace, are you not afeared that I will take the lead, and reprimand you for any inaccurate step?"

"No woman ever takes the lead with me," he replied firmly, guiding her expertly into the first steps of the dance.

Francesca could not resist the mischievous reply, "Oh but my lord, all Winchester knows by now that that is not quite the case. Why, Lady Alethia appears to be leading you a merry dance in her Journal!"

"Lady Alethia," replied the Duke with daunting self-control, "is in grave danger of becoming over-confident and over-reaching herself."

Wishful thinking, my dear Duke, thought Francesca, saying with a smile, "Indeed, yes. My sentiments exactly. And have you no notion, no suspicions at all as to who Lady Alethia might be?"

He shrugged, and said in a disinterested tone, "Oh it's obviously some embittered old crone. She is certainly very Poorly educated? Overblown and flowery? She queried flowery." As they made a turn, the Duke went on, "My, Francesca, we are a quarter of the way through a set, and you have not yet taken the lead! Is it too soon, do you imagine, for me to congratulate myself on achieving an all-comers record with you?"

Francesca stared straight ahead, not deigning to reply. Poorly educated? Overblown and flowery? she queried hotly. Well, after such critical remarks about my Journal, I have no intention of giving the Duke the satisfaction of complimenting him on his dancing!

It is quite infuriating, she told herself, the manner in which the Duke excels at so many things. He is, it has to be admitted, a fine dancer, managing to combine both grace and authority in his movements. He is an excellent horseman, he dresses impeccably, he is widely read and I have heard that he is one of the best shots in the county. It crossed her mind that he was probably also extremely accomplished in the art of love. Hastily, she pushed the thought aside.

Yet why, she wondered, has he never married? Oh of course, I know him to be such an arrogant individual that any woman misguided enough to marry him would endure the most miserable life. But he is, after all, a rich and handsome Duke. He could take his pick from the flower of Hampshire womanhood.

As they completed another turn, the Duke glanced round the ballroom and remarked, "I wonder if Lady Medway is here tonight?"

Francesca shook her head. "My aunt informs me that her son, the Viscount, was so shocked by the news of her runaway phaeton that he is confined to bed, suffering from a mild fever. Lady Medway is attending him, much to my relief I confess, as my aunt has it firmly in mind that I should become the next Viscountess Medway."

The Duke roared with laughter. "Heavens, Francesca, he would not be your style at all! Why, you would be obliged to spend your wedding night with a physician in attendance, lest your bridegroom's unaccustomed exertions caused him to collapse with fatigue."

"Your Grace, I am shocked!" protested Francesca, trying hard not to laugh, and hoping desperately that the other dancers in the set had not overheard.

The Duke would not be quelled. He went on in a low voice, "Ah, Francesca, there would be no sunlit kisses for you then. Your lovemaking would be confined to a heavily-curtained bed, smelling of embrocation."

Francesca shuddered. "Please do not talk of such things. You are putting me to the blush!"

"Nonsense. There was not the faintest tinge of a blush on your face when I began to embrace you on the Downs the other day. I noticed most particularly."

Francesca felt helplessly trapped. When, oh when would this interminable dance end? The Duke was clearly in a devilish mood, determined as usual to ruffle her self control. Then she decided that it was foolish to allow him to put her on the defensive. The more she wriggled and writhed, the more enjoyment he derived from her distress.

Accordingly, she changed tactics and went straight into the attack, "No doubt, my lord Duke, it would have amused you a great deal to have had your way, and kissed me that day on the Downs?"

He raised an eyebrow at her bold tone. "Yes," he replied, an unfathomable expression in his blue eyes. "It would have amused me very much, Francesca."

"Then I fear the entertainment would have been one-sided," she snapped back, "for I certainly have no desire to kiss you!"

"Indeed?" he said sardonically. "I do not recall much maidenly display of resistance?"

"There are times when one is so repulsed, that it induces a condition of numbed shock," Francesca informed him coldly, neatly timing her remark to coincide with the graceful curtsey she made to him at the end of the dance.

But as she glanced up into his eyes, she felt a shiver of apprehension. Merciful heavens, she thought. He is not at all chastened by my remarks. Instead, he clearly imagines I have issued a challenge! And from the steely glint in his eyes it is apparent that he intends to win!

★   ★   ★

The ball ended shortly after midnight. No sooner had the Rothersay carriage door been shut, than Lady Rothersay exclaimed in hushed, excited tones, "My, what a to-do with Lady Southport! I did not want to make too much of it at the time, of course. Lady Sombourne has ears like pitchers."

"But what ailed Lady Southport?" enquired Aithne, easing off her dancing slippers with a sigh of relief.

"It is all very sad," said Lady Rothersay. "She swooned on the terrace as you know. As I reached her, she was beginning to recover. And she was murmuring, *old, old . . . what to do*?" Lady Rothersay fussed with her hair and said complacently, "I had no notion that Lady Southport was so concerned about her advancing years. And it is not as if she is the most ancient woman in Hampshire. Why, we came out together, so she must have the same number of years as I. And I am most certainly far from decrepit."

"No, Mama."

"Indeed so, Aunt."

Well satisfied, Lady Rothersay smiled indulgently at the two girls. And did you both enjoy the ball?"

"Very much," said Aithne enthusiastically, "though the notion of the masks seemed somewhat absurd to me. Even before we all revealed ourselves at midnight, it was obvious to me who most of the masks concealed."

"Indeed?" said Lady Rothersay frostily. "In that case, Aithne, perhaps you would be so kind as to tell me the identity of the dark-haired gentleman who danced with you twice this evening."

Aithne's pretty face glazed. "Oh . . . I . . . really have not the faintest notion, Mama."

Lady Rothersay glared at her and continued, "And what of the Duke? Did he converse with you whilst you were dancing?"

"Yes, Mama. He was most civil."

"Civil?" spat Lady Rothersay. "Is that all?"

Aithne was almost in tears. "Really, Mama, you can hardly expect him to go down on one knee and propose to me right in the middle of the quadrille!"

"Aithne! How dare you speak to me in such an impertinent fashion!"

Francesca, admiring her cousin's display of defiance, hastened to Aithne's support. "It occurs to me that the Duke is not a man of excessive passions, Aunt. I assure you, when he danced with me he displayed a most barbed spirit. So the fact that he was so civil to Aithne could be taken as a sign of great affection."

It was utterly absurd, of course, but because Lady Rothersay wanted to believe it, she allowed herself to be mollified. Impatiently, she tapped her fan on the carriage door. "It distresses me that we appear to be making no progress with our marriage plans for you two girls. Oh, it vexed me beyond endurance observing Clorinda so smugly triumphant tonight with her new fiancé. But now it appears that we shall have to find someone else for Francesca, as Viscount Medway seems to have declined into a permanent state of ill health. And as for the Duke, well, I shall have to set my mind to inventing some way to make him come to the point, and declare himself for Aithne."

Francesca could hardly contain herself. How she would love to have seen the Duke's face had he been here to hear such a pronouncement!

"It is at times like this," sighed Lady Rothersay, "that I long for Lord Rothersay to return from London. If he were only here, he could have a few quiet words with the Duke over port at Buckhurst's. It would be a simple matter for him diplomatically to point out to the Duke the advantages of a match with Aithne."

"But Mama," said Aithne as they descended from the carriage. "How can you be sure that he holds any true feelings of affection for me?"

"You foolish girl," smiled Lady Rothersay. "Why do you think he now makes a point of gracing every gathering attended also by you? If he is being a little tardy in declaring himself, it is simply because the selection of a Duchess is a responsibility which he takes extremely seriously. A man in his position cannot afford to make a mistake." Her smile faded as she regarded her golden-haired daughter, standing in a pool of lamplight. "Aithne! The skin on your cheeks is quite dingy, child! Are you unwell?"

"Oh no, Mama. Just extremely fatigued after the excitement of the ball. I shall be fully restored after a good night's rest."

But Aithne did not go immediately to her bed. As Francesca sat in her nightshift brushing her long, shining dark tresses, there came a tap at her bedchamber door, and Aithne slipped quietly in.

"Francesca, I must ask your advice," she breathed, settling herself on a corner of her cousin's bed. "Do you really believe, as you said, that the Duke's civility to me this evening was really a sign of affection? Do you think he does want to marry me?"

"Heavens, Aithne, I have not the faintest notion what thoughts and opinions the Duke holds," replied Francesca lightly. "I only uttered those sentiments, you know, to prevent my aunt from scolding you for answering her so impetuously!"

She felt sorry for her cousin, huddled so miserably against the blue bedcurtains. "Dear Aithne, has the Duke, then, captured your heart? Is it torture for you, waiting for him to declare himself?"

"No!" Aithne exploded violently. "If he asks me to marry him I should die of fright! Oh Francesca, I cannot keep my secret a moment longer! You see," her blue eyes grew moist, "I am in love with another!"

Francesca almost fell off her stool with shock. Throwing down her hairbrush, she ran to her cousin's side, and took her trembling hand. "Why Aithne! How wonderful. How exciting! Tell me all. Who is this mysterious man you have given your heart to?"

Aithne shook her golden head. "I must not say, Francesca."

"But you can trust me, Cousin. I promise I will not breath a word to a soul."

Tears ran down Aithne's cheeks. "I gave him my word that I would not reveal his identity. You see, he is totally unsuitable. It would be quite impossible for me ever to wed him."

Francesca caught her breath. "He is married, Aithne! How tragic. What are you to do?"

"It is all quite hopeless," sobbed Aithne pitifully. "I love him so desperately, Francesca. I count the days, the hours, the minutes until I am able to see him again. But if Mama ever discovered the truth . . . "

Both girls sat silently, contemplating the parental wrath that would descend on Aithne if it were learnt that she had a secret, married beau!

"Tell me, Aithne," Francesca enquired curiously, "how long have you known that you loved this mystery gentleman?"

Aithne sighed. "Oh, for some time I have been feeling strangely elated whenever I was in his presence. But tonight, oh tonight, Francesca, he took me out onto the terrace, and kissed me in the moonlight! Words cannot express my turmoil of emotions, Cousin. But I knew then, without a shadow of doubt, that I was hopelessly in love with him!"

Francesca was furious with herself for not paying more attention to Aithne's dancing partners at the ball. Could the unnamed beau be the gentleman who Lady Rothersay had observed dancing twice with her daughter? Francesca cast her mind back and tried to conjure some details of him. He was, she recalled, dark-haired, of medium build and with the complexion of one who had been out a great deal in all weathers. But although there had been something vaguely familiar about him, she could not for the life of her put a name to the man.

"Francesca, I need your help," said Aithne urgently, wrapping her slender arms round her drawn-up knees. "Tomorrow I have agreed to tryst with him for an hour."

Francesca frowned. "Aithne, I do hope you are not contemplating anything foolish!"

"Oh no, be assured, Cousin," said Aithne earnestly. "We will simply walk together, and talk, in the way that lovers do. But of course, there is the question of Mama. She is certain to sleep late tomorrow after the ball. So would it be possible for us two to leave the house together, leaving word that we intend shopping in the High Street?"

It was an arrangement which, in fact, suited Francesca's purposes very well. For she had fixed to meet Sir Peter Jamieson at their secret place by the river, as he wished to discuss certain aspects of *Lady Alethia's Journal* with her. Aithne's hour with her mystery beau would give Francesca just the opportunity she required to keep her own assignation with Sir Peter!

"Very well, Aithne," smiled Francesca. "I agree to your plan. Though heaven knows what will befall us if my aunt discovers what we are about!"

"Oh, you will think of something to tell her," said Aithne confidently. "You are always so resourceful, Francesca."

When her cousin had gone, Francesca slid thoughtfully between the sheets. She left the bedcurtains open to allow the balmy night air to circulate freely in the room.

My, she mused, who would have dreamed that Aithne

would have possessed the spirit to defy her mother in such a manner! But who, who can this mystery beau be?

Francesca wracked her brains, considering and discarding all the dark-haired married gentlemen of her acquaintance in Winchester. Lord Sombourne? Oh surely not. He was bald and ponderous — though it had to be admitted that on all counts he was the man most calculated to send Lady Rothersay into forty fits if she ever discovered the truth. That Aithne should have fallen in love with the husband of Lady Rothersay's arch rival! Francesca gurgled with laughter at the notion.

Gradually, however, it dawned on her that the man to whom Aithne had so rashly given her heart must be Lord Sutton. She had heard whispers of his alleged philandering, and when she herself had danced with him at Lady Rothersay's charity ball, she had been obliged to take firm steps to prevent him becoming familiar with her as they passed behind one of the garlanded pillars. It was reported to my aunt that I was boldly taking the lead in the dance, recalled Francesca with a wry smile, but in truth I was simply escaping from Lord Sutton's unwelcome attentions!

It did not at all surprise Francesca that the young and very naive Aithne should have fallen for the rakish charms of Lord Sutton. She wondered where Aithne was to tryst with him tomorrow.

I do hope she has chosen somewhere extremely private, thought Francesca. For I have found to my cost that there are eyes and ears everywhere in Winchester, and there is very little that does not in due course find its way back to my aunt.

As she blew out her candle, Francesca reflected sadly on Aithne's love affair. It would end in tragedy, of course. Even Aithne, blinded with love as she was, could see that her happiness would be short lived, leaving her with nought but bittersweet memories. Yet Francesca knew enough about girls in love to appreciate that there was no point in attempting to reason with her cousin. Aithne thoroughly understood the hazards in romancing with a married man. But for the moment, her heart was ruling her head and she would have no truck with any chilling, common sense advice.

Aithne is in love, Francesca repeated to herself as she gazed into the dark. It is all quite doomed, and hopeless for her.

Yet even so, Francesca found she could not repress a pang of envy for the girl who would tomorrow run so eagerly into her lover's embrace.

★   ★   ★

Aithne was pale with apprehension as they left the house the following morning.

"You are sure there was no sound from my mother's apartments?" she asked for the tenth time.

"Rest assured, her maid has not yet drawn the bedchamber curtains," said Francesca soothingly. "And do stop fretting with those bonnet ribbons, Aithne. You look absolutely lovely."

They walked half the length of the High Street and stood for a moment under the great Guildhall clock which projected out over the street. Aithne glanced nervously up at the niche which held the splendid statue of Queen Anne.

"Oh dear, she looks so severe. It is as if she knows, and disapproves!"

"Calm yourself, Aithne! Now, how long will you be away?" asked Francesca.

Aithne studied the clock. "It is now ten minutes to noon.

I will meet you here in this very spot in two hours from now."

Francesca nodded. "Very well, Aithne. But do try not to be late!"

Aithne's eyes were shining as she took Francesca's hands in hers. "I am ever in your debt, Cousin. If there is ever anything I can do for you, you have only to ask!"

And with that she hurried away down the High Street, and soon her flowered bonnet was lost in the crowd. Francesca quickly made her way through the peaceful Cathedral grounds and on down to her favourite walk by the river, where the banks were misted by purple willow herb. At the Winchester end of the river the way was thronged with ladies and gentlemen taking the air, but as she progressed towards St Cross she soon found herself a solitary walker on the path.

To her relief, Sir Peter Jamieson was waiting for her on the old elm seat. He arose as she approached, his thin frame bending in a gallant bow.

"My dear Lady Alethia! I trust I find you well?"

"A little fatigued, to own the truth, after last night's ball," confessed Francesca with a smile.

"Ah!" he rubbed his hands in anticipation. "I am greatly looking forward to reading all about it in *Lady Alethia's Journal* next Friday!"

Francesca raised a mocking eyebrow. "You could not summon the courage, then, to brave the ball yourself? I had imagined that as it was a masked affair, you might have slipped in and amused yourself listening to the revellers' outraged comments about Lady Alethia."

He shuddered. "My nerve failed me. Clearly, there is a conspiracy amongst the ladies of the city to treat me with an icy disdain. I noticed Lady Featherstone crossing the street to avoid me yesterday."

"Oh dear. Does such treatment distress you?" enquired Francesca.

"Oh, I am cut to the quick," he said cheerfully. "And any passing irritation I may feel is soon dispelled when I study the circulation figures of my newspaper. Since your Journal appeared in the *Courier* the paper has sold more copies than ever before! Oh, before I forget — "

He reached into his pocket and handed Francesca two shining guinea pieces. "Talented writer though you are, I still believe this payment to be extortionate!"

"Nonsense," smiled Francesca, slipping the coins into her reticule. "I am worth every penny! Though to be frank, I have my doubts about how much longer I can continue with the Journal. It cannot be long before someone deduces that I am the culprit. So far, I believe I have managed to pull the wool over everyone' eyes by mentioning myself unfavourably in every Journal. But sooner or later, someone is going to tumble to the truth."

"The same notion had occurred to me," he said thoughtfully. "And I do believe I have devised a solution to the problem. You see, so far it has naturally been assumed that Lady Alethia is a lady. But if you managed to insert some scandal from Buckhurst's Club into your Journal, then that would widen the field of suspects to include all the gentlemen in the city as well!"

Francesca clasped her hands in delight. "Oh that is a capital idea, Sir Peter! What fun! You are a member of Buckhurst's are you not? It will be a simple matter for you to pass on the information to me for my Journal."

Sir Peter seemed suddenly intent on smoothing a stubborn crease from his beige breeches. "Ah . . . well no, I fear that would not do at all. You must remember that I am already regarded with great suspicion by the elite of the city. So far, I have pretended that I have not the first notion as to the identity of Lady Alethia. I allege that her handwritten column is delivered to me anonymously and that I am as much in the dark as everyone else."

"Naturally, no one believes that for a minute," smiled Francesca.

"Quite," he agreed. "But if, after I was present at a particularly roisterous evening at Buckhurst's, intelligence of the event appeared in your Journal, then all the gentlemen would be convinced that they had finally stripped the mask from Lady Alethia. And then my position in the city would be quite untenable."

"So how are we to elicit the information we need from Buckhurst's?" asked Francesca.

Sir Peter had difficulty clearing his throat. "I . . . well . . . I thought it might amuse *you* to attend the club one evening."

"Me?" shrieked Francesca, frightening a duck who had paddled up, hoping for some bread. "Sir Peter, Buckhurst's is an exclusively gentlemen's club." She laughed. "Surely you are not proposing that I masquerade as a man!"

He looked steadily into her amused grey-green eyes. "Yes," he said, "that is exactly what I am suggesting."

8

Horrified, Francesca could only stammer, "But — really this is too much to ask — the problems are immense — and if I am discovered — "

One by one, Sir Peter waved aside her doubts. "Consider the facts, Lady Francesca. You are tall, and strong-featured so you would easily pass as a young man when dressed in the appropriate clothes. On the subject of which, I will deliver to the tradesman's entrance of your aunt's house tomorrow a parcel of suitable attire for you. If you linger by the servants' door at ten of the clock, there will be no danger of the package falling into your aunt's hands."

Francesca was beginning to feel that events were running away with her. "And how do you propose that I gain entrance to Buckhurst's" she enquired acidly. "I happen to know that admittance is strictly by membership only. In fact, I have heard it rumoured that you yourself are to be blackballed from the Club!"

"If this little escapade ever comes to light then I shall most surely be drummed out in utter disgrace," he grinned. "No. I propose to have a letter delivered to Viscount Polesdon, announcing the arrival in Winchester of one oh, who shall we say . . . Lord Wingate from . . . Somerset.

That is a good long distance away, is it not? Lord Wingate will remind the Viscount of the acquaintanceship they struck up last year at Whites in London and suggest that it would be pleasant to renew the friendship over a bottle or two of claret. As Viscount Polesdon invariably attends Buckhurst's on Mondays, he is bound to agree to take you along there."

Francesca considered this plan. "You are depending on the fact, of course, that Viscount Polesdon is so stupid, and so often drunk, that he is unlikely to remember whether or not he did meet Lord Wingate whilst he was inebriated at White's."

"Precisely." Sir Peter picked up a stone and skimmed it over the surface of the water. "And if your face does seem familiar to him, well, he will assume of course that he vaguely remembers you from Whites. But you need have little fear on that score. The lighting at Buckhurst's is excessively dim."

"I have no worries on any score, Sir Peter," retorted Francesca, "for I am not at all sure that I agree to participate in this wild scheme. It is fraught with dangers. How am I to escape from my aunt's house at night, without her knowledge? And where are Viscount Polesdon and I to meet? He can hardly come bowling up to my aunt's house to wait on Lord Wingate!"

"In my letter, I shall state that I, that is Lord Wingate, am putting up at the George for a few days. All you have to do is linger in the inn for a few minutes whilst you wait for Viscount Polesdon to arrive. I shall be seated in a corner of the inn to keep an eye on you. But of course, I shan't be able to follow you to Buckhurst's, as it is vital that I am nowhere to be seen on that particular evening."

Francesca buried her head in her hands, and shook with laughter. "Sir Peter, you are incorrigible."

"Think what an experience it will be for you," he urged, scenting victory. "Why, I know no other woman in the world who would dare to invade a gentlemen's club! Imagine the insights you will receive into the workings of the male mind. What an advantage you will have over us mere males for ever more!"

"Yes," mused Francesca, "there is much in what you say. And *Lady Alethia's Journal* would positively crackle with scandal. The intelligence from Buckhurst's would certainly set the town on fire!"

"If you attend the Club on Monday, you would have time to write the Journal on Tuesday in time for that week's *Courier*," Sir Peter said encouragingly.

Francesca, who had never in her life been able to resist a challenge, turned to him then, her eyes sparkling, "Very well! I will do it. I shall be terrified out of my wits — but oh, if I succeed, what a coup!"

*   *   *

At two o'clock Aithne came tripping happily down the High Street. "I am so sorry I am late, Cousin," she beamed. "I do hope you have not had too tedious a time on your own."

"Not at all," murmured Francesca faintly. "I have greatly enjoyed myself strolling round the shops."

This last was almost true. She had left Sir Peter before one o'clock and devoted an hour looking at the shopkeeper's wares, wondering on what she might spend her hard earned two guineas. But those sixty minutes had been enough to turn her mood of defiant elation into one of shaking apprehension.

I must have been deranged to agree to such a scheme, she thought crossly, as she and Aithne started for home. True, I have listened long enough to the conversation of my father and brother to be aware of men's speech, and the topics they favour in conversation. I am well read, and adept with cards should I be called upon to play. Nevertheless, the dangers are immense. And should I be discovered, the scandal would rock all Hampshire.

But I have given Sir Peter my word. I should never be able to look him frankly in the eyes again if I lost my nerve now and refused to play my part.

She turned to her cousin and enquired. "Did everything go well for you with your gentleman friend, Aithne?"

"Oh yes!" breathed Aithne rapturously. "He is so kind and considerate. Yet he makes me laugh so much he brings tears to my eyes. I cannot thank you enough, Francesca for making it possible for me to enjoy such a happy hour with him."

Two hours, to be precise, thought Francesca. Hesitantly, she said aloud, "Strangely enough there is a little matter on which I require your assistance, Aithne."

"Name it," said the golden-haired girl promptly.

Francesca said, in a matter of fact tone, "I wish to leave the house unobserved on Monday night. Have you any notion how this could be arranged?"

Aithne gulped. "My, Francesca, whatever are you about? Oh, can it be that you too have a secret beau?"

"It is better that you do not ask any questions, Cousin," replied Francesca firmly.

Aithne took a deep breath. "As it happens, Monday is the one night which would present no difficulty for your plan. Mama is to dine with Lady Sombourne that night, to discuss the possibility of a joint charity ball later in the summer." She giggled. "Heavens, what a charade that will be!"

Francesca could hardly believe her good fortune. "So I

shall be able to slip out unobserved! And if by any chance Lady Rothersay returns ahead of time, it will be your task, Aithne, to declare that I retired with a headache and have requested not to be disturbed."

"Of course Francesca, you may rely on me." Aithne went on all in a rush, "I'm sorry I was so horrid to you when you first arrived in Winchester, Francesca. But I had never before encountered anyone with your freedom of spirit. At first I was deeply shocked, but now I have come to admire you enormously. I have the deepest respect for Mama, of course, but I no longer believe her to be right about everything."

"Nevertheless, you do realise that if she discovers about your beau, she'll skin you alive," warned Francesca.

Aithne nodded fearfully, "But you too will be boiled in oil if she learns you have been out at night, alone!"

Shivering with forboding, the two conspirators crept guiltily into the house.

★   ★   ★

As Lady Rothersay's carriage rolled out of sight round the corner of Upper Brook on Monday evening, the servants' door opened and an elegantly dressed young gentleman stepped out onto the cobbles. Feeling extremely self-conscious in the double breasted tail coat, and close fitting breeches, Francesca set forth towards the George, remembering to lengthen her stride and swing her shoulders in a jauntily masculine fashion.

After a few minutes, she realised to her relief that no one was turning to stare at her. Fashionable ladies in their carriages were not peering in amazement out of the window, exclaiming at the extraordinary sight of a young lady dressed as a man! I must truly look the part then, thought

Francesca, allowing herself an experimental twirl of her tortoiseshell-topped cane.

So far, everything had gone wonderfully according to plan. Sir Peter had delivered a package of clothes which Francesca had changed into that evening in a little-used old flower room at the back of the house. She rather admired Sir Peter's taste in attire, though when it came to tying the fiddly tapes at the back of the square cut white waistcoat, Francesca dearly wished she had the benefit of an accomplice to assist her. She left the top two buttons open to reveal the exquisite frilled shirt beneath, and enjoyed herself arranging the expensive lace in a slightly out of date manner, which she reasoned would be suitable for the rustically foppish Lord Wingate from his country seat in Somerset.

Aithne, though burning with curiosity about Francesca's mysterious assignation, had contained herself and asked no questions beyond what time Francesca imagined she would return home that Monday night.

"I am not sure, I may be late," Francesca replied, "so when everyone has retired for the night Aithne, you must creep down and unbolt the servants' door for me. And remember, if your Mama returns early from her evening with Lady Sombourne, you must pretend that I have a headache and desire not to be disturbed until morning!"

From Aithne's expression of horrified fascination it was obvious to the amused Francesca that she clearly imagined the worst of Francesca's secret tryst.

Francesca strolled down to a corner of the High Street and was soon within sight of the bustling George Inn which was ablaze with lights and the sound of merriment within. Taking a deep breath, she swaggered boldly into the main tavern, which was comfortably appointed and agleam with shining brass and polished wood. Hearing a discreet cough from a corner, she turned her head and observed Sir Peter sitting enjoying a glass of brandy. He gave her a slight nod. This she interpreted to mean that the letter from "Lord Wingate" had been safely delivered to Viscount Polesdon, who had replied that he would be delighted to meet his old acquaintance at the George on Monday.

Sir Peter's presence reassured Francesca, and she sat down in one of the window seats, opposite a crowd of young blades who were entertaining one of the actresses from the town. A serving girl approached, and Francesca, controlling her nerves, asked in a low voice for a glass of claret. Glancing at Sir Peter, she smiled briefly as she saw him raise his glass to her in an admiring tribute. She had uttered her first words as Lord Wingate! She looked the part, and now as the serving girl laid down the wine on the table, it was clear that she sounded the part also. Trembling with relief, Francesca took a well-earned sip of wine — but then, remembering her role, she threw back her head and downed half the glass in one gulp, just as Viscount Polesdon sauntered into the tavern.

Emboldened by the claret, Francesca marched straight across and slapped him on the shoulder. "Polesdon! Capital to see you again! My, what a fine town you have here. My room at the inn is excellent and I swear the fillies of the city are quite the prettiest in all southern England! Oh, but of course, you're no longer permitted a roving eye, eh? I read of your engagement in *The Times*. Delighted for you. Sorry to lose you from our bachelor ranks, though. My, what a night we had at White's — and afterwards eh? Tell me, was that the night we nailed a guardsman into his box and rolled him downhill . . . or was it the time we enjoyed a moonlight romp with those actresses in Green Park . . . "

Francesca rattled on as the bemused Viscount joined her at the window table and ordered himself a brandy. The Viscount, Francesca realised shrewdly, was an excellent choice of unwitting accomplice. Because he had always been so jealously guarded by his fiancée, Lady Clorinda, Francesca had been provided with little opportunity to converse with him at any length when they were in company together. This of course was now to her advantage, as her voice was not overly familiar to him.

The Viscount, however, was one of those genial souls who is only too happy to be amiable towards all his fellow creatures. (Francesca could well imagine what an easy task Lady Sombourne had had, easing the smiling Viscount into an engagement with Clorinda.) And now, side by side on the window seat with the engaging Lord Wingate, Viscount Polesdon was reluctant to spoil the friendly atmosphere by admitting that he could not for the life of him remember meeting the fellow at Whites!

Accordingly, when Lord Wingate declared, "Hope I'm not inconveniencing you, arriving unheralded and unsung as it were. I'd be mortified to think that you'd vexed your fiancée by ditching her for an evening on my account," the Viscount replied earnestly.

"Oh, not at all old chap! You couldn't have timed it better, for I always spend Mondays at my Club. Perhaps you'd care to come along? There's usually an excellent dinner, good company, and some deucedly fast cards."

Francesca declared this to be a capital notion, and the two gentlemen soon departed. If the serving girl thought it odd that the dark-haired gentleman winked at Sir Peter as he passed by, she gave it not a second thought. Serving in a tavern, you meet all sorts of folk, she told herself, wondering if she dare slip out for a few minutes to soak her aching feet in mustard and water.

Buckhurst's Club was an imposing Queen Anne building with a forbidding glossy black front door. As Francesca was hurried through a chilly marble hall she caught glimpses through open doors of sombre, dimly lit saloons, furnished with leather chairs and oil paintings of bleak country winter scenes.

The Viscount professed himself "mortal hungry", so the pair proceeded immediately in to dine. In the elegant dining room they sat down under the austere gaze of the six former presidents of the club, preserved in oils upon the silk-hung walls. Francesca felt a moment's trepidation as she saw they were to be joined by Lords Southport and Compton. But it soon transpired that the two lords were preoccupied with matters of their own.

Lord Southport was in a tetchy mood over the uncharacteristically temperamental behaviour of his wife:

"Dashed woman keeps having attacks of the vapours, swooning all over the house and alarming my dogs," he muttered irritably, splashing his asparagus in a pool of butter.

Lord Compton, meanwhile, was engaged in what was clearly a long standing feud with the footmen, and the Club's chef.

"Yes, my good man, I've no doubt these mushrooms were fresh picked as you say," he glared at the white-hatted, perspiring chef who had been summoned to the dining room in the wake of the fillet of veal with mushrooms. "But does that mean they were fresh this morning or fresh last Tuesday?"

Viscount Polesdon groaned, and muttered in a low voice to Francesca, "Quite ruins the appetite, doesn't he? I'm afraid Compton's so fastidious and pernickety, he always devotes the dining hour to a tirade against the chef, who he's convinced is trying to poison him. At home of course, Compton has a man who tastes all his food, but naturally, the fellow isn't allowed in here."

"Oh, naturally," concurred Francesca thinking that Lord

Compton's long suffering food taster must look forward with longing to a few hours freedom on Monday nights.

When he had demolished a large portion of apricot tart smothered in thick cream, the Viscount suggested that he and Wingate should take port in the gaming room. Francesca was only too glad to escape from the grumbles of Lord Southport and Compton. Nevertheless, the mention of port only served to increase her apprehension about the alcoholic aspect of her charade as a man.

Normally, Francesca drank very little, and so far this evening she had managed to take just a scant two glasses of wine. But Viscount Polesdon, released from the domestic leash for the evening, was clearly determined to put himself in the best of spirits. How then, was Francesca to appear to keep up with him in the drinking stakes?

All manner of ruses crossed her mind, only to be rejected. She had thought of surreptitiously pouring her port into her boot, or down her sleeve. But that would prove to be too uncomfortably messy — and how was she to explain herself should she be detected? She was too young to plead enforced temperance through gout. But clearly, she would have to think of something fast, for she knew that two glasses of port or brandy would speedily send her insensible under the table.

Thinking hard, she accompanied the Viscount into the card room, which after the ornate dining room presented an austere appearance. Francesca realised that this was due to the stark, bare walls, left naked of adornment presumably so as not to distract the gamblers' attention.

"What are you for, Wingate?" asked the Viscount. "I recommend the cognac, though the madeira's pretty fine too."

Francesca lounged against a side table, and drew a small tortoiseshell box from her waistcoat pocket. "Later, Polesdon! It is my custom after I have dined, to enjoy a little snuff. May I offer you some. It is King's Martinique, fine, light, one of my favourites."

Lord Polesdon declined, but Lord Sutton looked up with interest from the far table. "Prefer Brazil myself. Large grained. A good, robust snuff."

Francesca nodded with interest, watching him deal the full pack two cards at a time into two heaps, one on his left hand, one on his right. "I find the flavour of Brazil a might overpowering," she remarked, silently blessing her father for his expert instruction on the various blends, and also her brother Edward, for initiating her into the art of taking the snuff.

With the deal complete, Lord Sutton in his position as faro banker, paid out the stakes placed on the cards to his right hand, and smilingly collected the money due to him from the left hand deal. Francesca, meanwhile, nonchalantly tilted back her head and with a small flourish took her King's Martinique.

She then settled down to a game of *vingt-et-un* with Viscount Polesdon. Francesca was an adroit player, clever enough on this occasion to give the Viscount the pleasure of beating his opponent. But all too soon the brandy decanter was waved once more before Francesca.

"Come along now, Wingate! It's excellent stuff. I promise you!" declared the Viscount, somewhat unsteadily.

Francesca groaned with regret. "Don't tempt me, Polesdon! If you knew how I'm fair dying for a drop of the amber liquid! But I've a thousand guinea wager riding on my abstinence. Fellow at Whites wagered that I wouldn't be able to survive three months without a drop of spirits passing my lips. It's a wager I'm sorely regretting, I can tell you! But I'm determined to have the satisfaction of winning."

"Why, I should say so!" exclaimed the Viscount. "Three months eh? That's a cruel long time to go without the fire of brandy in your belly."

Lord Sutton nodded from the faro table. "Thousand guineas or no, it's not a wager I could have accepted! I admit I like to live dangerously, but going without brandy is tantamount to suicide!"

Francesca eyed the dark-eyed lord with interest, imagining him whispering sweet tender words of love to Aithne. My, what a scoundrel he was! Poor Aithne was bound to be grievously hurt, whilst to Lord Sutton the affair was simply an amusing entertainment.

Lord Southport held his port up to the lamp. "You're a wise man, Wingate, not to imbibe whilst you're at the tables."

"Stuff and nonsense!" exclaimed Lord Sutton, leaning back in his chair. "To my mind, there's nothing worse than fellows who take their gambling over seriously. Why, I was recently at the Silver Peacock club, where the lowest stake allowed was fifty guineas, and there were never less than twenty thousand guineas in the pot. And what a dour business it was! Members wearing leather sleeves to protect their lace cuffs, and one dandy even sported a nightcap to keep his curls in order!"

Viscount Polesdon nodded. "It is extremely intense at the Silver Peacock. They even have a special duelling room, with pistols or swords provided by the management in the case of disputes over the cards or dice."

"Bah! Duels should be fought in manly fashion, out in the open at crack of dawn!" Lord Sutton pronounced emphatically. "But to my mind, duels over gambling disputes are totally unnecessary. Most of the time its one fellow trying to Greek another, in which case the culprit should be blackballed."

Lord Compton flicked dust from his glass with his handkerchief, and muttered, "D'you recall that fellow I had blackballed for cheating at whist?" He turned to Francesca. "The blackguard had a code with his collaborator. If he blew his nose he had a good hand, and if he took snuff it was a bad one. But I'm up to all the tricks. I spotted the scoundrel within minutes. Dashed bad show."

There was a general murmur of agreement, "Almosh as worsh," slurred the Viscount, "is watching a fellow who can't take his loshes like a man."

Lord Southport vigorously shuffled the cards. "Most amazing sight I ever saw in that line was a chap who found himself absolutely ruined at the tables. Penury staring him in the face. What did he do? He quite suddenly seized the edge of the table between his teeth, clung on, resisting all attempts to remove him, and then proceeded to die in the act. His teethmarks are still in the table to this day!"

Lord Compton, who suffered greatly with falling teeth, looked extremely sour as he listened to this feat. Francesca relinquished her place at the *vinget-et-un* table to Lord Featherstone, and retired to one of the wall seats, quietly making mental notes on the conversations all around her. She sat with one breeched leg crossed easily across the other, and was now beginning to quite enjoy herself. With all the main hurdles crossed, and with herself clearly accepted by the gentlemen as one of them, she could now begin to take pleasure in her situation.

One thing is for sure, she thought, I am glad I was not born a man and obliged always to wear these uncomfortable clothes. Admittedly, the freedom afforded her by the breeches was a most liberating experience, but her frock coat was unbearably tight across the shoulders, in the fashionable mode, and she found the wealth of lace ruffles at her neck most irritating.

She took another pinch of snuff, and joined in the laughter as Lord Sutton recounted the tale of the Frenchman who, distraught because he could not pay his debts at the card table, rammed a billiard ball down his throat and choked to death in front of his infuriated claimant.

It was then, as she slipped the tortoiseshell snuff box back into her waistcoat pocket, that Francesca felt familiar eyes upon her. With pounding heart she looked up, and saw the Duke of Wexford standing in the doorway, his unfathomable blue eyes flickering over her. For one chilling moment she thought he was on the point of inviting her to the whist table. But as the Duke moved towards her, Viscount Polesdon threw down his hand and declared.

"Enough for tonight, Wingate! If I lose any more my fiancée's aunt will forbid me to come here on Monday nights. Come, let us retire to the saloon, and you shall tell me more of our uproarious nights at Whites!"

Francesca was so relieved to be escaping from the sharp-eyed Duke, she worried not a jot about the prospect of being obliged now to invent outrageous tales of her supposed exploits in London with the Viscount. But no sooner was she seated in one of the deep leather armchairs, than the Duke himself entered the saloon, with various of the other lords in attendance.

"Gaming room's too crowded tonight," grumbled Lord Southport, propping his gouty leg on a stool. "Half the menfolk of Winchester seem to be here, escaping from their wives."

Lord Sutton nodded. "All the ladies can talk about these days is that damned Lady Alethia and her impertinent Journal. But none of them are any closer to unmasking the viper amongst them who is the perpetrator of this ridiculous Journal."

"Why should the writer be a lady?" asked the Duke of

Wexford, looking at nobody in particular. "No reason why that *she* shouldn't in truth be a *he*."

"I've said before that we should blackball that fellow Jamieson," growled Lord Featherstone.

Lord Compton wagged a gloved finger. "Nonsense, Featherstone. One only blackballs a fellow for a *serious* crime, like cheating at cards."

"In any event, Jamieson is denying all knowledge of the identity of this Lady Alethia," said Lord Southport irritably. "But one thing's for sure, my wife hasn't been her normal robust self since that Journal started appearing." He turned to Francesca, "Are you married, Wingate?"

"Indeed no," demurred Francesca.

"Wise man," muttered Lord Southport. "How d'ye like them though, Wingate? Handsome, clever or rich?"

Francesca crossed her legs, and said thoughtfully, "Ah, well that's my dilemma, my lord. I have never understood, you see, why it is considered impossible to find a woman who is all three!"

The Duke of Wexford led the appreciative laughter. Lord Compton glanced across at him and remarked slyly, "If Lady Alethia is to be believed, marriage is very much on your mind at present, Wexford. Don't keep us in suspense. Who's the fortunate lady to be?"

The Duke lit up a cigar, and calmly blew the smoke towards the painted ceiling of the saloon "Since you are obviously such an avid reader of *Lady Alethia's Journal*, my lord, I suggest that you continue to keep an earnest eye on her writings. I seem to recall that the lady is confident of being the first to reveal to the world who my future Duchess is to be."

Lord Southport chuckled. "My wife was most intrigued by that particular paragraph. Putting two and two together and making five, in the way women do, she leapt to the conclusion that your sister, Lady Penshurst, must be the writer of *Lady Alethia's Journal*."

"I assure you, if that were so, Evelina would be quite incapable of keeping the fact to herself," smiled the Duke. "She is as open and honest as the day is long, and quite incapable of keeping such a monumental secret."

The port was passed round once more, and again Francesca declined.

"Come now, let me fill your glass," urged Lord Compton. "Pains me to see a man not drinking. If you don't incline to the port, let me recommend the brandy.'

Hastily, Francesca repeated her tale about the wager which prevented a drop of spirits from passing her lips. And she added, with a smile, "As for the brandy, my lord, even without the restriction imposed by my wager, I fear I am not feeling particularly heroic tonight."

Lord Compton scratched his head. "Heroic? You've lost me, Wingate."

The Duke of Wexford tapped the ash from his cigar, and said dryly, "I believe Lord Wingate is referring to a remark made by Dr Johnson. If memory serves me right, he said that *claret is for boys, port for men and brandy for heroes*." He glanced across at Lord Wingate, for confirmation, but the newcomer from Somerset was busily engaged in taking snuff.

"Port?" snorted Lord Southport. "I've had to give it up, dash it, because of this infernal gout. I stick to sherry now. Better for the health."

"Have you tried sea bathing?" enquired Francesca. "It is supposed to be most beneficial for gout."

Lord Compton broke in, "If you do make an excursion to Lyme or Brighton, Southport, take care not to have your wife accompany you. I hear that the loose ladies of the town have taken to bathing without stays beneath their bathing dresses. Their entire female outline is quite visible in the water. Quite appalling!"

"Mmm. Sounds quite delightful to me," said Lord Sutton with a rakish grin.

The Duke of Wexford arose. "Anyone care for a game of billiards? Wingate?"

Francesca paled with alarm. Her brother Edward had always steadfastly refused to allow Francesca into the billiard room, declaring that her impatient nature would only cause her to dig the cue into the green baize and ruin it.

She waved a careless hand. "Thank you, Your Grace, but I confess I am in an indolent mood tonight, and too lazy to move!"

"I'll be happy to give you a game, Wexford," declared Lord Featherstone, heaving himself to his feet. "This is valiant of me, under the circumstances, as I seem to recall that last time we played you made me look a green horn at the game."

As he passed by Lord Polesdon, who had fallen heavily asleep in his chair, the Earl gave him a hard poke in the chest. Lord Polesdon sat up with a jerk, and declared automatically.

"Yes, my dear!"

The entire company burst into laughter, and Lord Southport remarked, "Time enough for that sort of behaviour after you're married, my lad! Mind you, with my wife behaving so temperamentally at present, marriage is not an institution I would recommend to anyone."

"Too true," agreed Lord Sutton, not at all to Francesca's surprise. "But at least your wife is only going through a phase of fainting fits, Southport. Mine has fallen into the river, and attempted to hurl herself from an upstairs window. I can't imagine what ails her." He turned to Francesca. "Wingate, you bring a fresh outlook to our company here.

Have you any insight into the psyche of our ladies?"

Now the Duke had retired to the billiard room, Francesca felt considerably more relaxed. When he had been present, she had been stingingly aware of his eyes upon her, certain that at any moment he would expose her for the fraud she was.

With his departure, however, her confidence had risen, and she replied now to Lord Sutton, "All I can recommend, my lord is the old Fable about the female sex. Let me see now, how do the lines go:

> *To know the mistress' humour right*
> *See if her maids are clean, and tight;*
> *If Betty waits without her stays,*
> *She copies but her lady's ways.*
> *When miss comes in with boist'rous shout,*
> *And drops no curtsey, going out,*
> *Depend upon it, mama is one,*
> *Who reads, or drinks too much alone!"*

An aghast silence fell on the saloon. Lord Sutton, white faced, downed his port in one gulp and immediately held out his glass for a refill.

"I say, dash it all!" blustered Lord Southport. "I hope you're not implying, Wingate, that either my wife or Sutton's behaves in such a loose unladylike manner?"

"Of course that's what he was saying!" shouted Lord Sutton, gulping down more port. "It's outrageous!"

"But . . . but . . . I assure you. I spoke only in jest," stammered an alarmed Francesca.

"A jest in extremely poor taste," put in Lord Compton. "If I were you, Sutton, I'd call the fellow out!"

Lord Southport smashed his fist on the arm of the chair. "I'd call you out myself, Wingate, if it weren't for this damned crocked leg!"

Francesca felt as if she were strapped to a runaway horse

which was plunging towards a precipice. She was utterly powerless, in the hands of capricious Fate.

All eyes turned to Lord Sutton. He sat glaring at Francesca, a purple vein throbbing in his head.

"Honour must be satisfied," growled Lord Compton. "If word of this fellow's outrage ever reaches Lady Sutton's delicate ears, why, I shudder to think of the effect it will have on her!"

Francesca sat, terrified and transfixed as Lord Sutton, with hands trembling with rage, drew off his white glove. He stood up, took two paces towards her and slapped the glove across her cheek. "In defence of my good lady's name, I challenge you, Wingate, to a duel. Tomorrow, at dawn on Flower Down!"

9

An hour before first light, Francesca was shaken awake by Lord Polesdon.

"Rouse yourself, Wingate! I fear the hour draws near," said the Viscount, rubbing eyes that resembled poached eggs.

When he had left the room, Francesca pulled off her nightcap, and shivered her way across to the washstand. Gradually, the events of the previous night swam before her in full terrifying detail.

After Lord Sutton had declared his challenge, Lord Compton had promptly offered himself as a second. Viscount Polesdon had put himself forward to act as Francesca's second. Then there was the question of weapons. Viscount Polesdon agreed that normally Wingate, as the one who had been challenged, would have enjoyed the privilege of the choice of weapons. Francesca had in fact, been depending on that, for she knew herself to possess a reasonable skill as a fencer. But to Francesca's dismay, the Viscount explained that it was the custom in Winchester, if the duel was being fought over a lady's honour, for pistols to be the choice of weapon.

At this, Francesca had almost bolted from the room in

fright. Pistols! Why, she had never in her life held such an object in her hands, let alone learned to fire one!

Perhaps reading the expression on her face, Lord Compton had said hastily, "As his second, Polesdon, it will be your responsibility to ensure that Wingate is a man of his word, and does not take flight back to Somerset before dawn. It would be best all round if Wingate returned with you to your house for the night."

Francesca sat on the bed and pulled on her boots. The more she thought about it, the more she realised that had it not been for Lord Compton, she would not have been placed in this agonising situation. It was he, she mused, who goaded Lord Sutton into challenging me to a duel. He is a small man, with a small mind, who has not the courage to fight battles himself, but has no qualms about pushing others forward into the front line of the fray.

Lord Polesdon entered, carrying a pistol case under his arm, "Are you prepared Wingate? Then come very quietly. Duelling is strictly forbidden in Winchester, you know, so not even the servants must hear a whisper of what we are at."

As they rode, in gradually lightening darkness, out of the town and towards the incline which would lead them to Flower Down, Francesca could not repress a certain degree of wry amusement at her situation.

My, what capital Lady Alethia could make of all this! Here is Lady Francesca de Lisle, disguised as one Lord Wingate, challenged to a duel on Flower Down! That is rich enough. But, irony upon irony, the gentleman at whom she would soon be raising her pistol was none other than her own cousin's secret lover!

Francesca closed her eyes in anguish, imagining the delicate Aithne, peacefully asleep in her bed, blissfully unaware of the mortal danger facing the man she loved so fervently.

Francesca stifled a bitter laugh. Mortal danger! What fanciful notion was this? Why it was she, Francesca, who was in the most desperate situation. Lord Sutton, as Lord Compton had gleefully pointed out to her the night before, was a superb shot. And although, by all the honourable rules of the duel, he was supposed to shoot to wound rather than kill, Francesca knew she could not bank on it. She knew that even now, Lord Compton would be at his side, whispering in his weaseling way that Wingate should be forced to pay the ultimate penalty for his rash suggestions about the behaviour of Lady Sutton.

"I say, Wingate, I can't tell you how wretched I feel that all this should have come to pass," declared Viscount Polesdon as they began the climb up the chalk and flint path. "Trouble was, we'd all had a dashed sight too much to drink. Tempers flared. Everything got out of hand. My God, I just hope Lady Sombourne never gets to hear of this. If she knows I was involved she could make things extremely sticky between myself and my fiancée."

Francesca made no reply. She was by now so frightened that it was only with a great effort of will that she prevented her teeth from chattering loudly, and uncontrollably.

As they rode up onto Flower Down, the sky was streaked with the red and gold of a summer's dawn. Not surprisingly, Francesca gained no pleasure from the sight. Her hands were numb on the reins, and her legs ached with the unaccustomed effort of riding astride, instead of her normal ladylike sidesaddle.

"Ah, there's the spot!" exclaimed the Viscount, pointing towards a flattish stretch of turf, marked at each end by clumps of gorse bushes. And Sutton and Compton are already there, waiting!"

Straining at the leash, no doubt, thought Francesca her throat now completely dry.

"I'd offer you a nip of brandy from my flask," said the Viscount anxiously, "but of course you won't take it because of your wager, will you? Dashed nuisance. But a thousand guineas is not to be sniffed at, if you win. If you are still alive to win that is," he muttered gloomily, taking a long swig of brandy from the flask.

They dismounted, and received a curt greeting from Lords Sutton and Compton. The two seconds then retired, to choose the weapons and pace out a stretch on the dew spangled turf. Lord Sutton, meanwhile, stood with his arms folded and his back turned to Francesca, presenting a perfect picture of outraged innocence.

Francesca dearly wished she was wearing a dress, for her breeches revealed in the most shaming fashion that her knees were beginning to knock alarmingly. If only, she reflected, it had simply been a question of rushing up here to the Down, cocking our pistols and firing, all in the heat of the moment, I do believe I should not have felt so petrified. But the slow, drawn out ritual of it all is quite unnerving, and increases one's terror a thousandfold.

Then the preliminaries were completed. Lord Sutton and Francesca, having removed their coats, were presented with their weapons, and requested to stand back to back in the middle of the measured stretch.

"Ten paces forward, turn and fire," instructed Lord Compton, his face flushed with excitement. "Are you ready my lords?"

"Ready!" chorused the combatants, one in ringing tones, the other in a choked whisper.

Lord Compton raised his hand. In the tense hush, Francesca could feel her heart hammering against her chest. I am going to be killed, she thought numbly. These are my last moments on earth. Oh merciful God, I should be praying. I should be thinking of my father and my brother, but my mind is so frozen with fear that I can imagine nothing but the explosion of powder. Will it hurt much? Oh please let his aim be accurate so I do not suffer the indignity of lying writhing in agony before I breathe my last!

Lord Compton's hand dropped. "Onset!" he shouted, the word echoing through the quiet of the Downland dawn.

Francesca began to walk forward. Ten paces, she thought. Ten paces to death. She heard the squeak of her boots on the damp grass and with unseeing eyes watched the linnets flying out of the gorse bush ahead of her.

Six, seven . . . the pistol was far heavier than she had anticipated. She held it cocked to her shoulder and already she could smell the powder . . .

Eight, nine . . . the sun was coming up. My last sunrise. No! It can't be true! This can't be happening to me. Something — a miracle — must intervene to stop this madness!

Ten!

Taking a last shuddering breath, Francesca whirled round, aiming her pistol blindly at the man twenty paces from her. Steadying herself, she curled a finger round the trigger.

With an ear-shattering explosion a shot rang out. Lord Sutton screamed with pain, and fell to the ground. Francesca dropped her pistol in fright and stood stunned for a moment. Then she stumbled, bewildered, towards the injured man.

Lord Compton was there before her, kneeling on the turf. "Flesh wound in the arm," he muttered. Lord Sutton winced in pain as his second ripped away the bloodstained sleeve of his shirt.

"Dashed good shot," said the Viscount admiringly to the shaken Francesca. "Frankly, I had my doubts about you, Wingate. Thought you'd be lying there dead on the grass and me with a great deal of explaining to do back in town. Well, Sutton, I think you'll agree that honour's been satisfied?"

Lord Sutton sat up, allowing Lord Compton to bind his arm with the ripped sleeve of his shirt. "You've a cool nerve and a steady hand, Wingate. I'll give you that. Yes, honour satisfied, damn you! Here's my hand on it."

"One moment!" Lord Compton intervened as Francesca leaned down to shake her opponent's hand. "It is the duty of the seconds to examine the weapons after firing."

"Oh, what a fusser you are, Compton," exclaimed the Viscount irritably. "Let us consider the matter over and done with. Speaking for myself, its been a long hard night and I'm anxious for my breakfast!"

Lord Compton was unmoved. "As Lord Sutton's second, I insist that all the rules of fair play be properly observed. Are you standing in my way, Polesdon?"

"No, no," sighed the Viscount, turning to Francesca. "Where is your pistol, Wingate?"

Pale-faced, Francesca pointed to the spot on the grass where she had dropped her pistol. As Lord Compton marched towards it, she sank to her knees on the turf and closed her eyes in an attempt to blot out what was to come.

For Francesca knew, without a shadow of a doubt, that the shot which had wounded Lord Sutton had not come from her pistol! Yes, her finger had hovered on the trigger. But, before she had summoned the courage to fire, a shot had rung out, sending Lord Sutton slumping to the ground. Who could have fired the shot, or why, or from whence it had come, she felt too dazed to contemplate. After barely four hours sleep and a dawn filled with drama, she felt quite incapable of formulating a single clear coherent thought.

Lord Compton was but a step away from the pistol in the grass when there came a shout from the top of the Down.

"You there! For heavens sake, take to your horses!"

The rider came galloping towards them at a furious speed. "Why, its the Duke of Wexford," frowned Viscount Polesdon. "What the devil's afoot?"

They watched in alarm as the Duke thundered towards them, reined in his grey and hurriedly dismounted. "The Constabulary have got wind of the duel," he said breathlessly. "They are on their way here now! I managed to gain time on them by taking the short cut out of town, but I have only five minutes lead on them at the best!"

Lord Compton was already running for his horse. "Dash it, Compton, what about me?" exclaimed an aggrieved Lord Sutton. "I'm injured, damn you, and you're supposed to be my second!"

As the Duke assisted Lord Sutton into the saddle, Viscount Polesdon turned to Francesca, "Best if we go our separate ways, Wingate. There'll be all hell to pay with my fiancée's aunt if I'm discovered by the Constabulary in the company of a duellist. So glad to have renewed our acquaintance. Do contact me again if you are ever in Winchester . . . "

And with this false sentiment floating in the morning air, he followed the other two lords over the hill.

Francesca hastily gathered her wits. Rising to her feet, she executed a graceful bow and declared, "I regret that my companions did not pause to express their gratitude for your prompt action in alerting us to the Constabulary. My thanks, my Lord. Now if you will excuse me, I think it best that I too take to horse and quit this place with the least possible delay."

The Duke stood with hands on hips, gazing down at her. "For heaven's sake, Francesca," he said in tones of heavy resignation, "do stop growling at me in that absurd fashion. You will make your throat unbearably sore!"

"You knew!" cried Francesca, outraged and disappointed all at once. "You knew all along you rogue!"

He laughed. "No, you managed to deceive me for about five minutes last night. Whilst you remained seated in the card room, I admit I was unsure about you. But when you moved into the saloon, then I was certain that I recognised you. As you yourself once pointed out Francesca, one of the hardest things in the world to disguise is one's walk."

Francesca was furious that he had seen so quickly through what she had considered to be an excellent disguise. She began to move towards her horse. "Well if the Law are on their way here, we had best make ourselves scarce."

He strolled forward at an unhurried pace, so that he stood between Francesca and the horse. "Of course the Constabulary aren't on their way here, you foolish girl! It was the only way I could devise of making Compton and the others scatter as fast as possible. Really, Francesca you do land yourself in some impossible scrapes! Why, when I returned to the saloon last night after my game of billiards, and heard that Sutton had challenged you to a duel, I felt like throwing you over my knee and giving you a sound spanking for your stupidity!"

Francesca's eyes blazed. "Why, you impertinent creature! What right have you to pass judgement on my actions, and why do you always take it upon yourself to interfere in everything I do? Why won't you leave me alone!"

"Dash me!" he shouted, taking an angry step towards her. "You are without doubt the most hot-headed and ungrateful young lady I have ever encountered! I spend a most uncomfortable hour sitting amidst a clump of gorse bushes waiting for the duelling party to arrive. I almost die of boredom as Compton fusses in his old maidish way over the pistols, and the pacing out of the stretch. I then manage to fire over your shoulder, and hit Sutton in the arm. I retire down the hill, mount my horse, and gallop over the Down to announce in suitably agitated manner that the Constabulary are on their way. And you, Lady Francesca de Lisle, have the gall to accuse me, in most resentful tones, of unwarranted interference!"

Francesca hurriedly backed away, unnerved by the steely gleam in his deep blue eyes. "Pray do not misunderstand me, my lord. Natually, I am most grateful to you for rescuing me from a most fearful plight." A smile touched her lips. "Of course! I remember now that a flock of birds flew out of the gorse bushes during the duel. At the time I was too distraught to pay any attention, but I see now that it must have been you who disturbed them!"

The Duke retrieved Francesca's pistol from the grass, and slipped it into his saddle bag. "Now that is what I like to hear, Francesca! Maidenly expressions of gratitude, so sweetly expressed. I knew you could do it if you tried!"

"How typical!" flared Francesca. "It is not what you do which is wrong, but your attitude! You are always so impossibly arrogant. Why, only a few moments ago you were berating me for becoming involved in this duel. But you seem to forget that it was Lord Sutton who challenged me, not the other way about!"

The Duke replied with maddening self assurance, "None of it would have come about at all if you hadn't taken it upon yourself to masquerade as a man. Oh, and while we're on the subject — "

Without warning, he seized Francesca by the shoulder, bent her head down and untied the velvet ribbon holding her hair in a knot at the nape of her neck. "Ah, that's better," he smiled, as her beautiful raven tresses, shining in the early morning sunlight, tumbled free about her shoulders. Francesca turned away, unnerved by the touch of his hand on the sensitive skin at the back of her neck, which had sent a strange tingling sensation all the way down her spine.

"I couldn't think what else to do with my hair," she said, attempting a matter of fact tone. "Obviously, I couldn't wear a hat all night at the Club. Then it occurred to me that a gentleman from Somerset would probably not be *au fait* with the current fashion for cropped hair. After all, many country men still wear their hair longer, and tied back."

Naive babbling, she told herself. Stop it! She looked round for the Duke, and saw that he was sitting on a knoll with his back to her, looking at the mist gradually lifting in the valley below.

"I do hope," he said coolly, "that your experiences here this morning will prove valuable to you. Your descriptive powers will be tested to the utmost if you are to make your readers truly believe in the smell of powder and death in the dawn air."

"You knew I was Lady Alethia!" raged Francesca, rushing across and standing over him, her hands on her breeched hips. "Oh, this is too much! *How* did you know?"

He laughed. "It was a simple piece of deduction. There are only two women in Winchester with the wit, intelligence and nerve to take on such a task. One is my sister Evelina. She freely admits that had she thought of the notion first, she would greatly have enjoyed inventing *Lady Alethia's Journal*. So having satisfied myself that Evelina was not the mystery writer, I knew it had to be you."

"You would, you unsufferable man!" muttered Francesca.

"Damn it woman, I've just paid you a compliment!" he roared.

"That may be, but you always make your most flattering remarks sound remarkably like insults!" she retorted, tossing back her long, waving hair.

"That's rich, coming from you," he responded dryly.

"How dare you write all that nonsense about my alleged search for a bride? Why, you make me sound pathetic, the bachelor Duke, wandering soulfully through life pining for a soul mate."

Laughing delightedly, Francesca knelt on the grass, toying with a buttercup. "Mmm, I did enjoy writing those particular paragraphs. I feel I achieved quite a pinnacle of elegant prose — "

She moved hastily aside as his hand reached out to cuff her round the ear. "I see you are quite unrepetant," he observed. "But don't you feel it is time now to abandon Lady Alethia? It's all becoming extremely dangerous, is it not?"

"This morning's episode was exceptional," shrugged Francesca. "Besides, Sir Peter pays me handsomely for what I write, and I freely confess that I find the extra income extremely useful."

"If it is not an indelicate question, may I ask just what fee you command?" enquired the Duke.

"After some initial disagreement, he agreed to pay me one guinea for each of my Journals," said Francesca.

The Duke shook with laughter. "I take my hat off to you, Francesca. Poor Jamieson will be bankrupt if he continues paying you at that rate!"

"Not at all," protested Francesca. "And certainly, after a morning like this one, I regard part of my fee as danger money."

The Duke's face was grave. "There's no harm in you continuing to write *Lady Alethia's Journal*, Francesca. As long as you continue to be discreet about your identity of course. But I won't have you engaging in any more masculine charades like this one. I'm surprised at Jamieson's irresponsibility in allowing you to dress up as a man in the first place."

Francesca was practically at boiling point. "How dare you speak to me in terms of *allow* and *permit*. You would do well to remember that my affairs are no concern of yours, my lord Duke! I shall do as I please!"

She shot to her feet and stood glaring down at him, her figure trim and neat in the well-fitting breeches and white shirt, her dark hair gleaming in the sunlight.

"Don't be absurd, Francesca!" shouted the Duke. "Can't you see that it's dangerous for a young woman to go roaming the streets alone, after dark?"

"Dressed as a woman yes," snapped Francesca. "But I had the protection of men's clothes!"

"And your escapade ended in you being challenged to a duel! My God, you could have been killed. Now you must promise me never again to dress as a man."

"I will promise no such thing," stormed Francesca, her fists clenched in rage. "After last night's experience, I shall be a great deal more confident and wiser in my approach. Next time — "

He leapt up, his strong hands gripping her shoulders. "Next time? Never! I demand your word of honour, Francesca that you will never again do anything so foolish!"

"Demand?" exploded Francesca, struggling in vain to free herself from his grasp. "Oh you arrogant creature! I shall promise no such thing!"

"Oh yes you will," he said with quiet determination. "We have sparred long enough, you and I. The time has come, Francesca, for you to learn once and for all who is your master!"

He showed her no mercy. An experienced, dominating man, the Duke kissed Francesca with a passion that verged on the savage, ruthlessly stripping away all constraint and contention between them. His parted lips burned against hers and his hands boldly explored her, shameless in his determination to impose his will on her. Until at last, as he knew it would, her resistance melted and she yielded to him, abandoning herself then to the torrent of desire this man had aroused in her. As if possessed by a fever of rapture, she returned his kisses, meeting fire with fire, willingly and wantonly glorying in the ecstacy of his intimate embraces.

When they finally drew breath, and she stood pliant and trembling in his arms, Francesca heard his voice murmuring softly in her ear, "Now will you promise me, Francesca!"

At that moment, Francesca was in such turmoil that she would have promised him anything in the world. "Yes," she whispered. "I give you my word."

He held her close against his chest, and stroked her hair. "I know it pains you to ever admit that I was right, Francesca. But will you not confess that it was an enjoyable experience, to be kissed here in the sunlight on Flower Down?"

She tilted back her head and gazed into his eyes, "Yes you were right," she smiled, willing him to kiss her again.

"Ah, those splendid eyes," he said, gently drawing his finger along the dark line of her brows. "They were something else which gave you away at the Club last night. I have observed, you see, that when you are angry, they appear green. Yet on the rare occasions I have witnessed you in more tranquil mood, your eyes are more grey in hue. You may have affected masculine clothes and deepened your voice, but you were powerless to change the singular colour of your eyes."

His hands moved down her face, under her hair and stroked the back of her neck, making her shiver with ecstacy.

"I beg your pardon," he said, suddenly brisk: "You are

wearing that thin shirt, and must be cold. Permit me to fetch your coat, and then I must escort you home. Your aunt's household will be awake before long and you must be safely inside before then.''

As he courteously assisted her into her coat, Francesca required every ounce of self control to prevent her from hurling herself into his arms and begging him to kiss her once more, so that she might experience again that thrilling current of desire. But, somehow, she contained herself. They rode in silence over the Down and into Winchester, parting by mutual agreement at the corner of the lane which led to the servants' entrance of Lady Rothersay's house.

She slipped into the old flower room and changed into her dress, feeling strange now in a skirt after the freedom afforded her by Lord Wingate's breeches. Then she hastened upstairs and wrote a scribbled note to Aithne, asking her to see that she was not disturbed until midday. She pushed the message under Aithne's bedchamber door, ran back to her own room and fell into bed.

But of course she found it impossible to sleep. Francesca was by nature an honest straightforward girl and she was especially ruthless with herself when it came to examining her emotions. She would allow herself no evasions, no turning away from the truth.

And the truth is, she thought, sitting bolt upright in bed, that I have fallen in love with the Duke of Wexford! I suppose I knew deep down all along that he was the one man with the power to make me surrender to him. But I relished my freedom, so I fought him every inch of the way. For I suspected that once I gave in, his victory would be absolute. And I was right.

She shuddered with happiness as she recalled the fire of his lips on hers on Flower Down that morning. He was utterly determined, she thought, bringing me to my knees in an agony of desire for him. Yes, oh yes, I love him! No other man has ever aroused such a fever within me. I feel afire with longing for his kiss, and the touch of his hands upon me. I want him. Oh, how I want him. Here. Now, beside me, in this bed, taking me in his arms, his breath caressing my cheek as he unties the ribbons of my nightgown . . .

With a wail of fury Francesca flung her pillow hard upon the floor.

You fool, Francesca! she railed at herself. My, if he could see you now, if he could read what is in your mind, how he would laugh! Can you not imagine his triumph at the realisation that he had tamed you to such an extent that you are now whimpering with love for him?

For you must face facts, Francesca. He most certainly does not love you. Oh yes, he kissed you. Passionately and thoroughly, as he has all along hinted that he would. But it was not because he loved you. You were nothing more than a diverting challenge to him. Do you not recall how, at Lady Sombourne's ball, he told you that he would indeed find it most amusing to kiss you one summer's day, out on the windblown downs.

Amusing!

Francesca choked over the word. Thank heavens, she thought, I had the presence of mind this morning not to reveal how much his kiss had affected me. How wretched I should feel now if I had followed my instincts and let him see how much I desired him. I should never have been able to look him squarely in the eyes again. As it is, it will be nervewracking facing his mocking smile across my aunt's drawing room. I expect he is at home now, enjoying an enormous breakfast, feeling extremely satisfied with his morning's work.

The voice of reason intervened then, advising Francesca

that he had, after all, devoted considerable time and effort that day to protecting her interests — her life even. Irrationally, Francesca brushed the notion aside. He merely wanted to prove his dominance over me, and boost his own self-esteem into the bargain, she told herself. Nevertheless, she could not repress a feeling of admiration for the cool manner in which he had hidden in the gorse bushes and fired a shot of such unerring accuracy over her shoulder at Lord Sutton. Had he fired his pistol a second too late . . . had Lord Sutton moved, or fired first, then she, Francesca, would have been lying on the turf in a pool of blood.

Before he took his leave of her, the Duke had quietened Francesca's fears about news of the duel being common knowledge all round Winchester before the day was out.

"Remember duelling is strictly forbidden. You will find that amongst the gentlemen of the city, a most effective conspiracy of silence will come into operation. Of course, I do regret that it will also be essential for the all-seeing Lady Alethia to remain in blissful ignorance of the duel."

Francesca retrieved her pillow, and lay back with a sigh. She had promised Sir Peter that she would deliver her latest Journal to him by six o'clock this evening. And she had yet to write a line of this week's happenings!

How Winchester would be agog if she could only write the truth about this week's events! About her disguise as Lord Wingate, and the ensuing duel. How within the walls of 11 Upper Brook two girls were desperately in love — but were unable, for different reasons, to declare their passion to the world.

Francesca could well imagine Aithne's cries of alarm when she learned of the injury to her lover. Lord Sutton would no doubt declare that he had found himself in the way of a poacher's pistol, and Aithne would rush to sympathise and admire his bravery.

As for me, thought Francesca sleepily, I must devote all

my energies to preventing the Duke from realising my feelings for him. If he even noticed a glimmering of the truth, I should die of shame at the mocking laughter in his eyes.

Still burning with desire, she tossed restlessly between the sheets. "Damn you, Wexford," she whispered vehemently, "Why, of all the men in the world, did I allow myself to fall in love with you?"

10

As it happened, Francesca's dilemma over what to include in that week's journal was solved for her, in the most unexpected way, by Lady Rothersay. When Francesca entered the Drawing Room early that afternoon, she was greeted with warm concern by her aunt.

"My dear Francesca! I was so distressed to learn of your headache. Are you quite recovered? You look dreadfully pale and my, those dark circles under your eyes! Was the pain so bad that you were unable to sleep?"

Feeling the most appalling fraud, Francesca made the necessary replies and enquired after her Cousin.

Lady Rothersay waved her hands. "She is out riding all day with Lady Clorinda. Really, I am at a loss to understand Aithne's sudden enthusiasm for riding. I keep telling her, if she continues to spend so many hours in the saddle she will become as broad across the beam as Lady Featherstone and then there will be no chance at all of the Duke wanting to marry her."

Francesca busied herself rearranging a bowl of pink roses. It was obvious to her that Aithne was once more in the company of Lord Sutton, no doubt at this very moment sympathizing over his wound.

"I find it particularly vexing Aithne being out this afternoon, because I have so wanted to tell someone my news!" exclaimed Lady Rothersay, patting the seat beside her on the sofa.

Realising that this was the reason for her aunt's unaccustomed warmth towards her, Francesca obediently subsided onto the sofa and gave her aunt her full attention.

Lady Rothersay drew from her reticule a letter, which from its creased appearance had apparently been read, reread and refolded many times that day. "It is from Lord Rothersay!" she declared, her face glowing in pride. "He informs me that he will be returning home in three weeks time, and will be here for the rest of the summer!"

"Why that is wonderful news," responded Francesca with polite enthusiasm.

"Wait! There is more!" Lady Rothersay was so excited she could hardly spill out the words. "He is bringing with him no less a personage than the Prince Regent himself!"

Francesca was truly impressed at this intelligence. "The Prince is to stay here, in this house?" she asked, wide-eyed.

"No, no," said Lady Rothersay impatiently. "When the Prince is in Winchester he always resides at Wexford Hall with the Duke."

To Francesca's furious dismay, at the mention of the Duke's name she could feel a blush tinging her cheek. Fortunately, Lady Rothersay was too immersed in her own affairs to notice.

"The Prince will be in Winchester for a week," went on Lady Rothersay breathlessly, "and the highlight of his visit will be a banquet, attended by the elite of the city. What is more, he has requested that at the banquet the six golden goblets of Charles II should be used. Is that not a charming idea?"

"Why yes," agreed Francesca. "Will this be the first time

since the days of King Charles that all six goblets have graced a banqueting table at the same time?"

Lady Rothersay nodded. "It will be one of the most glittering occasions that Winchester has ever known. Lady Sombourne, who of course is not privileged to own a King Charles goblet, will be simply livid that she will not be invited to sit at the top table with the Prince and the Duke!"

"And will it be your responsibility to organise the banquet, Aunt?" enquired Francesca. Lady Rothersay modestly cast down her eyes, and sighed.

"No doubt the burden will fall upon my shoulders, yes. If the Duke were married, it would of course be a different matter. His wife would naturally act as hostess for the occasion. I suppose Lady Evelina could step in, but in her condition it would be most unsuitable."

Francesca hid a smile, imagining Lady Evelina's horror at being requested to take charge of such an enormous banquet.

"Unfortunately, two of the ladies who own goblets are no longer residing in Winchester," frowned Lady Rothersay. "I must write to them post haste and urge them to return. Lady Beddows has buried herself in Westmorland, and Lady Montfort is enjoying the bracing east winds of Norfolk. I spoke to Ladies Sutton, Featherstone and Southport about the matter this morning, but to be frank I found their reaction extremely disappointing."

Francesca raised a surprised eyebrow. "But were they not delighted at the prospect of such a banquet and the presence of the Prince?"

Lady Rothersay tapped her fan on the side table. "Lady Southport fainted clean away at the news. I understand from Lord Southport that this is now an alarmingly regular occurrence, and I must say he is being extremely unsympathetic about it. Instead of dashing off to your Club, I told him, you should spend some time with your wife and reassure her of your affection for her. He replied, with some asperity I might add, that it was difficult to murmur tender words of love to a woman who spent most of her time unconscious on the floor."

Francesca twisted the tasselled edge of the sofa into a knot, relishing this exchange between the crotchety Lord Southport and Lady Rothersay. "What about Lady Feather-stone, Aunt? Surely she was pleased at the news of the banquet."

"Admittedly, I did call on Lady Featherstone at rather an inconvenient moment," confessed Lady Rothersay. "Her stables had just caught fire, and she was quite distraught at the fear of losing her best hunter. I've never before observed Lady Featherstone in such a hysterical condition. But there you are. Even as a young girl she always insisted on Cook preparing special portions of food for her nursery rocking horse. So I then proceeded on to Sutton Lodge, where I found Lady Sutton in a very strange mood. She was quite short with me, and even went so far as to dismiss the notion of the banquet as romantic nonsense!"

Before Francesca could phrase a suitable reply, Lady Rothersay swept on, "But of course, I know what's behind Lady Sutton's strange attitude. The poor woman has obviously heard a whisper of her husband's latest indiscre-tion. Oh, he is the most unreliable man! No doubt it's one of the laundry maids again. It's extraordinary the number of men who seem to have a particular penchant for laundry maids. I suppose the only thing you can say about it is with all that soap, water and steam, at least one knows the girls are clean, if nothing else!"

Francesca could bear it no longer. She knew if she remained a minute more in the company of her aunt, she would dissolve into uncontrollable laughter. Accordingly, pleading extreme fatigue after her restless night, she escaped to her bedchamber where she straightaway set to work on *Lady Alethia's Journal*.

Later that afternoon she slipped from the house and made her way down to the river to meet Sir Peter. Making her escape had proved easier than she anticipated, because the Rothersay household was in a turmoil over the dinner to be held there that night. Lady Rothersay had invited the Ladies Sutton, Featherstone and Southport to a council of war, "to thrash out once and for all" as she put it, details of the arrangements for the Prince Regent's banquet.

"Lady Sombourne has also been invited to the dinner tonight," Francesca laughingly informed Sir Peter, "even though she is not one of the six elite who own the celebrated King Charles goblets which will be used at the banquet."

"I take it that Lady Sombourne has been invited solely in order to put her nose properly out of joint," smiled Sir Peter, eagerly taking the handwritten pages of *Lady Alethia's Journal* from Francesca's hands.

Francesca had remembered to bring some bread for the ducks and busied herself throwing cubes to the flotilla now advancing down the river.

"Mmm, this is capital stuff," said Sir Peter, scanning the closely written pages. "I admire your astringent snippets about Buckhurst's, and the intelligence about the Prince Regent's banquet strikes just the right waspish tone! By the way," he lowered his voice, though there was no one in sight on the riverside path, "I heard about your duel. My word, what an exciting evening you had, Lady Francesca!"

"Exciting!" exclaimed Francesca crossly. "I was very nearly killed, Sir Peter! I have never been so terrified in my life."

"But my information was that you acquitted yourself superbly," protested the dark-haired man. "Lord Sutton, one of the best shots in the county, wounded by a young rustic from Somerset! That is stirring news indeed. In fact, I am surprised there is no mention of the duel in your Journal. There would be no need to name names, of course. But surely you could have given some hint of the drama that morning on Flower Down?"

Francesca shook her head and said vehemently, "I should prefer to forget about the entire episode, Sir Peter!" My, she thought, if you knew the whole truth about that fateful morning, what news that would be for the *Winchester Courier*! It would set the entire town abuzz with speculation.

Perplexed, Sir Peter scratched his head. "You disappoint me, Lady Francesca. I expected a more fighting, defiant spirit from you! However, after your evening at Buckhurst's you must admit that the notion of you disguising yourself as a man is a capital one. I had it in mind that on the next occasion — "

"No," said Francesca quietly, but firmly. "There will be no next time, Sir Peter."

He stood up, and paced the path in front of her. "Really, Lady Francesca, it is most unlike you to display a yellow streak! Why, we have established the perfect cover for you in Lord Wingate. I assure you, after your success in the duel, your name is spoken of with awe in the city! We could have you elected to Buckhurst's in no time at all. My, what a splendid jest that would be! A woman elected to a gentleman's Club! Come now, Lady Francesca. Where is your spirit of adventure?"

With all her heart Francesca longed to confess that she agreed totally with Sir Peter. Normally she would have regarded it as a capital coup to have herself elected to Buckhurst's. The notion appealed strongly to all her headstrong reckless instincts.

But I gave the Duke my word that I would never again masquerade as a man, she thought, blushing at the memory of the manner in which that promise had been extracted from her. And although she believed that promises made under duress did not count, she knew in all honesty that the Duke had not forced her to do anything against her will. At that moment, she admitted, there in his arms with his lips on mine, I would gladly have promised him the sun, moon and stars.

And besides, Francesca reasoned, it cannot be denied that he did save me from the most terrible fate up on Flower Down. If he ever discovered that I had broken my word to him, and dressed again as a man, he would be very very angry indeed. Francesca shivered. Sparring with the Duke, as she often did, was one thing. But she knew she would go to any lengths to avoid incurring the full furious measure of his wrath. He was not a man likely to show mercy to any woman rash enough to overstep the limits he himself had laid down.

"I'm sorry, Sir Peter," said Francesca, standing up and brushing bread crumbs from her skirt, "but I will never again stride through the streets of Winchester as Lord Wingate. My mind is quite made up."

He sighed. "Ah well, it is a great pity — but I have come to recognise that particular note in your voice, Lady Francesca. It means that you will not be moved, and all my arguments, charm and powers of persuasion would be completely wasted."

Francesca laughed. "Poor Sir Peter. What a dismal life you lead! Will I see you at my aunt's Thursday Afternoon this week?"

"Hardly!" he responded dryly. "I am still very much *persona non grata* amongst the elite, you know."

"Oh dear," murmured Francesca. "Clearly, the ladies do

not believe that you are unaware of the identity of Lady Alethia. I do hope you are not ostracised to such an extent that you feel yourself to be a social outcast?"

He gazed into the water, and smiled. Much later, Francesca was to remember that smile, and kick herself for her stupidity in not realising what lay behind it.

"My newspaper is my life," he replied blandly. "It provides me with all the fulfilment and excitement that I require."

Francesca stood for a moment regarding him. She had no doubt that his position as proprietor of a newspaper secured him an interesting and eventful life. But what of romance, she wondered. A newspaper cannot cover your face in kisses, or take you in its arms and make you quite dizzy with desire.

But of course, this was neither the time nor place for her to voice such thoughts to Sir Peter. Although he had always treated her with the utmost respect, nevertheless she was aware that every time she met him like this, unchaperoned, she was increasingly placing herself in a compromising position. And she had no intention of adding fuel to the flames by introducing the subject of romance! Far wiser, she knew, that her relationship with Sir Peter should remain cool and businesslike.

Accordingly, she politely took her leave of him and they parted as was their custom, each walking in a different direction. After ten minutes or so, Francesca left the river path, crossed over the bridge and made her way up the narrow side street which provided a convenient short-cut back to her aunt's house.

She saw the anonymous, grey-painted carriage standing in the cobbled road, but paid it no heed. There was just room for her to squeeze by. Keeping close to the high wall, she began to edge her way past, silently remarking how inconsiderate it was of the coach driver to have blocked the narrow road with his vehicle.

She was allowed to proceed no further. The carriage door was suddenly thrown open, effectively barring her way forward. Alarmed, she took a pace back, and cannoned into a very large, burly man with a nose which had obviously been broken far more times than was good for!

Frightened now, Francesca opened her mouth to scream. Too late. The man's hand closed round her face and she found herself bundled unceremoniously into the carriage. There a second man, small but possessing a wiry strength, quickly knotted a grimy handkerchief round her eyes.

"If you make so much as one whimper of noise, my lady, I'll be forced to put a gag round your pretty mouth," he said menacingly. "And I should warn you that I'm a rough, clumsy creature by nature — so you'd probably end up half suffocating as well." Francesca suddenly felt his rough fingers pinching her cheek. "Do you understand what I'm saying to you?"

Francesca nodded, her masked eyes stinging with tears as she gritted her teeth in an effort not to cry out with the pain he was inflicting on her. She was pushed back into a corner of the carriage which then began its jolting progress out of Winchester. Francesca knew they were leaving the city, because it was impossible to depart from Winchester without ascending a hill. The pull of the horses told her that they would soon be out in open countryside — but of course she had no notion in which direction they were travelling or, indeed, why she had been abducted by these ruffians.

What was the meaning of it all? Was she to be held to ransom? In which case, why kidnap me, wondered the terrified Francesca. It is no secret that the de Lisles have little family fortune. Surely Aithne would have commanded a far higher price?

Perhaps it is all an elaborate jest, Francesca thought hopefully. Could Sir Peter be behind this charade, intending to provide her with more exciting drama for *Lady Alethia's Journal*?

Francesca burned with indignation. If indeed he does prove to be the culprit, she resolved, then he will feel the full lash of my tongue and no mistake! I am beginning to share the Duke of Wexford's opinion of Sir Peter. He is indeed a man without scruple or sense of responsibility.

She sat up in her seat, suddenly alert as the carriage jerked to a halt. The door creaked open, and she was hustled out along what she took to be a grassy or mossy path. All her senses were fully alert as she tried to determine where she might be. Her two captors had remained completely silent on the journey, obviously acting under orders to prevent her gaining any clue to their identity, or her whereabouts.

Then there came the sound of a latch being raised. As she was pushed forward, the air changed from that of a grass scented summer's afternoon to something more musty, indicating that she was in a damp, little-used dwelling.

Her ears pricked as she heard a croaking voice whispering "Take her blindfold off, and wait outside the door."

As the handkerchief was torn away, Francesca rubbed her eyes and saw that she was standing in the parlour of a tumbledown cottage, hidden away, she suspected, somewhere on the Downs. The room was sparsely furnished, with just a rough wooden table, two chairs and a tattered piece of cloth over the window.

Sitting at the table was a man, his face completely covered by a frightening black hood. All that was visible was a pair of cold blue eyes. The table was bare, apart from a pistol. Francesca had no doubt that it was loaded with powder.

"Pray sit down, Lady Francesca," whispered her captor.

"I am sure you are sensible enough to realise that this is no time for a display of heroics. My men are positioned outside the door. They are simple minded, lusty creatures and there is nothing they would like more than to tumble an attractive young lady such as yourself in the grass. And," his gloved hand toyed with the pistol in front of him, "I myself should have no compunction in using this. Although, of course, I would not claim to be such a good shot as young Lord Wingate!"

His laugh sent a shiver of apprehension through Francesca. She knew then that she had not been brought here by Sir Peter, in jest. This man, whoever he might be, clearly had more chillingly serious designs on her.

She lifted her dark head and demanded boldly. "Who are you? How dare you abduct me in such a manner? And why do you hide behind that mask? You are nothing but a coward and a rogue, and I insist that you release me immediately!"

"Bravo!" he whispered sarcastically. "Spoken as bravely and as stoutly as a man, my dear! But then you have had considerable experience of masquerading as one of my own sex, have you not?"

Francesca gazed straight over his head as she replied, with distant disdain, "To be sure, I have not the faintest notion to what you refer."

"Don't trifle with me, girl!" he growled. "I know all about your little act as Lord Wingate. I was out one morning, you see, riding across the Downs and suddenly my eye fell on such a charming scene! A raven-haired young girl, clad in shirt and breeches. And what was she doing? Yes, well might you have the grace to blush, Lady Francesca! You were clearly so enamoured of the Duke of Wexford that you neither saw nor heard me pass by!"

Francesca sat with downcast eyes, her hands clenched in

her lap. Oh, what misfortune! So she and the Duke had been observed. And as ill luck would have it, the passerby that morning had been this brutal rogue.

"What is it you want?" she demanded coldly. "If you have it in mind to attempt to use this information against either the Duke or myself then I must warn you — "

"Be silent!" he hissed. "You are in no position, Lady Francesca, to warn me of anything! You will kindly sit patiently and quietly until I have finished my little tale. For there is more to come."

She sensed him smile beneath the dark hood. Oh, how she loathed him! But she knew it was important to keep her wits about her, and remain on the alert for any clues, however small, to his identity. His voice was certainly giving her no help, for his assumed croakey whisper was further muffled by the silk hood. As he was seated, she had little notion of his height. And he was clad in a voluminous dark cape which revealed nothing of his physical form.

"Intrigued by what I saw on Flower Down," the man went on, in an infuriatingly slow tone, "I had you watched. I feared that my men would be obliged to endure a long vigil before you led them into an interesting situation. But no! This very day I receive word that you are trysting with yet another gentleman. Sir Peter Jamieson no less. My, what a very hot-blooded young lady you are, Lady Frances-ca! Secret assignations with two gentleman and all in the same day! I am quite overcome with the romance of it all!"

"Don't be absurd!" snapped Francesca. "You completely misunderstand the situation. Yes, you are right, I did pose as Lord Wingate. But that was just intended as a harmless prank. Something to write and entertain my brother with at Eton. Then, whilst I was on Flower Down, some grit blew into my eye. What appeared to you to be an embrace was merely the Duke looking in my eye to see where the piece of grit was located."

"I see," mused the hooded man, his tone dry with disbelief. "And what of Sir Peter Jamieson? My intelligence is that you were handing him a love letter."

"Then your intelligence is wrong!" flared Francesca, enraged that she should be obliged to defend and explain her actions to this unscrupulous blackguard.

"Calm yourself, my dear young lady," said the man silkily. "Naturally, I am prepared to take your word on the matter. It is my belief that the document passed from yourself to the newspaper proprietor was something far more interesting than the sentimental ramblings of one turtle dove to another. It was, in truth, the latest pages from the celebrated *Journal of Lady Alethia*, was it not?"

"What . . . what a ridiculous notion!" stammered Francesca, knotting her hands to prevent them trembling.

"Indeed? I think not," the voice whispered on, with maddening self-assurance. "But the truth will be revealed on Friday, will it not? If I open my *Winchester Courier* and find that Lady Alethia is revealing a surprising insight into the latest intrigues prevalent at Buckhurst's Club . . ."

His voice tailed away. In the fraught silence, Francesca was sure he must hear the terrified hammering of her heart.

"Knowing you to be a young lady of quite extraordinary initiative," her captor continued blithely, "let me advise you that my spies are everywhere in Winchester. Both you and Sir Peter will be under careful surveillance from now until Friday. So there will be no point in you attempting to send him a message, requesting that certain paragraphs be omitted from the Journal."

Stubbornly, Francesca said nothing. She was caught and she knew it. But she utterly refused to give the vermin on the other side of the desk the pleasure of hearing her admit the truth. Besides, she reasoned quickly, today was Tuesday. Even allowing for the fact that her Journal would be set into type by the printer long before the edition on Friday, there was still time — somehow — for her to send word to Sir Peter. There was time and therefore there was hope.

"Ah, how refreshing to see you sitting docile and sub-dued," murmured the man. "You realise, I take it, the seriousness of your position. And being a sensible girl, I am sure you will listen most attentively as I give you your instructions."

It was all the seething Francesca could do not to jump up and fly at him. How she longed to rip off his mask and claw his face until it bled!

But she knew she was powerless. She could not, single-handed, defeat a man with a pistol and two heavyweight rogues to protect him.

"What I want you to do," the man said quietly, "is quite simply to procure something for me."

Some of the anxiety left Francesca's face. It had occurred to her that the masked man, intrigued at the sight of her passionate embrace with the Duke, might be intending to demand similar intimacies with her. Now to her relief she realised that it was not carnal lust which motivated her kidnapper. He was more like a common thief and no doubt wished her to steal a few of her aunt's trinkets. From the man's accent she had already determined that he was of high birth. A gambler, she surmised, someone who has squan-dered the family fortune and now seeks to re-line his coffers by stealing from the wealthy of Winchester.

"What is it you want?" she enquired scornfully. "Am I to snatch my aunt's pearls from her neck?"

"Oh, nothing so crass, my dear Lady Francesca," he shuddered. "No, what I desire you to obtain for me is a simple drinking vessel. I refer, of course, to the golden goblet given to the Rothersays by King Charles."

"Are you quite mad?" exclaimed Francesca in horror.

"Why, if I took that there would be the most terrible scandal! The hue and cry would be never ending. My aunt would have no compunction about insisting that every house, from the humblest shepherd's cottage right up to the Duke of Wexford's mansion, be searched from top to bottom. Rest assured, Lady Rothersay would run that goblet to earth, and you with it!"

Again, she sensed that he was smiling beneath the mask. "Naturally, your aunt will be upset. But I shall not be at hand to witness her distress. By the time the loss is discovered, I shall be across the Channel to Europe and a certain Italian merchant who will pay me handsomely for my prize."

Francesca shifted on the hard wooden chair. "It seems to me that you are going to a great deal of trouble for a not very great reward. The goblet is valuable, certainly, as is any object fashioned so exquisitely of gold encrusted with diamonds. But the real value of the goblets lies in the fact that there are six of them, each of course adorned with a different jewel. If you owned the complete set, they would be more than valuable, they would be priceless . . ." She gasped as the truth dawned on her. "Oh my word! I see it all now! You *have* secured the other goblets, haven't you?"

He steepled his fingers, and remarked with pride, "I have indeed! What a remarkably clever girl you are, Lady Francesca."

She stared at him, her mind working furiously. So much was explained now. The hasty departure of Ladies Beddows and Montfort to their estates in Westmorland and Norfolk. Lady Sutton's accidents, when she fell into the river and almost stumbled from a third floor window. But of course, they weren't accidents at all, thought Francesca. The distraught woman was clearly beside herself with anxiety over the loss of her family heirloom.

Then there was Lady Southport's sudden oncourse of fainting fits. What was it Lady Rothersay had reported she had said when she fainted on the terrace at Lady Sombourne's ball? Something agitated about her increasing years. But of course, she wasn't saying *old*, but *gold*, Francesca realised. Heavens, these poor ladies must have been frantic with worry. And all because of the avarice of this man holding me captive now!

Francesca longed to give him a piece of her mind. But for once in her life, she kept a strong curb on her impulsive nature. I have no hope of winning by making a forthright attack on him, she thought. That will only infuriate him, and in consequence he will deal even more harshly with me.

Accordingly, remembering that note of pride in his voice, she set out to flatter him. "You have been most ingenious, Sir," she said admiringly, though the words struck in her throat. "As you so rightly say, I am quick-witted by nature. But you, it appears are quite my master!"

"You are young," he replied kindly. "I am twice your age, my dear, and so have many more years experience."

Francesca lowered her eyes to mask her triumph. So, I have discovered if nothing else that he is not a man in the first flush of youth!

She tilted her lovely head to one side and said slowly, "But however did you manage to inveigle these ladies to part so easily with their families' most treasured possessions? I am sure if I thought for a year, I could not devise a scheme of that sophisticated degree of cunning."

Her captor's gruff voice trembled with excitement. "Ah, but every family has its skeleton in the closet, my dear Lady Francesca. And in a city like Winchester where propriety is very much the order of the day, the most elite and respected families will go to any length to prevent that murky closet door being opened for all the world to see!"

"Blackmail!" breathed Francesca, managing just in time to disguise the disgust in her voice.

"No no! Please! Such a vulgar expression. I prefer to think of it as gentle persuasion. And it was not all that difficult. I discovered, you see, that both Lady Beddows and Lady Montfort — flighty damsels in their youth — had been rash enough years ago to dally with gentleman other than their husbands. Then there was Lady Sutton. Or rather, Lord Sutton. We are all aware, of course that he had a devilish eye for the ladies. But as I pointed out to Lady Sutton, it would be too distressing if all Winchester was to learn that his indiscretion with the laundry maid had borne fruit in the shape of a pair of extremely boisterous twins."

Francesca paled, imagining the dire consequences if this evil man ever discovered about Lord Sutton's latest flirtation — with poor gullible Aithne! Hastily diverting him from the subject of Lord Sutton, she enquired:

"And what of Lady Southport? Surely she has never taken a lover? And from what I have observed of Lord Southport, he is more concerned with cossetting his gouty leg than engaging in intimate caresses with the laundry maid."

"Quite so. As always, your perspicacity does you credit," said the voice which Francesca was coming to loathe with every fibre of her being. "No, Lady Southport has another very worrying little problem. Next time you embark on a shopping expedition, take note of the singularly large reticule carried by the good Lady Southport. At the end of the morning, you will hear her declare that not a single article has caught her eye. Yet her reticule will be bulging in the most interesting fashion."

Francesca's eyes widened. "You mean she takes articles from shops without paying for them, or having them charged to her account?"

"Most distressing," whispered the hooded man. "The poor lady would be quite suicidal if ever the news was made public."

Francesca was appalled yet fascinated all at the same time. Naturally, she deplored this hooded rogue's attempts at blackmail. Nevertheless, his revelations proved what she had always suspected. That beneath the elegant veneer of this ancient town lurked a snakepit of scandal, deceit and intrigue.

Her curiosity thoroughly whetted, she could not restrain herself from challenging: "Which leaves the formidable Lady Featherstone! A widow. Even in the unlikely event of you discovering any scandal about her family, I am confident that had you dared give utterance to what you knew, she would have come at you with her shotgun!"

The man's gloved fingers made a soft drumming sound on the wooden table. "Quite so. I admit, I was unable to discover anything damaging about Lady Featherstone. If there is a skeleton in her family closet it is guarded as strongly as the Tower of London. No, I fear I was obliged to employ a different method with Lady Featherstone.

Francesca gazed at him from beneath her thick, dark lashes. "That stable fire," she said slowly. "Were you responsible for that?"

"I regret yes," sighed the man. "I did warn Lady Featherstone, I told her if she refused to give me her King Charles goblet, then I would be forced to relieve her of one of her prime hunters. As it turned out, during the stable's blaze she managed to save her damned horse. But the incident was enough to make her realise that I would stop at nothing. I am happy to report that the Feathersone goblet was delivered to me with no further fuss or delay. So now I have five. Only the Rothersay goblet is missing from my collection. And what a godsend you will be to me in this respect, Lady Francesca!"

Francesca spread her hands in a helpless gesture. "I don't believe you understand the complexity of what you ask! The goblet is a family heirloom. It is not left lying carelessly on the sideboard. It is kept in its own locked glass case in its own small locked room. The only person with access to the keys is my aunt. Stealing it would be monstrously difficult."

"You are a young lady of great initiative and originality, Lady Francesca. I am confident that you will find a way. By next Tuesday, if you please. One week from today."

"And if I refuse?" asked Francesca defiantly.

He shrugged. "Then, to my own great personal distress, I shall be obliged to inform your aunt, and all of Winchester society, about your journalistic activities on the *Winchester Courier*, and also about your very interesting trysts on the Downs with the Duke of Wexford."

Francesca swallowed hard. Wriggle and writhe as she might, she could see no way out of this trap. If the hooded blackmailer revealed her to the town as Lady Alethia, Francesca knew that her Aunt Cecilia would be not only mightily angry but also put most embarrassingly to the blush. For a lady like Lady Rothersay, to whom propriety and social etiquette were all, to have her own niece exposed in such a manner would be a kind of living death. Francesca shuddered at the notion of inflicting such shame upon her aunt.

The masked man called for the two ruffians to re-enter the room. "I must delay you no longer, Lady Francesca, or you will be late for your aunt's dinner party."

Francesca said no more, but allowed herself to be hustled out of the cottage and into the carriage. Although she had refused to betray such an emotion to the loathsome blackmailer, she was at heart filled with despair.

What am I to do, she thought frantically. My aunt will raise the roof if that goblet goes missing. But if I refuse to steal it and one of her family is exposed as the scandalous Lady Alethia, then it will bring my aunt to the edge of suicide. Worse, if it is suggested to her that I, whilst a guest under her roof, have attempted to engage the affections of the man she has ear-marked as Aithne's fiancé . . . oh, the repercussions will be terrible indeed!

The thought of the Duke only increased Francesca's misery. I am in the hands of a reptilian blackmailer who will clearly show me not a shred of mercy. And I am desperately, hopelessly, passionately in love with a man who loves me not in return. Oh, how I wish I had never, ever set foot in Winchester!

11

"Francesca, where have you been?" gasped Aithne, bursting into the blue bedchamber where Francesca and a maid were working at breakneck speed to complete her toilette in time for dinner. "I was frantic when I returned home from my ride and discovered you absent from the house! Fortunately for you, Mama is in such a state of ecstacy over the Prince Regent's banquet that she did not realise you were missing. But what have you been doing? What happened last night? Where — "

"Thank you, Ellie," said Francesca hastily to the maid, "I can manage perfectly well on my own now." When the maid had retired, Francesca seized her hairbrush and attacked her tangled tresses, exclaiming tartly to Aithne. "Where have *I* been? What about you? I don't believe for a moment that you were out riding with Clorinda all afternoon!"

A dreamy expression on Aithne's face told Francesca that she had hit on the truth. Pulling her hair up into a knot of curls on top of her head, Francesca said anxiously, "Aithne please please take my advice and have the courage not to see this man again! Believe me, you will bring a mountain of misery tumbling down upon yourself if you continue with these secret meetings."

"I know you are speaking with the best intentions,

Cousin, but I should prefer not to discuss the matter further," said Aithne with dignity. "Anyway you are hardly in a position to lecture me! I am not the one who stays out all night and who then disappears for several hours in the afternoon as well!"

"You don't understand!" exclaimed Francesca, smoothing down the lace at the neck of her soft green muslin dress. "All is not as you imagine, Aithne."

Aithne retorted, her cheeks flushed, "Well if you are not prepared to confide in me, Cousin, you can hardly blame me for my reluctance to reveal my secrets to you!"

There came a tap on the door, and a maid poked her head into the bedchamber. "Beggin' your pardon, ladies. But Lady Rothersay requests that you join her immediately in the Drawing Room as the guests are due to arrive at any minute."

The dinner was a nightmare for Francesca. Seated round the oval mahogany table were all the ladies of the Winchester elite with the exception of Lady Beddows and Lady Montfort, who were still ensconced at their country estates. And only I know why, mused Francesca, well able to imagine the fright in the hearts of the two ladies who, each unbeknown to the other, had fled the city for fear that their marital indiscretions, and the blackmailer's possession of the King Charles' goblets, would be revealed.

Under the circumstances, it was not surprising that the only person at the table to show any enthusiasm for the forthcoming Prince Regent's banquet was Lady Rothersay herself. Ladies Featherstone, Sutton and Southport were unusually subdued, wincing every time Lady Rothersay mentioned the goblets. She would bring up the subject of them all being on display at the banquet, for the first time since King Charles was on the throne.

Lady Sombourne, who of course had never had the

honour of possessing a goblet in the first place, affected an expression of indulgent fatigue, as if she were listening with kindly tolerance to a group of nursery-age children discussing a forthcoming doll's tea party. And Lady Evelina, seated next to Francesca, confessed to her in a whisper that she felt quite out of it all.

"Charles is adamant that on this occasion I must curb my love of flouting convention. He will not permit me to appear in public before the Prince Regent whilst I am *enceinte*." She sighed, and continued in a resigned tone. "He is a wonderful husband and allows me a great deal of freedom. But when I hear that particular steely note in his voice I know it is useless to argue, and I must do my wifely duty and obey him!"

Francesca, preoccupied with her own thoughts, hardly heard what Lady Evelina was saying. Normally, she would have been highly amused by the cross-currents of tension at the dinner table. But because she understood only too well the gnawing despair of three of the ladies present, she found herself in consequence growing more and more sick with anxiety as the meal progressed.

She was also upset over the unfortunate scene in her bedchamber with Aithne. It was all my fault, she owned. Had I spoken to my cousin in a quiet, sympathetic tone I am sure I could have persuaded her to listen to reason, and abandon this precarious relationship with Lord Sutton. But I was in such a turmoil after all the events of the night and the day, that I spoke recklessly and harshly to my cousin. Naturally she felt resentful and alienated. No doubt at this moment she is seething at my ingratitude, for she was, after all, kind enough to cover for me with my aunt whilst I was out masquerading as Lord Wingate. Had my aunt discovered what I was about, the repercussions would have been almost as dreadful for Aithne as for myself.

Accordingly, she caught Aithne's eye across the table and gave her an apologetic smile. Aithne raised her glass, and smiled in return, much to Francesca's relief. With everything else so awry in her life the last thing she wanted was a foolish squabble with her cousin.

After dinner the ladies assembled in the Drawing Room and, over tea, talk turned to the organisation of the banquet itself.

"Naturally, there are certain standards which must be maintained," declared Lady Rothersay from her vantage point on the velvet sofa. "Lord Rothersay, who of course is one of the Prince's closest advisers," she smiled regally at the company, "informs me that, in London, the Prince is accustomed to a considerable amount of ceremony. When he comes to Winchester, I am determined to provide him with an evening to remember."

It will certainly be that, mused Francesca as she stood by the copper tea urn. Imagine the calamitous scene when he calls for the King Charles goblets to be brought before him, and none are forthcoming!

"What had you in mind, Lady Rothersay?" enquired Lady Evelina politely, smiling her thanks as Francesca pushed a low stool under her feet.

Lady Rothersay opened a copy of the *Winchester Courier*. "I noticed a report in here of a magnificent London fête hosted by the Prince. I will read it aloud to you so that we may obtain a notion of what the Prince will expect of us in Winchester.

" . . . *the night was most serene; and the multitudes who had been honoured with his Royal Highness's invitation were enabled to reach Carlton House without annoyance.*"

She paused. "A most important point, that. We must have the streets cleared of riff-raff so the carriages will be free to pass."

"But my dear, the entire town will be thronging the streets, agog to see the Prince," protested Lady Sutton.

"Then they must be roped off," declared Lady Rothersay with a dismissive wave of her hand. "Now, where was I. *The Palace was a scene of enchantment. Along the centre of the table, about six inches above the surface, a canal of pure water continued flowing from a silver fountain . . . At the head of the table above the fountain, sat his Royal Highness the Prince Regent on a throne of crimson velvet trimmed with gold.*"

"A canal?" boomed Lady Featherstone. "Don't be absurd, Cecilia! Why, the whole table will be awash with water in no time. We shall all be drenched!"

"Do you not think, Lady Rothersay," said Lady Evelina hastily, "that, as by now every society hostess will have read the account of the Prince's fête, he will soon be excessively bored with the canals and fountains spouting from every dinner table? Perhaps we should try to think of something novel which will surprise and delight him."

The argument raged on, but Francesca paid no heed. She took her tea across to the window seat, trying desperately to think of a solution to her own problems. But try as she might, she returned inevitably to the conclusion that the blackmailer had won. She had no choice but to steal the Rothersay goblet for him.

It would help of course, if I had the faintest clue as to the identity of the hooded man, she mused. But he was so well disguised and the light in that cottage was so dim, that I was unable to unearth a shred of information about him. Of course, once I have handed him the sixth goblet, the matter will soon be resolved. He freely admitted that he intended taking the collection of goblets to a merchant in Italy. So whichever prominent Winchester gentleman suddenly disappears will inevitably be the culprit. But by then, she sighed, it will be too late.

"Then there is the question," Lady Rothersay was saying, returning to her favourite theme, "of which beverage we should choose to grace the wonderful golden goblets. It seems to me that champagne would be the most suitable choice."

Lady Sombourne sniffed. "How commonplace, Lady Rothersay! Surely the Regent's Special Punch would be more appropriate."

Nothing on this earth would force Lady Rothersay to confess that she had never heard of the Regent's Punch. "Er . . . refresh my memory, Lady Sombourne. What exactly are the ingredients of this concoction?"

Lady Sombourne took a deep breath. "Three bottles of champagne, two of Madeira, one of Hock, one of Curacao, one quart of Brandy, one pint of Rum and two bottles of seltzer water flavoured with four pounds of bloom raisins, Seville oranges, lemons, white sugar candy and diluted with iced green tea."

"Oh how shockingly inebriating," breathed Lady Rothersay in horror. "I hardly think — "

"I do believe," said Lady Evelina sweetly, a mischievous glint in her eye, "that the Regent's Punch was in fact named after its creator."

That, of course, settled the matter. After another half hour of heated debate about the music, the flowers and the menu, Lady Evelina arose, pleading fatigue. "But pray do not disturb yourself, Lady Rothersay. I am sure Lady Francesca will be kind enough to escort me to my carriage."

Out in the street, Lady Evelina took a deep breath of the scented summer night air. "My, I am beginning to feel mightily relieved that I shall not be attending the banquet after all. Whilst all the other ladies are growing tipsy and argumentative on Regent's Punch and falling into fountains of gushing water, I shall be peacefully curled up on my sofa at home, immersed in a new romance from the Circulating Library!"

"Yes, indeed," said Francesca listlessly.

Lady Evelina touched her arm. "Why not ride out and visit me tomorrow? Charles will be in London attending to stuffy financial affairs with his broker so I shall be excessively glad of some company."

It was a notion which greatly appealed to Francesca. A ride over the Downs would help to clear her mind. And she always enjoyed any sociable association with the lively Lady Evelina.

★   ★   ★

Lady Rothersay was late down to breakfast the following morning and appeared dressed in an elegant dark blue carriage gown.

"I shall be calling on Lady Medway, to advise her of the latest developments over the banquet," she announced. Her eye fell speculatively on Francesca, who had eaten practically no breakfast, "I had expected by now that Lady Medway would have asked to see you, Francesca. I must confess to a slight feeling of foreboding over the prospect of your betrothal to Lord Medway. I do hope lady Medway's silence does not indicate that she has changed her mind over the match."

Francesca sat with downcast eyes, praying fervently that this was indeed the case.

"I feel it my duty, you known, to send you back to Dorset as an engaged girl with your future settled," said Lady Rothersay firmly. "It is unfortunate that for the next few weeks I shall be immersed in preparations for the banquet so your matrimonial plans will not receive the attention I should have wished."

Francesca dare not look up, for fear that the relief would show in her eyes. She said quietly, "Lady Evelina has invited me to call on her today, Aunt. May I have your permission to ride over to Penshurst Lodge?"

"Oh, I should so much like to go too!" cried Aithne. "May I, Mama?"

"Of course. It is an excellent notion for you to be as much in the company of the Duke's sister as possible. She exerts a considerable influence on him, I am sure."

But as Francesca had anticipated, no sooner were the two girls clear of Upper Brook than Aithne reined in her horse and declared her intention of setting forth for her own, private destination. Francesca took a deep breath, determined to try one last time to make her cousin see sense.

"Aithne, please don't misunderstand me, or be annoyed at what I am about to say. But you must see that the longer you persist in these secret meetings, the worse your fate is bound to be. Why, you told me yourself that your relationship with your beau is doomed."

"Yes," said Aithne, pushing back her golden curls, "it is all quite hopeless. But I love him, Francesca! And I am determined to snatch every hour, every minute, every second with him that I can. My love for him is akin to a fever, you see, which takes total command of me! It makes me reckless and foolhardy, but I cannot help myself. Nor do I want to! I want only to be in his arms." She smiled. "I have shocked you, Cousin! But how can I make you understand? You have no notion of what it is like to be so passionately, so rapturously in love!"

And with that she raised a hand and cantered away, leaving Francesca staring after her with tears in her eyes. She blinked them away and turned her horse towards the Downland path.

I don't know what it is to be passionately, rapturously in

love? whispered Francesca. Oh Aithne, what irony! How your opinion of me would change if you had a glimmering of the long, sleepless nights when I lie restless in my bed, yearning to feel the Duke's lips on mine once more. Why, even the very mention of his name is enough to set me afire with longing for him.

On her arrival at Penshurst Lodge, a footman informed her that she was awaited in the garden. Eagerly, Francesca hurried out onto the terrace which overlooked the lawns and well-stocked flower beds. She was looking forward enormously to a few hours of cheering conversation with the lively Lady Evelina who was, Francesca realised, the only lady in Winchester with whom she felt completely in tune.

A figure was seated on the low wall which bordered the terrace. But it was not Lady Evelina. Francesca's heart turned a somersault and she was furious to find herself blushing as the Duke of Wexford arose and strolled towards her. With trembling fingers, she put up her parasol, the better to shield her expressive face from the man she loved.

"I . . . I was invited to call on your sister," she stammered, cursing herself as she realised how foolish she must sound. Why else, after all, would she be calling at Lady Evelina's home?

The Duke inspected a piece of honeysuckle climbing up the house wall. "She is at Wexford Hall this morning. The Prince Regent, as you know, will be residing with me for the duration of his stay in Winchester, and Evelina has taken it upon herself to organise a massive cleaning and refurbishing operation in his honour. When she told me that you were expected here, I was only too delighted to escape from the artillery of mops and brooms and come and spend a few hours in your company."

Francesca would not meet his eyes. She was not deceived

for one moment by his speech. *He has been thinking over that episode between us on Flower Down,* she reasoned. *He was worried that because he kissed me, I might assume that the next step would be a proposal of marriage. Hence he has taken the opportunity this morning to make it quite clear that his sister is firmly in charge of his household at Wexford Hall and therefore, by implication, he has no need of the services of a Duchess!*

The silence between them lengthened. The Duke, nonchalantly at ease, stood looking down at her. She, uncomfortably aware of his gaze, twirled her parasol round and round as she gazed with unseeing eyes out over the sunlit garden. She wished she had never come. She wished he would go away. Above all, she wished she could quench the raging, overpowering desire she felt for him.

"Francesca, what is wrong?" he enquired quietly.

She pulled the parasol further down over her face and contrived a brittle laugh. "Wrong? Why nothing! Whatever can you mean?"

"You seem unusually subdued today," he informed her, his penetrating blue eyes not leaving her for a second.

Francesca affected an amused little sigh. "I am merely in a contemplative mood. There are times in life, you know, when it is most pleasant simply to remain quiet, and observe the — "

She gasped as he seized hold of her parasol and flung it out over the terrace and onto the lawn. Then his hands were in her hair, tilting her face up to his.

"That's better," he muttered grimly, "Just as I thought. Your eyes are grey and troubled. They give you away every time, you know!"

The feel of his hands on her face was almost the undoing of Francesca. She knew if he continued to touch her for much longer, she would not be able to prevent herself from throwing herself into his arms.

With a monumental effort of will, she wrenched herself free. "Your concern for my welfare is most touching, Your Grace. But I am sure you have many matters demanding your attention back on your estate. Pray do not allow me to detain you."

"Listen to me, you stubborn girl," he said levelly. "I heard from Evelina that you looked distinctly distraught at your aunt's dinner last night. You ate hardly a morsel of food, and paid scant attention to anything which was said to you. Evelina was intending to be here when you called this morning, in the hope that you would confide in her and unburden your worries to her as a friend. But," his voice deepened as he stretched out a hand towards her. "As I believe I have a notion as to the cause of your troubled state of mind, I took it upon myself to come here and talk to you myself."

She stared at him, consumed with dread, willing him not to continue.

He held her hands in his, "Francesca, when I took you in my arms on Flower Down and kissed you — "

But she refused to stand and listen to that which she most feared to hear. Whirling away from him she ran from the terrace and out across the lawn, hot tears of humiliation stinging her eyes.

Oh no, she thought miserably, this is too much! He has come to make a gallantly defensive little speech with the underlying message that his kiss meant nothing to him. He fears that I misunderstood his motives and believe him to be passionately in love with me. He wishes to establish now, once and for all between us, that what happened on Flower Down was merely a *divertissement*, a brief, amusing little flirtation to which I would be foolish to attach any deeper emotion!

The embarrassment of her situation made Francesca shake with rage. When the Duke came striding across the lawn towards her she turned on him, her knuckles white, her eyes blazing, "You are without doubt the most arrogant, self-centred, self-important man I have ever met! How dare you assume that because of a single, insignificant kiss I am in a state of the vapours over the matter. How dare you!"

His eyes narrowed as he regarded the furious girl in the blue sprigged muslin dress. "I thought you might be alarmed in case anyone had observed us on Flower Down and reported the matter back to your aunt."

Francesca was in such a frenzy of fury that all self-restraint was cast to the winds. "You are too late! Someone did see us! That's the whole point!" she blurted. "And the consequences will be disastrous for my entire family!"

Distraught at having said so much, she flung herself down on the garden seat. After a moment, the Duke seated himself beside her, and said. "Francesca, you must tell me what this is all about. You know I will help you if I can. And you know also that, even though you may regard me as the most arrogant man that ever walked this earth, you can at least trust me."

She sat with her head in her hands, accepting that what he said was true. He had kept his silence over many matters in the time she had known him. And yes, he had been generous with his help, too. Why, she could not imagine. To add a little amusing spice to his life she supposed. But the fact remained that he was a man of honour. And, she had to admit, it would be such an overwhelming relief to share her burden with someone.

She took a deep breath. "Very well. You may find this difficult to believe, but the fact is that there are six ladies in this town who are being blackmailed. Six ladies. One of whom is myself."

She told him then most of what had happened to her from

the time the two ruffians had bundled her into the carriage, to the moment when they had released her in a quiet backstreet of the town. The Duke's face was dark with anger by the time she finished her tale, saying helplessly,

"He wore a voluminous cloak and a hood so it was impossible for me to gain an inkling as to his identity. And, of course, he spoke in an assumed, croaky whisper of a voice."

The Duke looked at her with concern. "I wish you had come to me immediately with this intelligence, Francesca. My God! That you should have been obliged to endure such treatment!" His fist smashed on the garden seat. "He shall be caught and horsewhipped, Francesca. I give you my word on that."

"I fear that the other ladies have suffered more than I," said Francesca. "Why poor Lady Sutton was driven twice to attempt suicide. Only by purest accident was she saved each time right at the last moment."

The Duke stood up and restlessly paced the lawn. "Francesca, I want you to tell me again about your encounter with the blackmailer. Don't leave anything out, however insignificant it may seem. I want to know everything, from the size of his hands to the colour of the cloth covering the window."

It seemed a pointless, time-wasting exercise to Francesca. During her hour at the cottage she had, after all, been listening and looking with every nerve on the alert for clues. But to the best of her knowledge, apart from the fact that the blackmailer was not a young man, nothing else of value had been forthcoming. And she, after all, had been the one who had been there. She could not imagine what the Duke hoped to learn from another account of the episode.

However, he was adamant, so she cast her mind back,

telling him of the mossy path, the smell of damp, the man's woollen cloak and silk hood . . .

The Duke interrupted her many times, quizzing her on the blackmailer's gestures, his attitude, his response to her defiance, his attitude towards his ruffian accomplices.

When she had finished, the Duke was silent for a while. Then he remarked calmly, "There is something missing, Francesca. There is something you have not told me."

Francesca gazed down at the lawn, cursing his sharp intelligence, He can read me like an open book, she thought resentfully. It is quite impossible to conceal anything from him, anything at all!

He said gently. "Come along now, Francesca. Stop wriggling your toes and wishing me a million miles away. Out with it!"

She gave a nervous laugh. "Oh, it was just something very silly and unimportant. As you know, the man was blackmailing me over *Lady Alethia's Journal*, and my natural reluctance to have my aunt mightily embarrassed in her social circle by the truth about her niece's activities becoming common intelligence in Winchester. But, er, the blackmailer also had, as he imagined, a second string to his bow."

"Go on," said the Duke drily.

"Well, having observed us, er, together on Flower Down he jumped to the conclusion that we were engaged in something of a grand passion and he threatened to tell my aunt of my trysts on the Downs with you. Of course, this was one threat which did not worry me in the least, because I could in all truth and honesty have assured my aunt that there was nothing between us whatsoever and — "

"Trysts!" the Duke cried sharply, cutting through Francesca's embarrassed flounderings. "Are you quite sure, Francesca, that he said trysts and not tryst?"

Her brow puckered. "Yes," she said finally and firmly. "I am quite sure. I remember that he had a way of hissing when he pronounced an s. It was quite distinctive."

The Duke slapped his thigh, "Then I am almost sure I know who the blackmailer is," he said softly. "You see, I saw him spying on us on the Downs that day."

"You saw him!" exclaimed Francesca. "But why did you not say so immediately? Who was he?"

"At the time, it did not seem important. And I had far more pressing matters on my mind!" He looked at her in a manner which made her blood race. "In any case, such was the position of the sun that I could not see the man's features, only his silhouette. And, most significantly as it turns out, in the few seconds that my attention was diverted from you to him, I could observe the manner in which he handled his horse. The appallingly *rough* manner . . . "

Perplexed, Francesca shook her head. "I don't understand. You seem to be talking in riddles."

"Trysts, Francesca," prompted the Duke. "Who has seen us on another occasion when we were alone on the Downs? Whom did I take to task on that occasion for his bad horsemanship!"

"Lord Compton!" breathed Francesca in amazement. "He was responsible for the phaeton carrying Lady Medway to break away! And he was furious with you for making his culpability plain!" Her fingers drummed on the wooden seat. "Yes . . . but of course! I remember now. As I was about to be released from the cottage, he reprimanded one of the ruffians. He was shocked by the grimy condition of the handkerchief being used to bind my eyes, and insisted that one of his own clean ones be used."

The Duke nodded. "It all fits, does it not? Lord Compton is celebrated for his fastidious tidy-minded ways. I suspect in fact, that he returned to Flower Down that morning with the intention of retrieving the duelling pistol you had dropped in the grass. The swine! I shall take great pleasure in bringing him to justice over this!"

"But don't you see, our hands are tied!" protested Francesca. "How can we expose him as a blackmailer without the indiscretions of Lord Sutton, and Lady Beddows and the rest becoming common knowledge all over town! And while we're on the subject, what puzzles me is how he obtained all his information about his victims."

Thoughtfully, the Duke rubbed his chin. "Mmm, I do believe, Francesca, that this is one part of the puzzle which is easy to solve. Easy, that is, now we know that the blackmailer is Lord Compton. I have no proof of course, nothing to guide me but my own instincts. But I do believe that Lord Compton was obtaining his information from Lady Medway."

"But she is seen only very rarely in society," protested Francesca. "If you remember, I wrote a teasing paragraph about her in my first *Lady Alethia's Journal*."

"And if you recall," said the Duke, "it was shortly after that item in the *Courier* that the lady was goaded from the refuge of her house."

"You imagine, then that Lord Compton paid frequent visits to Medway and these rides across the lonely part of the Downs were a common practice?"

The Duke nodded. "It was only due to Lord Compton's bad management of the horses that day, that we saw them at all. Otherwise they would have gone undetected. And you see, you must remember that although Lady Medway rarely enters into society, that does not prevent society from calling on her."

"Of course!" exclaimed Francesca. "Why, this very morning my aunt expressed her intention of calling on Lady Medway to inform her of the arrangements for the Prince

Regent's banquet. And because she is something of a recluse, it is highly likely that the ladies of the town would have confided their secrets to her."

"It is one of the follies of human nature," smiled the Duke. "That we choose to believe what we want to believe. Because Lady Medway is not observed promenading along the High Street, indulging in whispered tittle tattle with her contemporaries, the ladies of the town imagined her to be above all forms of gossip. All the while, of course, Lady Medway had found her own confidant in Lord Compton."

"Do you truly imagine them to be in league?" breathed Francesca. "Is Lady Medway condoning his endeavours at blackmail?"

"Oh no, I am sure a lady of Lady Medway's quality would have no truck with such low activities. She is quite unaware of his darker motives. It is my opinion that she regards him simply as a sympathetic companion. Compton is a great favourite with the middle-aged ladies of the town, you know."

Francesca let out a great sigh and lifted her face to the sun. "Oh, what a relief it is to have told you all this, and to have discovered the identity of the blackmailer! I feel as if a great weight has been lifted from me." Then she leaned forward and said eagerly, "Now, the next problem is, how do we put an end to Lord Compton's scandalous activities, without at the same time exposing the blackmailed ladies to embarrassing public scrutiny? What shall we do?"

"*We*," replied the Duke with heavy emphasis, "are going to do nothing. *You* are going to return home and play your part as the dutiful niece with nothing more pressing on her mind than which dress to wear to the Prince Regent's banquet. *I*, meanwhile, shall deal with Lord Compton."

"But how?" cried Francesca, leaping to her feet. "He told me I must deliver up the Rothersay goblet to him by

Tuesday at the latest. And today is Wednesday. That leaves so little time!"

"Yes," he agreed, "especially as I shall be away from home for a short while as from tomorrow. However, Lord Compton is always present at Buckhurst's on Mondays. So I shall deal with him then."

"But *how*?" repeated Francesca, in a frenzy of curiosity. "What will you do? How can you possibly deal with him without making public his blackmailing activities, and thereby sorely embarrassing his female victims?"

The Duke strolled across the lawn and retrieved Francesca's parasol. "Rest assured, Francesca. Everything will be under control."

She regarded him contemplatively from beneath her long lashes. But, as if reading her thoughts, he said severely, "No, Francesca! Let us have one thing quite clear, under no circumstances will I tolerate you masquerading once more as Lord Wingate in order to be present when I give Compton his come-uppance!"

"But that's unfair!"

"Be sensible, Francesca. I shall have enough on my mind to worry about without being obliged to keep a watchful eye on your charade as well. Besides," he went on, observing the defiant gleam in her eye, "you did give me your word, you know, that you would never again masquerade as a gentleman."

Trembling, she turned away. Yes, she had given her promise. And she had a strong feeling that if she continued now to defy the Duke, he would take her in his arms and kiss her again, with the intention of forcing her to confirm that promise. And if he should kiss me again, thought Francesca, her blood racing, he would know then without a shadow of doubt the depth of my feelings for him. For at the touch of his lips on mine, I should be unable to control my emotions. The truth would be laid bare between us, and I should then have to suffer the humiliation of his gallant rejection of me!

He stepped forward, and handed Francesca her parasol. "Return home now, Francesca. And try to be patient. On Tuesday morning you will receive word of the events at Buckhurst's."

Francesca took the parasol. "Yes, my Lord," she murmured demurely.

12

Naturally, the spirited Francesca had no intention of being excluded from the drama which was to be enacted on Monday night at Buckhurst's. Return home and wait patiently indeed, she thought indignantly. How typical of the Duke! Does he not realise by now that it is simply not in my nature to sit quietly at my embroidery waiting for news of the adventures of others? No, I will not be patronised in this manner! If there is excitement afoot, then I desire to have a part in it, whatever the risks and dangers! And after Lord Compton's disgraceful treatment of myself and the other ladies of Winchester, it will be a moment of great delight to me to see him receive his come-uppance.

The problem is, she mused, how do I gain entrance to a gentlemen's club, when I have promised the Duke that I will never again dress myself as a man?

Over the next few days, Francesca pondered on what she could remember of Buckhurst's, the size and arrangement of the main rooms, the positioning of the doors and the windows. Being an imaginative girl, she was not devoid of ideas as to a method of securing admittance to the Club. She could be carried in at the bottom of a laundry basket . . . or disguise herself as a scullery maid. All manner of fanciful notions danced before her. But she rejected them all as too complicated or too dangerous. Simplicity, she told herself, is all. She remembered that the card room and main saloon were situated at the back of the building, overlooking the terraced, walled garden. If it is a fine night, she reasoned, the windows will be opened to release the cigar smoke from the rooms. It will be a simple matter then for me to hide behind the long curtains at one of the windows. Because of the obstruction of the curtain, and the dim lighting in the Club, I may not have the best of views. But I will surely hear every word that passes between the Duke and Lord Compton! The vital thing is that Monday night remains fine. A downpour of rain will drench my plans for sure.

On Monday, Francesca approached Aithne and warned her that she felt another of her headaches was imminent, necessitating that she retire to her room after dinner, not to emerge again until morning.

Aithne sighed. "Really Francesca! Surely you are not intending to stay out all night again!"

"Not all night," Francesca reassured her. "And this will be the last time I shall require you to cover for me. I promise you."

Aithne's eyes were round with curiosity but, when Francesca steadfastly refused to answer any more questions, she was obliged to content herself with the tart rejoinder, "You take it upon yourself to lecture me about my beau, Francesca, but at least I do not engage in night-time trysts with him!"

To Francesca's relief the evening, though dull, appeared settled and there was no hint of rain in the air. After retiring to her bedchamber with her "headache", she slipped into a dark green dress and threw a black shawl round her shoulders. It was dusk as she slipped from the servants entrance of the house, and ran through the backstreets to the lane that skirted the Club gardens. She pushed open the gate, and stood for a moment, savouring the heady scent of roses and honeysuckle rambling up the high wall.

Directly in front of her was the imposing ediface of the Club, softly aglow in the lamplight. Francesca smiled as she observed the open window. After checking that there was no one abroad in the garden, she hurried across the grass, up the steps and flattened herself against the wall near the tall windows of the main saloon.

Peering in, she observed Lord Featherstone snoring in a deep armchair, and Lord Medway glancing through *The Gentleman's Magazine*. But as there was no sign of the two gentlemen she sought, she inched her way along the wall until she was outside the card room. A shiver of triumph ran through her. There they were! The Duke stood with his back to Francesca, watching Lord Compton and Lord Southport who were engaged in a game of backgammon.

Holding her breath, Francesca eased herself into the room, positioning herself behind the long dark red damask curtains. She was relieved that the Duke was positioned with his back to her. Had he been facing me, she realised, with a shudder of apprehension, I should have been convinced all the while that those sapphire blue eyes of his were penetrating right through these curtains, and exposing me!

It amazed her that the atmosphere in the card room had such an air of normality. When, she wondered impatiently, would the Duke make his move? Oh, how could he stand there so calmly, sipping brandy and looking as if he had not a care in the world!

The Duke seemed totally absorbed in the game of backgammon being played out before him, but each rattle of the red dice only served to increase Francesca's agitation. Time was drawing on.

Lord Compton won the game, and Francesca's heart sank

as she heard Lord Southport challenge him to another. But the card room door opened and Lord Featherstone declared, "Dispatches, just arrived from the war! There's most encouraging news from the front. General Mace is to read the dispatches to us in the library."

Francesca was furious as she watched the gentlemen abandon their tables and quit the room. The Library, she knew, was situated at the front of the house and provided her with no convenient vantage point.

Lord Compton was amongst the last to move towards the door. But he was detained by the Duke, who said pleasantly, "Before you leave, Compton, could I trouble you for a sight of the dice you were using in your backgammon game?"

Perfectly at ease, Lord Compton reached into his pocket. "Surely. But they are just my usual red dice, Wexford. I find red a lucky colour. Sutton, now, disagrees. He will play with nothing but ivory dice!"

Grave faced, the Duke closed the door. With the red dice lying in the open palm of his hand, he said quietly "These dice are loaded, Compton."

Lord Compton turned purple. "This is outrageous, Wexford! Retract this instant or I'll have you blackballed from the Club."

Ignoring the older man's outburst, the Duke held one of the dice up to the light and remarked, "Ah, as I thought. A short pig's bristle has been inserted into one corner, adding extra weight, and ensuring of course that the dice falls more often on one side than the other. Most ingenious, Compton!"

Behind the damask curtain, Francesca stood with her hand over her mouth, hardly able to contain her mirth. Clearly, the Duke had switched the dice. Just how, Francesca could not imagine, but she suspected that in his youth on his Grand Tour, the Duke had taken the opportunity to learn a trick or two in many of the more disreputable gaming clubs of Paris. Lord Compton was hopping from one foot to the other, obviously burning to take a swing at his accusor, but wisely refraining in view of the Duke's superior height and muscular power.

"You are not denying, Compton, that these are the dice you used in your game with Lord Southport?"

"I don't deny it," snapped the shorter man. "But someone must have switched them!"

"Let's have this quite clear," thundered the Duke, "are you accusing a member of this Club of Greeking on you, Compton? That's an extremely serious charge!"

"Yes — no — " blustered Lord Compton. He paced the room, struggling for control. Then he rounded on the Duke. "You! You must have switched them, Wexford. If you persist in taking this matter further I warn you I shall defend myself, and point an accusing finger at you!"

"Believe me," murmured the Duke, "If necessary I shall not hesitate to lay the whole disgraceful affair before the other members of the Club. It will be your word, of course, against mine. But you admit that these are the dice you used in your game and, I would remind you that even if it is found that the case is not totally proven against you, the memory of the accusation will remain in the members' minds. No smoke without fire, they will think . . . "

Lord Compton's eyes narrowed. "All right, Wexford. You've made your point. Just what's behind all this?"

"It is really quite simple," smiled the Duke. "I am prepared to seal my lips over the incident of these loaded dice. On two conditions. One, that you quit Winchester and travel abroad for a while. Two, that you give into my safe keeping, tonight, the five King Charles goblets which you obtained by blackmail."

A bitter laugh echoed round the card room. "So! The Lady Francesca came running to you for aid, did she? Foolish girl! And what is to stop me whispering a few choice words in her aunt's ear about your clandestine activities with Lady Francesca up on the Downs?"

The Duke's voice was low, but steely. "If you attempt to cast any slur upon the name of the Lady Francesca de Lisle, you will have me to answer to, Compton. I shall take you to a quiet, lonely place and I shall, quite literally, reduce to you pulp."

Lord Compton gulped. "And . . . and if I refuse to accept your conditions?"

"Then I shall have no option but to reveal to the others members the matter of the loaded dice. I have no doubt they will accept my word over yours, and by midday tomorrow all of southern England will be aware that you have been blackballed from Buckhurst's. Socially, you will be a total outcast, Compton."

The older man slumped against the wall. "Very well. I will return home immediately and have the goblets sent to Wexford Hall."

"On the contrary, Compton," said the Duke levelly. "I shall escort you home, and take possession of the goblets personally. My God!" he suddenly exploded, "what a dastardly blackguard you are! Even now, you are displaying no remorse for your despicable behaviour. What made you entangle yourself in these blackmailing activities, man? Tell me that."

"Boredom," sighed Lord Compton. "All those salons, drinking tea and making polite conversation with all those conventional Winchester ladies . . . it was simply that my activities in securing the goblets provided an entertaining diversion in an otherwise excessively tedious life."

"Come," ordered the Duke looking scornfully at the

broken Lord Compton, "let us away. Whilst you are writing your letter of resignation from the Club, I will take possession of the goblets. They will be returned, anonymously, to their rightful owners."

Behind the curtain, Francesca's eyes danced with laughter and admiration. My, how very astute of the Duke, she thought. By threatening to have him exposed as a card cheat, and blackballed from the Club, the Duke has hit on the one thing likely to terrify Lord Compton into submission. For, with this particular breed of English gentleman, it would not matter a toss to them if they were publicly denounced as embezzelers, frauds or wife beaters. They would shrug, and simply laugh the matter off. But to expose a man as a Greeker, to have him blackballed from his Club, why that was the worst imaginable fate, like being condemned to the fires of a worldly Hell.

With the drama over, the two men were now preparing to take their leave. Francesca, confident that there was nothing further to be heard, was on the point of slipping away across the garden, when she heard the voice of Sir Peter Jamieson. He sounded most aggrieved.

"I say, Wexford! Don't dash off. I thought it was a deuced poor show your missing our appointment last Friday. I don't mind telling you, I was mightily put out when your steward informed me that you were away from home, and you had not the courtesy to leave me a word of explanation for breaking our engagement."

"A thousand apologies, Sir Peter," said the Duke gravely. "It was indeed most remiss of me. It had, I confess, quite slipped my mind that we were to race your new hunter against mine that day. All I can say in my defence is that I had other matters very much on my mind last week . . . "

There was a slight pause and then he continued in a low tone, "Matrimonial matters, as it happens."

"Indeed?" said Sir Peter curiously. "May I enquire the name of the fortunate lady?"

"I regret that I have not yet secured her permission to make our engagement public," smiled the Duke.

Sir Peter laughed. "Keeping you dangling for a while, is she! Well that won't do you any harm, Wexford. I say! Whatever ails poor old Compton? His face is quite corpse like."

"He is not in the best of health," said the Duke. "I am attending him home, and shall recommend that for the sake of his health he should reside for a while in warmer climes. But I'm glad I ran into you, Jamieson. Bring your hunter up to the Hall tomorrow and I'll make amends for last week. We'll spend the afternoon racing and then, at dinner, I'd like your opinion on some rather fine claret laid down by my grandfather."

"Capital notion! Until tomorrow then!"

Francesca turned away from the window, let herself out through the garden gate and ran at a furious pace all the way home. By the time she flung herself onto her bed she was gasping for breath over the stabbing stitch in her side. But that pain was nothing, compared to the despair searing her heart.

★　　★　　★

Over the next few days, an inexplicable air of gaiety suddenly pervaded the stately city of Winchester. Lord Southport was delighted to find that his wife no longer spent most of the day in a state of swoon. Lady Sutton and Lady Featherstone were positively skittish, and to everyone's surprise and delight, the Ladies Beddows and Montfort returned from their country estates, their glowing complexions and sparkling eyes attesting to the benefits of good fresh country air.

At 11 Upper Brook, Lady Rothersay was pleased to discover that she now had the full, enthusiastic support of the other ladies over the planning of the Prince Regent's banquet. Not a day passed without the ladies of the elite gathering in Lady Rothersay's Drawing Room, to discuss details for the floral displays, the Prince's favourite music, their own gowns, their hairstyles, fans, slippers, jewels, perfume. Everyone declared in breathless tones that they simply could not wait for the day of the banquet to dawn.

Only Francesca remained withdrawn, eating little, saying less, taking no interest in the fever of excitement all around her. Lady Rothersay was too occupied with all her preparations to notice Francesca's unhappiness, but Aithne's blue eyes were more observant.

"Francesca why do you spend so many hours alone in your chamber? I can tell that something is dreadfully wrong. Will you not confide in me? I would do anything to help you."

"It is a kind thought, Cousin," replied Francesca listlessly. "But there is nothing anyone can do. Please, I should just like to be left alone!'

Lying on her bed, gazing with unseeing eyes at the blue rosettes on the cornice, Francesca felt as if she were truly in Hell. She burned with longing for the Duke. With all her heart and soul she yearned for the man she loved — the man who would shortly be announcing his betrothal to another lady.

Oh, how Francesca loathed the Duke's mysterious fiancée. Who is she? Francesca raged. The Duke was away for several days, so it is likely that she lives in another county — or London! Yes, that would be it. He is to marry some elegant, sophisticated London beauty, who no doubt will be highly amused by his story of the rustic girl from Dorset, and how he entertained himself by kissing her on Flower Down.

Francesca's nails razed the counterpane, I hate her! she thought passionately, her eyes blazing with jealousy. But oh, thank heavens I was not so foolish as to give the Duke a clue as to my true feelings for him. If he knew how much I loved him, I think I would die of embarrassment.

The days seemed endless to her. But the nights were worse. Oh, those long, balmy summer nights, fragrant with the scent of roses, newly scythed grass and honeysuckle. The scents of romance, drifting in from the starlit, indigo sky to torture her with thoughts of what might have been . . . if only, oh, if *only*!

Such was Francesca's state of utter despair that she could summon none of her customary secret amazement over the arrival of Friday's *Winchester Courier*, containing the latest epistle from the pen of Lady Alethia. As usual, Lady Rothersay was seated at the head of the breakfast table, her face taut as the newspaper was borne into her on a silver salver. The servants were dismissed from the room, and Lady Rothersay made a pretence of glancing through the Court circular, intelligence of Parliament, and London society.

Aithne and Francesca sat in silence as at last, Lady Rothersay turned resolutely to the page dominated by "that woman's hysterical ravings," as Lady Featherstone had once put it. Lady Rothersay was normally outraged by one or more paragraphs of the Journal. But on this particular Friday as she scanned the first paragraph, she sat white-faced, as if turned to stone.

"What is it Mama?" asked Aithne anxiously. "What does Lady Alethia say?"

The colour flooded back into Lady Rothersay's face, as she struggled for words. "Why, this is perfectly scandalous!" she choked, clawing at the pearls at her neck. "This is monstrous! I have never in my life encountered such impertinence, such deceit, such reptilian behaviour!"

As her aunt sat trembling with rage, Francesca hastily cast her mind back to the items she had included that week in her Journal. She had, as she remembered, started with an amusing anecdote concerning the physician's indiscreet revelations about Lord Medway's chilblains but surely that was not sufficient to reduce her aunt to such a state of apoplexy? Francesca suspected that Sir Peter, exercising his editorial control, had probably taken it upon himself to alter the order of her paragraphs. Could he have placed at the head of the column the item about Lady Southport insisting on taking precedence over Lady Sutton at the Prince Regent's banquet?

Was it that which had so shocked her Aunt? Lady Rothersay, rapidly gaining control of herself, was returning to full whiplash tone. Waving the impatient and understandably curious Aithne to silence, she began to read, as if quite unable to believe her eyes:

"*Faithful readers of this Journal will recall how, in my first humble paragraphs in this august publication, I made mention of one of our most celebrated Winchester residents, the Duke of Wexford. The Duke, I revealed, having decided to embrace the responsibilities and delights of matrimony, was casting his eye upon the elegible ladies of the city. I gave you my word, dear readers, that once his choice was made, it would be here, in my Journal, that you would first learn the name of the future Duchess of Wexford. There is joy in my heart today as I pen these lines, for I am about to keep my promise to you.*"

Aithne gasped. "The Duke is to marry? But who Mama? Who?"

Lady Rothersay's voice was icy. "Quiet, Aithne. Pray permit me to continue with this disgraceful saga! *Most delightful of all is the intelligence that the lady to whom the Duke has given his heart, is a member of one of our oldest and most respected Winchester families. She is none other than the charm-*

ing," Lady Rothersay glared at the two girls, *"the charming and most attractive Lady Francesca de Lisle, niece of the Count and Countess of —* "

"Francesca!" shrieked Aithne, dropping her knife with a clatter to the floor. "Francesca is to marry the Duke?"

"But I — you don't understand — I didn't," stammered Francesca, her face scarlet.

"Be silent!" ordered a furious Lady Rothersay. She turned to her daughter, stretching out her arms in a gesture of anguish. "My dearest girl! I accept full responsibility for this dreadful event. I have failed, yes failed you as a mother! It was I who invited Francesca to Winchester in the first place. It was a disastrous mistake, I see that now. But how was I to know that she would treat us so shamelessly? That she would be so underhand as to steal your beau from you! Oh Aithne, I can well imagine the black despair within your poor young heart!"

Aithne viewed her mother's histrionics with a remarkably placid eye. "Do not fret so, Mama. I assure you, the news does not upset me in the least."

"How brave! How noble! But what is to become of you now, Aithne! With your cousin stealing the glory by walking up the Cathedral aisle with the Duke, I fear there is nothing for it but to hide away in a Nunnery."

"Nonsense, Mama. You do not understand the situation at all," said Aithne. She paused and turned very pink, as if she were holding her breath. Then she blurted, in a galloping succession of disjointed phrases. "I don't want to marry the Duke . . . HeisafinemannodoubtbutIdon'tlovehim . . . IaminlovewithsomeoneelseMama . . . IaminlovewithSir-PeterJamiesonhehasaskedmetomarryhimandIhaveaccepte-dIknowyouwon'tapprovebutifyouwon'tletmemarryhim—I'll*die*!"

Forgetting herself completely, Lady Rothersay sat open

mouthed, staring aghast at her daughter. "What . . . w . . . kindly repeat all that Aithne. Slowly!"

But Aithne, *little fire*, had burnt herself out. Her courage exhausted, she mutely appealed to Francesca for help. Francesca, stunned with shock at Aithne's amazing revelation, hurriedly cleared her throat and said in a matter of fact tone to her aunt.

"Er, I think what Aithne was trying to say was that she is in truth in love not with the Duke, but with . . . well, Aithne is in love with . . . with Sir Peter Jamieson."

"But he's a tradesman!" screamed Lady Rothersay. "No member of our family has ever married into trade! The notion is insupportable!"

"I don't care!" flared Aithne. "I love him. Anyway, he's not a tradesman, he's a newspaper proprietor. But if it were a fish stall he owned, I'd still be determined to marry him."

"Oh, you wicked ungrateful girl! Your father — "

"Sir Peter intends formally to ask my father for my hand as soon as Papa returns from London," said Aithne, her napkin twisted into a series of tight little knots.

Lady Rothersay moaned. "This has been quite the worst morning of my entire life! I must return to my apartments, I must lie down. Oh, when Lady Sombourne hears about this she will be crowing from the roof tops! Clorinda marries a Viscount and my own daughter desires to marry a common tradesman!"

She rang the bell for her maid, and was supported upstairs to her darkened bedchamber. In the Breakfast Parlour, the two girls regarded one another, and breathed a mutual sigh of relief.

"Well really, Aithne!" exclaimed Francesca, pouring them both more tea. "I was completely taken in by you. Why, you told me yourself that your secret romance was doomed because your lover was married!"

"I told you no such thing," protested Aithne indignantly. "It was you and your vivid imagination jumping to conclusions, Francesca! No, I believed our love to be hopeless because of course Mama disapproves so violently of Sir Peter. But he says we must be brave, and firm. He intends speaking to my father and if permission is still not forthcoming then we shall elope!"

"But how did your romance start?" asked Francesca, thinking furiously.

"At the first of Mama's Thursday Afternoons attended by Sir Peter," replied Aithne, smiling at the memory. "He came and talked to me for a long while, and oh, Francesca, he is the first man I have ever met who didn't make me feel like a brainless idiot. Usually I can never think of anything to say to a man, but with him, because he seemed so genuinely interested in me, it was all so easy!"

Francesca nodded. Of course, it was soon after this that Sir Peter became *persona non grata* in the Rothersay household, because of the publication of *Lady Alethia's Journal*. But how cunning of Sir Peter not to have breathed a word to me about his romance, during our meetings down by the river, mused Francesca. She remembered one meeting in particular, when she and Aithne were both allegedly shopping in the city, and Aithne had rushed off to join her lover for a stolen hour. That rogue Sir Peter met me first by the river, hurried through our business pertaining to Lady Alethia, and then sped off to meet Aithne, Francesca realised. And all the time, I was congratulating myself on duping all Winchester with my Journal. Heavens, my subterfuges were as nothing, compared to the machinations of Sir Peter!

Aithne giggled. "The most amusing time was on the night of Lady Sombourne's masked ball. Sir Peter knew he would be lynched on sight if he were recognised, so he wore padding underneath his evening coat, and stained his face to a more swarthy hue with vegetable dye!"

"Some of which, as I recall, found its way onto your cheek," laughed Francesca, remembering Lady Rothersay's disparaging remarks at the end of the evening about her daughter's somewhat grubby face. She went on warmly, "I am relieved beyond measure that the man you love is not the married man whom I imagined him to be. I wish you every happiness with Sir Peter, Aithne. It is wonderful to see you so radiantly in love. But my, what a pair of dark horses you are!"

"Oh Francesca," exclaimed Aithne, "You are one to point the finger! Why for all these weeks, you have been secretly trysting with the Duke of Wexford! And now we learn that you are actually betrothed to him!"

"No, no, Aithne," said Francesca hurriedly, "Lady Alethia is wrong. It is all a dreadful mistake. I — "

But Aithne was not listening. A footman had entered and was trying to engage her attention. "Lady Rothersay requests that you attend her in her apartments immediately, Lady Aithne."

"Oh dear," muttered Aithne, rising reluctantly to her feet. "I do wish Sir Peter were here to support me. This is going to be the most difficult interview. But I am quite determined, Francesca. I shall not allow Mama to cow me!"

Francesca gave her a hug of encouragement. "I am sure once she has recovered from the shock, and realises how much in love you are, she will relent. Remember, Aithne, Love Conquers All!"

Half an hour later, Francesca was mounted on her favourite chestnut, riding out of Winchester along the old Roman road. 'Love Conquers All', she had said encouragingly to Aithne. But Francesca could find little comfort in the thought. Sadly, it simply isn't true, she realised. I am desperately in love with the Duke but he is shortly to become betrothed to another. And now I have the highly humiliating task of presenting myself before him, to explain that the extraordinary paragraph in *Lady Alethia's Journal* predicting that he would make me his Duchess, was most certainly not penned by me!

Francesca's cheeks flamed as she imagined the Duke's reaction when he read that item. Oh, it is too dreadful, Francesca thought in an agony of embarrassment. He will be furious with me for putting him in such a difficult position. All Winchester will be calling to congratulate him, and he will then be obliged to issue a denial, and the newspaper will be forced to print a retraction . . . and I, through no fault of my own, will most certainly be sent home in disgrace for bringing down so much shame upon the family.

It was obvious to Francesca that the person who had penned those lines about the Duke and herself was none other than Sir Peter Jamieson. Once more he is up to his old tricks of making mischief, Francesca fumed. But this time, he has gone too far! Poor Aithne, I wonder if she realises the real nature of the man she so passionately desires to marry. Life for her will not be dull, true enough, but has she any notion of how unscrupulous a character the beast has?

On her arrival at Wexford Hall, Francesca was informed that the Duke was down by the river. The Steward did not specify on which stretch of the river bank the Duke was to be found, but instinctively Francesca made her way to the shaded inlet in which she had so rashly bathed on her first morning in Hampshire.

Stepping lightly down the dry path, she pushed aside the bushes and saw the Duke lying full length on the bank, tickling for trout.

Before she could help herself, Francesca heard herself

saying in a challenging tone, "I did not think it was considered very sporting to attempt to catch the fry."

He glanced up, looking not at all surprised to see Francesca there. "I was only practising. In the unlikely event that I had caught anything, I should have put it straight back." He stood up, brushed the grass from his breeches, and remarked conversationally, "You have arrived a little earlier than I anticipated."

Francesca's eyes fell on a copy of the *Winchester Courier* lying on the bank. Oh, but this interview is going to be even more worse than I anticipated, she thought nervously. He obviously imagines that having written about our engagement in my Journal, I have come here this morning to convince him of my undying love! He, in turn, will be obliged gently to keep me at a distance, whilst he informs me of his true engagement to his society beauty in London.

The Duke was regarding her, a strange light in his deep blue eyes. Francesca was dressed from head to foot in green. Her riding habit was a deep forest green, whilst the cravat at her neck was a soft, subtle shade that beautifully complimented her lustrous grey-green eyes. She had chosen to wear this colour today because she usually found it calming. This morning, however, she found herself in such a state of apprehension that she was convinced she would never feel tranquil again.

Taking a deep breath, she made haste with her prepared speech about that morning's Journal. "Your Grace, I rode up here this morning because . . . that is, I felt I must explain immediately . . . I want you to understand that I was utterly appalled . . . I feel totally put to the blush . . . " Francesca clenched her hands behind her back, cursing herself for stuttering like an incoherent love sick girl. She gazed at a point somewhere to the left of the Duke's broad shoulder and went on crisply, "I felt I must come to assure you, on my word of honour, that I did not write that first paragraph in *Lady Alethia's Journal* this morning. I can only assume that it was inserted by Sir Peter himself, as a jest — a jest in extremely bad taste!"

The Duke was seated on an old tree stump, his long legs stretched out, his eyes never leaving Francesca's face. "Of course Sir Peter didn't write that paragraph," he said. Then he smiled. It was a smile Francesca was never to forget. "I wrote it, Francesca."

The colour drained from Francesca's face. "You! But why!"

He stood up. "I should have thought that was obvious. Because I love you. Because I want to marry you. And because I thought such a novel form of proposal would amuse you."

"Amuse me!' shouted Francesca, her relief and joy taking the form of shocked anger. "Why, I have been to Hell and back this morning, wondering how to explain that paragraph to you! Oh you beast! You cruel, callous, ruthless, arrogant — "

She was allowed to continue no further. Laughing, the Duke swept her into his arms and kissed her with a masterful intensity which made her heart sing with joy. Mindless of time, all that mattered to her now were his kisses, his caresses and the soaring realisation that he loved her. Yes, he truly loved her, and was kissing her in a manner which proved the fact conclusively!

"I am beginning to realise," the Duke murmured, "that in order to gain any peace and quiet in our marriage I shall be obliged to kiss you a great deal. I confess, I am greatly looking forward to it!"

Francesca tossed her head. "Well really! How dare you assume that I am so desperate to marry you?"

Smiling, he tenderly traced the lovely line of her face. "The manner in which you responded to my kisses was hardly that of a young lady deeply affronted by them!"

She closed her eyes, defiantly refusing to allow him to see the love shining within them. "It is customary, I believe," she said with a shaky attempt at *hauteur*, "to approach the young lady's father, and gain his approval of the match. I am not convinced that my father would consider you a suitable husband for me!"

"On the contrary," he said, kissing with exquisite tenderness first her left eye and then her right. "Your father and I have established an excellent rapport. I rode down to Dorset last week and formally requested permission to marry you. Your brother Edward was home from Eton, and your father was good enough to open a bottle of his finest cognac to welcome me into the family."

"Oh!" gasped Francesca, beating her fists against his chest. "Of all the underhand things to do! To go behind my back in such a fashion!"

He seized her hands and held them firmly behind her back, rendering her immobile against him. "It's your own fault for being such a headstrong young woman! I had fully intended proposing to you, in finest romantic tradition, on the terrace of Penshurst Lodge that day when you came to call on my sister and found her not at home. But the moment I made mention of that very memorable kiss on Flower Down, you took flight. Then I learned of Compton's dastardly attempts at blackmail, and of course with that on our minds the climate was hardly suitable for a proposal of marriage!"

Trembling, she gazed up at him, "So you decided to propose to me publicly, in the columns of the *Winchester Courier*! Oh, if you could have witnessed my aunt's face when she read that item! Fortunately, her attention was diverted from me to my cousin. Did you know that she is in love with Sir Peter Jamieson?"

He nodded. "Jamieson confided it all to me. I believe he will make your cousin an excellent husband."

"Oh are you sure?" asked Francesca anxiously. "Does he truly love her?"

"With all his heart," the Duke assured her. "He is a wealthy man, and will provide Aithne with every comfort and luxury. But at the same time, because he possesses a refreshingly unconventional spirit, he will never permit her to become a dreary Winchester matron. She will lead an eventful, fulfilling life with a man who would lay down his life for her."

Francesca trusted the Duke's judgement completely. "I am so glad. I was so concerned about Aithne. It is a relief to know that everything has turned out so well for her."

"And for us," he said, his hands moving up her shoulders and into her beautiful hair. "Come now, Francesca. Tell me you will marry me!"

With all her heart Francesca longed to yield. But she could not resist teasing him a little longer. "You realise that I have no dowry, and no feminine accomplishments. I cannot paint, I sing out of tune and my embroidery looks as if it has been executed with my left foot."

"My!" he mocked. "What a disaster. I knew the moment I set eyes on you, here in this very river, that you would bring me nothing but shame and disgrace."

"How ungallant of you," she said pertly. "I had imagined that you were about to tell me that you fell wildly in love with me at first sight."

"No, it took about an hour longer. I was intrigued and infuriated with you that morning when we first met. But it was when you came into my house and sat over breakfast with me in total silence that I thought, here is a woman I could share my life with. She is docile, tranquil and serene. Everything I have ever wanted in a wife. Of course," he sighed heavily. "I was not to realise then quite what a hot-headed minx you are."

"You are impossible. Quite impossible!" cried Francesca. But she could not repress a nostalgic smile at the memory of the breakfast they had shared together. She remembered very well the wonderful sense of companionship between them. Although they were strangers, it was as if they had known and loved one another since time began.

"Why do you think," the Duke said softly, "that I suddenly began once more to take part in the Wincester society which I had for so long avoided? Because I wanted to lose no opportunity of being with you. Only Evelina realised the truth. In fact, she told me a long time ago that if I didn't hurry up and marry you, I'd kick myself for the rest of my days."

Francesca laughed. "I like your sister enormously."

"Yes," he muttered dryly. "I can see that with the two of you in tandem within the family my life is going to be a continual series of upheavals. I do believe that Penshurst and I will be obliged to leave you ladies here in Hampshire whilst we devote our attentions to our London Clubs."

"You will do no such thing!" flared Francesca. "If you dare to leave my side for one unnecessary minute I shall assume my disguise as Lord Wingate and hound you round those London Clubs. You see if I don't!"

She drew up short at the expression in his deep blue eyes. "Yes," she said shakily. "Oh yes, I do love you! With all my heart I love you. And yes, please, please, marry me!"

His arms tightened around her. "I shall, of course, be obliged to insist that as Duchess of Wexford, you abandon your activities as Lady Alethia."

"Insist? Why you — "

"Francesca!" he said commandingly in a tone which melted the last flickering flame of her resistance. "Defiant to the end, aren't you. Am I obliged then, to make you give me your promise?"

Her lips parted as she gazed into his eyes. "Oh yes," she breathed ecstatically, "make me promise!"